Caspar Walsh is a successful author and dramatist. His
worory
Vinc... cu-
dram... *Prison Father*. His work as a freelance journalist
includes a regular column on crime and rehabilitation for
the *Guardian* and an arts column for *Resurgence* magazine.
He runs Wilderness and Writing programmes for prisons,
the probation service and rehabs using his experiences to
help inspire change. *Blood Road* is his first semi-autobio-
graphical novel, following his highly acclaimed memoir
Criminal.

Praise for *Criminal*:

'While peppered with hair-raising accounts of scrapes with
the cops, violence and abuse, *Criminal* never loses its sense
of optimism . . . characters are vividly brought to life' *News
of the World*

'An extraordinary autobiography. Vibrantly written with
one of the most compelling characters in Caspar's father
that I've come across in a long time . . . A masterful
portrayal of the two sides of a man' Minette Walters

'This is a fine, unsparing book about what addiction does
to all the lives it touches . . . If you want to understand why
our prisons are bulging, and where some hope for the
future may lie, read this book' Helen Dunmore

'Thankfully, Walsh's abused, drug-crazed, sham-glam
criminal childhood landed him in prison rather than the
morgue. The journey from there to where he is now is
redemptive, fuelled by a quiet heroism that is deeply
moving' Peter Florence Di............... Festival

BLOOD ROAD

Caspar Walsh

headline

The right of Caspar Walsh to be identified as the Author of the Work
has been asserted by him in accordance with the
Copyright, Designs and Patents Act 1988.

First published in Great Britain in 2010 by
HEADLINE PUBLISHING GROUP

First published in paperback in 2011 by
HEADLINE PUBLISHING GROUP

1

Cataloguing in Publication Data is available from the British Library

ISBN 978 07553 1751 6

Typeset in Giovanni book by Avon DataSet Ltd,
Bidford-on-Avon, Warwickshire

Printed and bound in Great Britain by
Clays Ltd, St Ives plc

Headline's policy is to use papers that are natural, renewable and
recyclable products and made from wood grown in sustainable forests.
The logging and manufacturing processes are expected to conform
to the environmental regulations of the country of origin.

HEADLINE PUBLISHING GROUP
An Hachette UK Company
338 Euston Road
London NW1 3BH

www.headline.co.uk
www.hachette.co.uk

This book is dedicated to the memory of my father,
who gave me a crooked eye on the world
and ceaseless passion for life.

The biggest thanks goes to my incredibly supportive and patient editor Claire Baldwin at Headline and my amazing wife Emma for their help in shaping this book into what it is. It would not be what it is without you.

Thanks also to my ever-patient and caring agent Broo Doherty. You have so many angles about you!

Could I thank everyone that helped me in the writing of this book? Not in name, but you know who you are and you have my gratitude and love.

Prologue

Vincent Cracknel parks his Mercedes in the lay-by just outside the village of Westfield. He switches off the engine and looks out into the black of the two a.m. winter night. Sleet curls in front of the windshield. He takes out his mobile phone, lays it on the dash, lights a cigarette and waits.

Tiredness is heavy in his bones.

I'm too old for this.

He looks around. No cars pass. Across the field to his left he sees the light from the bungalow a half a mile or so away. He could drive there. The walk will do him good. Fresh air for his diseased lungs.

The mobile trills out a polyphonic 'Waterloo Sunset'. He puts it on loudspeaker, keeping it as far away from his ear as possible. 'Milton. How are you, sunshine?'

'Cold. There's no fucking kettle here . . . and no cups.'

'I've got a flask of coffee. He with you?'

'He's colder than I am.'

'Be with you in about twenty minutes. I'll walk the last half-mile.'

'You're insane, mate. It's fucking five below.'

'My legs are stiff . . . from the drive. Be good to get some air in the old lungs.'

Vincent hangs up, stubs the cigarette and gets out of the car.

He takes a small holdall from the boot, clicks it gently shut and heads for the gate leading into the field.

Milton opens the door as Vincent walks into the drive. They head into the bungalow in silence.

The man sitting in the far corner of the living room looks up as Vincent walks in.

'Evening, sunshine.' Vincent pulls over a chair and straddles it. 'Won't say it's good to see you.' He looks around. 'Bit fucking Spartan in here. Could do with a woman's touch.'

Vincent takes out the flask and two cups; pours one for himself, one for Milton. Milton gets himself a chair.

The two men sit opposite the twenty-something man and look at him in silence as they drink.

After the second cup, Vincent stands. The man pulls back a little.

'How many times have I asked you?' Vincent looks expectantly at him.

No reply.

He continues, 'How many times have I asked you to keep things sustainable? And how many fucking times have we had this conversation? You know you can only take so much from your patch. That's the first thing I taught you.' Vincent looks across to Milton who continues to sip his coffee. 'Know where the word ambition comes from?'

Milton shakes his head, uninterested.

'From the word "ambit". The distance over which something extends, like a boundary. In the Middle Ages, each year, a chief would have to walk the boundary of his kingdom, the ambit. See, if it was too big, if he was unable to walk it, he'd become too ambitious, unable to protect his people, defend his kingdom.' Vincent looks down at the steam rising from his cup and continues to talk. 'I gave you Peckham. Asked you to walk your patch every once in a while, get you out of that stupid fucking car of yours, keep your feet on the ground. You did well. But you rolled out the cliché and got greedy. I was thinking our chat last summer had sorted all this out. But then I hear you've been stretching the boundaries again . . . getting a little too . . . ambitious.' Vincent walks up behind the silent man and tightens the bound cotton scarf holding the tennis ball in his mouth. The man moves a little. Vincent rests one finger on his head. He stops moving.

'So you've been making more money than has been checked in and seeing as you tried to convince Milton nothing was amiss we are forced out here in the middle of a freezing fucking cold night in Surrey to try and find out just where you've put it all. You know how I hate looking for money that's owed, money that's mine, and you know I hate unnecessary violence. This is what we do for a living. Why would you want to fuck around with that? Risk tipping the balance of a good system, something that benefits all of us? Why would you do that to me, ey, why? After all my generosity.'

Sweat trickles down the bound man's forehead into his eye. He blinks it out, keeping his focus on Vincent.

'So where is it?' Vincent asks, calmly.

The man shakes his head.

'One more time. You tell me where you put it and we'll forget all this. You'll be taken off the street for a few months, pack you off to sunny Spain for some reflection and we'll have you back working Peckham by spring.'

He looks at Vincent blankly. The almost imperceptible cocky shrug is all Vincent needs. He stands, walks over to the window, opens it, leans out and looks up. The stars are sharp and bright. He draws in a lungful of the cold air. It hurts. He looks up at the low-hanging eaves and gutter and reaches his arm out, snapping off an icicle. He leans back in and walks over, opening the palm of his hand, showing the man the ice: five inches long, irregular in shape, tapering to a sharp point. The cold of it in his hand is refreshing. Small drops of water fall, darkening the concrete floor. Gently rolling it between the warmth of index finger and thumb, Vincent sharpens the point further.

'Check the rope will you,' he tells Milton, who follows the order without question, checking the man's bound arms, body and legs.

Vincent rests the sharpened point of ice on the man's face, running its tip down the side of his temple and around his left eyebrow. He turns it, continually honing its tip on the heat of the man's skin. The man closes his eyes, squashing icy, saline tears between lashes.

'Open your eyes, sunshine.' He squeezes them shut. 'Eyes.' Vincent brings the icicle to the corner of the man's tightly shut eye. He pushes the tip gently into the upper orbital ridge.

'No sudden movements, ey. You could have someone's eye out with this.'

Milton snorts a laugh and runs his hands through his hair.

The man's legs begin to shake.

Vincent continues, 'I read in a book once that ice is a perfect weapon.' He pauses for effect. 'All you have to do after you've inflicted your damage is let the evidence melt. Nice and tidy, ey.' Milton walks over, grips the man's head and pulls his eyelid back. Vincent takes hold of the back of his head and gently drives the sharpened length of ice just beneath the bone of his eye socket and over the top of his eyeball. The man bucks his body as much as the rope will allow. His wails are muffled behind the tennis ball. He tries pointlessly to move his head. The rope holds fast. His eyelid is now held open by the ice spike. It continues to slide into the gap between bone socket and eye. It reaches its destination at the back of his optic nerve and continues through. Vincent watches him closely, listening to the deadened, prolonged scream, then twists it slowly. He snaps the spike in two. A long moan like the howl of a distant dog tries to make it out of the man's muzzled mouth. Virtually no sound is heard, certainly nothing beyond the walls of the Spartan room. Streaming tears turn pink then dark red.

'Kind of beautiful,' Vincent remarks.

Milton lets go his hold and sits back down. Thick drops of blood fall silently on to the man's bound, quaking hands.

Vincent coughs a small round of his own cancerous blood into his handkerchief. He watches intently as his protégé drifts into unconsciousness and the last moments of his life.

One

Nick Geneva closes the door with forced gentleness. He wants Emily to know he's the grown-up. It took all he had not to slam it off its hinges and scream at her like a kid. Leaning back against the flaking paint of the door frame, he closes his eyes, enjoying the warmth of the old house.

He'd stood on the freezing cold doorstep for less than a minute taking his two sons from their pissed-off, monosyllabic mother. This is what he's ended up with: weekends and parts of the holidays. It's left him feeling bitter, drunk and victimised. She looked him in the eye like she always did these days and accused him of being stoned again, unfit to look after her kids. But she handed them over anyway.

Nick's love for Emily faded years before they split. Like most of their friends their age, they'd ground the bones of their relationship to dust for the sake of the kids. They dragged out their partnership in grim determination until being together was more damaging than separation. The pain of being alone for Nick was far easier to bear than the

7

daily drama of living with Emily. He takes an in-breath trying to calm the rush of anger inside him.

'Why are you always nasty to Mum?' Zeb leans against the wall heater trying to mimic Nick's pissed-off pose.

'Not all the time, only when she pisses me off.' Nick heads into the kitchen, Zeb follows and continues to question him.

'Never used to be horrible, not when I was smaller, you used to cuddle and stuff.'

Nick looks at him and smiles. 'You're still small. Everything's changed. You know that.'

Nick looks out the window through the bare, street-lit trees. Right now he'd do anything to get out of London. He knows his time is fast running out. The police have been trying to nick him for the last ten years. If he ran now it would have to be alone. So he's staying. Jake and Zeb are the only reason he remains and risks being busted in his own front room day in, day out. He's tired of running. Tired of watching over his shoulder. He's got no one to blame but himself, he knows that.

'Where's Jake?' he asks Zeb.

He isn't really interested in where Jake is. Zeb stands close to Nick looking up at him with a mixture of curiosity and anger. He pauses for effect.

'Said he didn't want to fight with you cos you're stoned. Went upstairs to toss himself off.'

'Why does everybody think I'm stoned?'

'Cos you are,' Zeb replies flatly.

Nick always hopes it will go unnoticed. It never does. He brings his hand to his desiccated mouth and massages his jaw. He smiles to himself and crouches down in front of Zeb, resting his hands on his thin shoulders. He kisses him on the forehead.

'I'm sorry, kid.'

'What for?' Zeb looks confused.

'Fucking it up.'

'It's not your fault. Still got a mum and a dad and now I got two bedrooms, double toys.' Zeb blows his fringe out of his eyes. 'Just stop being nasty to her.'

Nick puts his arms round him and hugs him. He breathes in his son's scent. He hates that Emily baths them so much. Zeb smells better when he's been running around in the woods.

'Dinner.' Nick releases Zeb and stands up.

'What is it?' Zeb asks excitedly.

'Spag bol. That'll get your brother out of his shit stinking room.'

Zeb runs up to the stove, lifts the lid on the pan and draws in the smell.

The kitchen walls, much like the rest of the house, are covered in Persian and Afghan rugs. Candles flicker on most surfaces. An ancient, enamelled Coca-Cola advert with Santa Claus standing by a grandfather clock is nailed to the wall by the door. Zeb and Jake use it for airgun practice. Santa's grinning face is ripped up and pockmarked. Striking photographs of the Highlands and lochs of Scotland line the far wall. The large kitchen table is the most used space in the house.

Nick starts to roll a joint. He licks the papers nonchalantly, looking at the photo of the whitewashed cottage by a loch resting beneath the sprawling mountain landscape. He never tires of the image. If he had the courage he would go there tomorrow. He turns to watch Zeb stir the pasta.

'Did Mum pick up your inhaler refills?'

'They're in my school bag.'

'She gets some things right.'

Zeb picks up a strand of spaghetti from the boiling water and hurls it at the wall. It slides down the back of the cooker. He shrugs and carries on stirring. Nick takes his shoes off and puts his feet up on the table. He lights the joint then starts to massage his foot. 'Where you wanna go for half term then?'

Zeb tuts at the stupidity of the question. 'Disneyland, doughnut.' He takes a block of cheese out of the fridge.

Nick tokes on the joint. 'Anywhere a little less expensive?'

'Not bloody Center Parcs.'

'You swear too much, kid.' Nick flicks his ash neatly into the ashtray.

'I just do what you do innit. Chillax.' Zeb puts the cheese on the table and sits down in front of Nick, instantly bored. He rests his chin in his upturned palms.

'Why not Center Parcs?' Nick asks, knowing the answer.

'Bogus, seen pictures. Pikeys from school go there. I ain't going where stinking Pikey bastards go.'

'What about Scotland?'

'You always say that. You promised Disneyland.' Zeb starts eating the cheese.

Nick looks at the blackened end of the joint and relights it.

'There'll be snow on the mountains.' Nick knows it won't happen. Emily wouldn't let it.

'Can we watch *The Simpsons* after?' Zeb gets up, forks a single piece of spaghetti out of the boiling water and slings it at the wall. It sticks.

Nick relights the joint. 'Get Jake, I'll lay the table.'

Zeb runs up the stairs followed by repeated banging on Jake's bedroom door.

Zeb shouts through it. 'Stop tossing off, you wanker!'

Nick hears a muffled 'fuck off' from the other side of Jake's door.

Two

The large Georgian house is lit at the front by a wide-reaching green light illuminating the ornate pond. In the centre stands a laughing stone boy pissing frozen water. The pond is a tomb of ice. Three of the windows of the house are lit with no movement inside.

The Belgravia street is quiet, no cars passing. Those parked are covered in snow. The snow has thinned to sleet, leaving a grey slush on pavements and kerbs. Nick and Warren Sykes sit in Nick's beat-up Rover. They look straight ahead, smoking, silent, dressed casual, black sweatshirts under Gore-Tex jackets, balaclavas in pockets. They wait a further fifteen minutes. The last person to walk past was an old man, drunk, lurching, dog dragging him along the icy pavement.

Nick and Warren get out of the car. They head round the back of the building in silence. Warren goes first, as always. His heavy body and skill with his hands are essential in the first stages.

Nick finds the wires leading to the alarm and cuts them. The patio doors to the garden and windows are screened with shutters from the inside. Warren takes out a cheap jar of honey and smears the window with half of it. He drops the jar and takes out a roll of newspaper sticking it to the honeyed glass. He begins to push, letting his upper body weight do the rest of the work. The glass snaps in a quiet, wide arc, big enough to get his arm through. He lifts the sash window up and forces the shutters forward, busting the flat steel bar fastened on the other side. They listen for a response, alarms, dogs. Silence. Warren steps in first.

It's obvious to Nick the owner of this oversized house has a lot of money and little taste. The sitting room is a kitsch mix of Habitat plastic, overpriced antiques and too many English oil paintings of sportsmen, their horses and dogs. Nick sees through the facade. He knows the house is owned by a working-class thief made good. No genuine culture in sight, just money. The show of wealth alone is enough to piss him off into wanting to strip Vincent Cracknel of everything he's earned, stolen or borrowed. If only to bring him back to earth. Vincent's name and address were given to Nick in exchange for half an ounce of well-cut coke. The junkie in need of the powder had suffered more violence than was called for at the hands of Cracknel. He was happy to hand him and his house over for a few grams.

Nick and Warren remain silent in their work.

Nick puts the torch in his mouth, heads out into the hall and up the main stairs. Warren heads for the downstairs rooms.

* * *

Nick walks into what must be the main bedroom. He smells perfume and the stale stench of sex. He walks over to the bedside table and lifts up a silver gilt framed picture of a half-naked girl in the arms of an aging man with an over-the-top tan. From the description, Nick knows this is Vincent. The woman, clearly a teenager, smiles excitedly from the prow of a black speedboat.

Nick chucks the frame on the bed.

The décor and photo sum up the man being robbed, cementing Nick's commitment to rip him off for everything of value he can haul out. He moves calmly, systematically through the drawers and cupboards, enjoying the slow surge of adrenalin. He uses his breath to keep calm and focused; something Warren taught him when they were kids. He listens to Warren opening and closing doors and cupboards downstairs. He's reassured by his presence on the job.

Nick loves and hates this work in equal measure. Too far gone in this career to get anything legal, pay taxes, put something aside for a pension, he chose this line of work soon after he arrived back from Scotland with Emily in the autumn of 1993. Two years before Jake arrived, nine before Zeb. He curses her again for dragging them back to London away from the croft in the highlands of Wester Ross. Curses her for not taking his childhood pipe dream to be a writer seriously enough. She never stopped hassling him to get a proper job. When he got one she hassled him when the proper job didn't bring in enough money to live on. So he went back to crime, this kind, turning houses over to make a better living. After a few years driving cars for a psychotic armed robber, Nick grew into wanting something calmer, more befitting his age. For all its drawbacks, his paranoia, the daily fear of arrest, he loves the peace of this work. Anything for a quiet life. Always more welcome than being around people, save Warren and the kids.

He continues to move through the room and comes to a painting of country landscape with three hunting dogs and a squire walking thoughtfully along a river. He pushes the bottom right corner with his finger. He finds what he is looking for. He wonders why they always choose wall safes covered by cheap replica paintings. He lifts it off the wall. He's presented with a three by two empty hole in the wall, no safe; a job half done.

The last place he heads for is the walk-in wardrobe. He slides the doors back to find a rail of expensive suits. He drops to his knees and starts to remove the neatly stacked high-shined shoes from the floor, chucking them into a pile in the middle of the bedroom. He taps the carpet with his torch listening for the change in sound. He finds one and puts the torch back in his mouth, looking for the seam. After a few seconds he finds it and lifts up the carpet. The safe in the floor is bigger than usual but it is still going to be easy to remove. He needs Warren's tools. He backs out into the bedroom on his hands and knees.

What stops him is a sound he knows shouldn't be in the room. Every other noise has its place: clock, boiler, the wind outside. His mind and memory search for what the new sound could be. He tells himself to relax but knows something is wrong. His heart rate increases, the adrenalin now less comforting. He finally figures it out. The sound behind him is breathing. Warren is still searching down-stairs, he can hear him. In the fraction of a second it takes to edge two feet further out of the wardrobe he realises what kind of breathing: a panting, waiting dog. Rapid, panicking questions. How big? Why the fuck didn't it bark when they bust in? He inches round, torch in mouth. He comes eye level with the unblinking Staffordshire pit bull five feet in front of him, mouth open, teeth glistening ragged and grey in the man-made light.

Nick has been bitten by five dogs in the last ten years. Two of these were more of a nip leaving nothing but a bruise. The hyped-up mongrels chased him out of the houses with relative ease. The other three, all pedigree breeds, Rottweiler, Dobermann and wolfhound weren't so straightforward. One sunk his teeth so deep into Nick's thigh he had to stick his finger up its arse to force it to let go. The other two attacked Nick's hand and left arm respectively. Warren threw one out of a closed dining-room window. Nick nearly went with it. Nick stabbed the other in the eye with his pen torch.

Nick loves dogs. Killing the wolfhound brought his thieving to a stop for over a month; until the rent was due.

The aging pit bull lets out a low gurgle and coughs something up on to the carpet. It looks down at it for a moment, confused, then looks back up at Nick. It takes a step forward trying to force a convincing growl.

'You're an old fucker, aren't you?' Nick backs steadily into the wardrobe. 'No sudden moves ey, don't want any trouble. Just gonna take your old man's safe and that'll be it.'

Surprisingly, the dog stops in his tracks, apparently calmed by Nick's words. Nick holds his breath. Then the animal lunges at his face, sinking its smaller, sharper front

17

teeth into his nose and cheek. Nick jerks back automatically, tearing flesh and skin. It rips into three jagged pink flaps. Warm blood runs down his cheek and neck. His arms flail around above him searching for the clothes above his head. He tries to pull himself up. Then the chaos of falling suits, snapping jaws, teeth and blood. Nick prays for intervention.

His plea is met by a high-pitched yelp, followed by the sound of dry retching. Nick stumbles forward catching the first glimpse of Warren outside the wardrobe. He can see Warren's hands clasped firmly round the stricken dog's bollocks. It continues to dry heave, shoulders jerking, eyes wide until it finally throws up into the scattered pile of penny loafers.

'Where the fuck did he come from?' Warren shouts at Nick then at the dog. The dog doesn't respond. It stares down shocked at its last meal.

'Let go of it, Warr, fucking thing looks like it's gonna have a heart attack.'

'I'll give it a fucking heart attack. Chuck the cunt out the window.'

Nick stands up and steadies himself. Warren looks down at the dog and squeezes a little tighter. It screeches, attempting to growl between bouts of retching.

Warren looks Nick up and down. 'You got blood all over you, mate.'

'Keep it down for fuck sake, you'll wake the neighbours.' Nick walks over to the mirror, points the torch at himself and leans forward. He touches the flayed flesh. The adrenalin disguises the pain he knows will come later.

'Can't feel my fucking nose.' He looks at Warren in the

mirror, who is considering his next move with the dog.

Warren talks to Nick's reflection. 'Get some tissues. Over there by the bed. I'd do it but I got me hands full.' He brings his face close to the stricken dog. Nick walks over to the bed.

'Lively one for an old fucker, ain't ya boy,' Warren teases. The animal responds with a low whine.

'Think I know why Spike here didn't come say hello when we first knocked.' Nick dabs the blood from his nose.

'Enlighten me.' Warren kneels down to get a closer look at the animal.

Nick holds the tissue down to clot the blood.

'Old bag of bones is deaf.' Nick manages a half smile.

Warren laughs, finally releasing the dog from his grip.

The dog staggers around for a few seconds, finds his feet then launches teeth and jaws into Nick's bollocks. Nick staggers back, then swings his left foot out. His boot catches the animal square on the jaw.

'Fuck sake Nick you're gonna kill the poor bastard!'

The dog coughs once, collapses and stops breathing.

Nick slumps on to the bed, raising his palm to his forehead. 'Not another one. Only wanted to rob the fucking place. I'm not violent.'

'Nor am I, mate!' Warren looks at Nick, theatrically offended.

'You just killed the man's dog.' Nick rests his head in his hands.

'Hang on a minute, you just booted it in the head, that's what killed it.'

'Not arguing.'

After a moment's silence Nick looks up at Warren, saying nothing.

'What?' Warren is becoming visibly agitated.

'Let's bury it.'

'You're joking.' Warren looks down at the animal without pity.

'I want to bury it,' Nick says solemnly. 'Poor thing deserves more than being left in a pile of boots and puke.'

'You can fucking bury it.' Warren sits down on the bed next to Nick. He checks Nick's eye and nose. 'Found the safe?'

'In the wardrobe; the floor. By the time you get it out I'll be back, help you carry it downstairs.' Nick kneels down on the floor and slides his hands under the dog. He lifts it up with some difficulty. Warren doesn't help. Blood breaks through the clot in his nose and trickles down his face. He heads silently downstairs, out the patio doors and into the garden.

He puts the dog down and walks to the shed at the bottom.

He comes out a few minutes later, spade in hand, looking around the garden for a place to dig.

Warren and Nick head out to the front of the house. As they reach the car the drunkard with the dog saunters past again. He nods at them both.

Nick and Warren get in the car.

'Should we worry about that?' Warren asks.

Nick shakes his head. 'Old cunt's out of his box. He'll be lucky if he makes it home in that state.'

Warren starts the car.

As they drive away the drunkard fumbles in his pocket, dog pulling, takes out a pen and an old envelope and scrawls down the number plate of the Rover P5 as it turns the corner.

Three

Zeb stands in the school playground staring straight ahead. One week to go before half term. He wishes it were Friday and he was in the car with Nick and Jake driving away from this shit tip of a school.

The two boys in front of him are both over a foot taller, one white, one Asian, both scruffy, wearing the remnants of school uniforms. The Asian kid puts his hand on Zeb's shoulder, squeezes hard, grinning down at him.

'You'll be fine Zebadiah shit for brains; won't starve, mate. Anyway your wanker of a dad can pick you up in his stupid old car and buy you a McDonald's after school, innit.'

'Don't eat McDonald's. Ain't giving you my lunch money so fuckoff.' Zeb stares down at the asphalt, waiting for the strike, holding back the tears, trying not to let them see his shaking legs.

The white kid kisses his teeth. 'Raas. Boy's got a mouth on him for a half-pint prick stick. You get five strokes of the wood from Mr Peters for lip like that.'

'Why do you always try and talk like a black man,

Trevor? I'm not giving you my lunch money so piss off.' Zeb knows Nick will come and bash them after school if he asks. It's all he has to do. Pick up his mobile and Nick'll be there.

'Ain't about you having a choice you scrawny fucking hippie.' The Asian kid yanks Zeb's bag off his shoulder. Zeb grabs the strap and yanks it back. The white kid pushes Zeb to the floor.

Zeb feels the impact on his arse. It starts to sting immediately. He looks up, eyes glistening. He can feel his lungs constrict. His breathing quickens.

'Not gonna cry are you Zebadiah? Please don't cry, I won't be able to sleep tonight,' the Asian kid mocks.

Zeb reaches into his bag, scrabbling around inside for his inhaler. He finds it, takes it out and draws on it. His lungs relax.

'Sweet one, blood.' The white bully slaps the Asian kid on the back and nods his head. This is swiftly followed by him getting slapped across the back of the head by a tall, slender black girl, authentically kissing her teeth loud enough for the entire playground to stop ignoring the bullying and start watching.

'Pussy face white boy picking on kid this small deserve a *real* beating.' The white kid holds the back of his head, bent down.

'Come on Joyce,' he protests. 'Was only messing with him, didn't hurt 'im.'

'Don't look like messing to me.' Joyce raises her hand to strike him again. He flinches. She stops mid strike and laughs down at him. Silence falls across the playground for a moment then erupts into laughter as the shamed white kid walks away, head down, followed silently by his friend. Joyce helps Zeb up and gives him his bag.

'You all right?' Joyce asks.

Zeb nods silently.

'Got to stand up to these cowards,' she tells him.

'They're bigger than me,' Zeb protests.

'I'll walk you to the canteen, make sure you get some meat for dem skinny bones.' She smiles at him.

Zeb walks half a step behind her the whole way.

This is the second time Joyce has stepped in to deal with the bullies for Zeb. Jake used to look after him until he went to secondary school. The hyenas take advantage of any opportunity. Zeb is smart outside of school, knows how to keep out of danger. He's grown up in this part of London and is comfortable on the streets day or night. But he struggles with school every day. Classes bore him. He gets a poor report each year. Nick isn't bothered but Emily is. Zeb spends more time staring at the trees outside the first-floor classroom window than he does the chalk on the blackboard. Mostly he's thinking of the end of the day, the week, the term.

His only respite is Sarah Tindle who sits three rows back. Smart, beautiful, almost as tall as Joyce. Zeb thinks about Sarah when he's alone. Especially when he's up in the crown of the trees in Hyde Park. He avoids eye contact with her when he's in class; much as he can. She notices him, smiles at him and sits next to him when they do art. He doesn't know why he likes her or why she sits next to him. Jake teases him to fever about her. Zeb can see her body is nice, curved like a cartoon. He doesn't toss himself off like Jake does. What he likes best about Sarah is the way she moves her lips silently when she reads to herself in reading time. She's always reading, any spare time she gets, in the playground, on the bus, walking to lunch. She's a good reader, better than Zeb, the best in class. She got a prize last year, book tokens for WH Smith. When it's time to read out loud in class she always goes first. She's read in assembly three times. Her voice is sweet. Zeb closes his eyes when she reads out the words, shutting out all other sounds. This is easily the best thing about school. He wishes he could walk with her in Hyde Park. Take her to the big oak by the Round Pond and climb it. The one he sits up in on his own, looking out across the park, imagining what it's like outside London.

'Everyone's talking about it.' Zeb is startled from his thoughts. 'Those nasties bash you again?' Sarah Tindle sits down next to him. He feels his legs and bum tense up. His bum still hurts. She talks like a grown-up. Zeb wishes his voice was deeper, like Jake's.

'Did Joyce help?' she continues. 'She's good with bullies.'

'Yeah.' Zeb is too ashamed to look at her.

'What's up?' She looks at him with concern.

'Nothing.'

'Yes there is, they hurt you? I'll get my brother on to them?'

She leans forward and peers through his fringe. He cannot help breaking into a smile.

'Only my bum . . . they pushed me on the ground. Got

an attack but I had my inhaler.' Zeb still doesn't look up. 'My trousers are ripped.'

'Would you like to come to my house for my birthday party this weekend?'

Zeb thinks his heart just stopped. He sneakily puts his hand on his chest to check.

'Not everyone can come but you can.'

He finds his heartbeat and finally manages to look at her. 'I'll ask my dad, we're staying with him this weekend.' He starts to get his books out of his bag.

'Good. I'll tell Mum you're coming.'

She looks over to two of her mates who lean in shoulder to shoulder, whisper to each other, look at Zeb and start giggling. His face flushes red. The girls break into uncontrolled laughter.

Sarah ignores their reaction, turns the pages of her book and starts to read to herself.

The immaculate, burgundy Rover P5 pulls slowly into the driveway, past the frozen pond to the front of the house where it stops, engine running, lights on. The two passengers sit silent and still, looking at the house.

'S'up, gorgeous?'

The young blonde sitting next to Vincent Cracknel touches his leg with her overmanicured hand; the same blonde grinning naively from the framed photo now lying on the bedroom floor of the house Vincent is now scrutinising.

'Someone's been here.' He looks ahead.

'No one's been here, love. Jasper makes sure of that.'

'Where is he then?'

'Who?'

Vincent takes a breath to stop himself from shouting at her.

'For fuck sake . . . Jasper.'

'He's probably asleep gorgeous, he's old and a bit deaf, ain't he.'

'Why do you always do that?'

'What, love?'

'Every time something's wrong you try an' make it right.'

'Come on, let's go and see, everything's fine, you'll see.'

They get out of the car. Vincent heads to the boot, opens it up and takes out a large bag of golf clubs and two holdalls. His wife takes the holdalls.

He stops and listens a full minute before sliding the key in the lock. He takes a flick knife from his inside pocket and pushes the door open.

'Wait here,' he commands.

He heads upstairs, straight for the bedroom.

He smells the vomit from the landing. As he walks in he puts his hand over mouth and nose and surveys the scene without reaction.

Instinctively, he walks over to the window and looks out across the lawn, along the line of trees, bushes and empty flower beds. At the far end of the garden near the compost heap he notices a raised mound of freshly dug earth, neatly patted down. A spade is propped up against the back fence.

'Thoughtful,' he whispers to himself.

Vincent knows this is no standard break-in. Whoever it was took their time. Confident. He heads to the walk-in wardrobe and looks down into the empty space in the floor. The sound of clacking across the tiled floor downstairs shakes him from his anger.

A few moments later, the pad of his wife's bare feet on the carpet of the upstairs landing.

'Christ, what's that bloody smell?'

Vincent stands by the window. 'He's in the garden.'

'Who's in the garden?'

'Jasper.'

The sound of her cussing and shouting fades. Background noise to the quickly rising grief and rage. He thought he would go before Jasper. He would've preferred it that way. Jasper is worth a hundred safes. He'll get the money back. The violence will come easy. It's one life skill he has in spades. DC Stringer will be useful. Payback for his beloved dog will be another, trickier matter. It will require more than an apology from a thoughtful burglar-cum-gravedigger.

Jake leans against the wall of the main entrance to his school, one foot flat against the graffitied concrete. He does his best not to look interested in any of the girls walking past. He wishes he had his shades. The Marlboro cupped and hidden in his gloved hand is all but finished. He enjoys the last of its heat.

The snow has stopped. The roads have been cleared from the heat of the cars, trucks and buses. He looks up, hating the sky. The chill bites through the ripped knees of his jeans and his legs tremble. He hums 'Don't wanna go to Rehab' to distract himself.

Two teenage girls click-clack past in dangerously high

shoes, look him up and down and tut. Just as he works out a decent dis, Carlos turns the corner and walks towards him. Jake offloads his humiliation onto him.

'Where the fuck have you been?'

'Easy, star. Only getting you the finest weed in town. Chill your boots, blood, this stuff will ease your troubles.'

'Been waiting over a fucking hour! Mr Winston's been hassling me to get me into woodwork.' Jake pushes himself away from the wall and offers his upturned palm to his mate.

'Hope you told the cunt to fuck off.' Carlos slaps him a low five and offers his palm in return.

'You wish. Keys?' Jake quietly prays it will be a yes.

Carlos nods, takes out a packet of cigarettes and offers Jake one.

They start walking. Carlos leads the way.

Mr Winston leans out of the classroom window shouting Jake in. Jake ignores him without difficulty, head down, looking forward to their visit.

Nick drives up to the top end of the lane, stops a moment and looks around calmly. Comfortable with the quiet he reverses the car up past the long line of broken-down garages. As he approaches the end of the lane, Warren emerges from the small door of the lock-up.

Nick flips the boot and gets out. Neither of them speak. Warren checks the end of the lane. The last of the day's light makes it hard to see anything more than the fading outlines of garages and cars.

They take hold of Vincent Cracknel's unopened safe, lift it out of the boot and get it through the garage door in under ten seconds. Both men are out of breath. Nick fingers the dressing around his nose and cheek, smoothing down the medical tape.

'How is it?' Warren asks.

'Sore.' Nick leans down and looks closely at the safe. 'Burn it or blow it?' he asks, eyes fixed on the sturdy-looking box.

'Nothing to blow it with. I'll get the torch.'

Warren heads over to the cabinet and takes out the oxyacetylene torch. Nick continues to inspect the safe, hoping the contents will cover the rent, maybe get him a new car. This size safe usually only carries jewellery, objects, stuff he can sell. Extra work but it's money.

Warren bends down, turns the valve on the burner and takes out his lighter.

It takes less than ten minutes to remove the combination lock. The soft click of the door is a welcome replacement to the roar of the torch. They're greeted by a small pile of papers, and a cloth bag.

'Why does no fucker use cash these days.' Nick shakes his head, taking out the bag. He looks inside. The tacky necklace and earrings were clearly made to fit round the teenage girl's neck. Nick drops them back into the bag and removes the wad of papers. Receipts for sales; he flicks through them.

'Any good?' Warren asks.

'Not much. Stones'll get us a couple of grand. Rest is receipts.' He flicks through them. 'Check this out. Muhammad Ali's fucking boots. Joe Frasier's gloves. Henry Cooper's gumshield. Bet they're fucking fakes. Hasn't this fucker got anything better to do with his time?' Nick chucks them on the floor. Something doesn't fit. He checks the safe again. He looks into the empty space then reaches in and taps the back.

'Bring us over the chisel,' he asks Warren.

Warren chucks over two chisels.

Nick runs the blade along the back of the safe and jams it forward. The plate comes loose.

'Sneaky fucker.' Nick reaches forward, pulls the plate out and sees what he knows are four tightly packed stacks of pink notes.

'What's he got?' Warren asks.

'Fifties. Lots of them.'

Nick takes a small pile for Warren and one for himself, stashes the rest in a carrier bag and puts it into a box behind the cabinet.

'How much?' Warren asks.

'Least thirty grand.' Nick knows this is the job he's been praying for. Now that it's here though, he's left with a bad feeling. The money will get him a lot more than a new car.

'That's more like it.' Warren smiles broadly, slapping Nick on the back.

They tidy away the rest of the mess. Nick puts the jewel bag in his pocket and burns the receipts.

The two men head back to the car. Plans quickly form in Nick's mind.

Jake watches Carlos wrench back the sheet of rusted corrugated iron wide enough for them to get through.

'Better be warm in there, blood,' Jake whispers.

'Build us a fat cone. Warm us up good.' Carlos smiles back at Jake as he climbs through. Jake follows him to the back of the building. Carlos takes out the keys and unlocks the heavy decaying door. The two teenagers disappear inside.

Jake remembers this place as a busy, trendy restaurant when he was a kid. His mum and dad used to take him here every Saturday, before Zeb was born. He remembers the times clearly; sweeter, happier, trouble free. He smells the memory of the food. Same meal, same drink, same cake, every week. The routine made him feel good. Safe.

They walk through what was the main restaurant area, checking out the blackened mirrors, dead wall lights and piled-up furniture. The bones of a huge palm tree droop, long dead, in the far corner. Tables and chairs are stacked up high in the middle of the room covered in dust and debris. No working lights, no electricity. Carlos opens up a drawer by the bar, takes out a candle, sticks it in a glass and lights it. He continues to lead the way, heading out back, up two flights of broken stairs.

Jake hasn't been here since it shut down. There'd always been music, looped, a bit shit but it went with the place. He didn't like this silence.

'Dad stayed here when he worked late.' Carlos's heavy frame looks unsteady to Jake. 'Shagged this damn waitress up here while he was still with Mum. Prick.' Carlos laughs to himself. Jake knows the laugh is covering up anger.

Jake hears rapid splintering followed by Carlos's foot disappearing into one of the stairs. He cries out grabbing the banister.

He shouts out in pain. 'Fucking place's a shit tip!!'

'Fuck that shit. You all right bro?' Jake puts his hand out. Carlos steadies himself then wrenches his foot out.

Carlos bends down, checking his leg, monkey like, looking at the long rip in his darkening skin.

'Shit.' He pulls his sock up and they carry on up the stairs.

They reach the first landing and head in through the first door.

The room is damp, airless and dark. Empty white squares where paintings used to hang mark the walls. The dirt on the windows acts as a solid curtain to the last of the outside light.

'Got some skins?' Carlos sits down heavily on the manky sofa.

'None, bro. Run out.'

'Don't fuck me about.' Carlos rubs his wound.

'Serious.'

'How the fuck we gonna get mash up with no skins?'

Jake shakes his head solemnly. 'Sorry, bro. I fucked up.'

'Damn straight you fucked . . .' Carlos sees the smile break as Jake reaches into his pocket and takes out two new packets of Rizla.

'You wanker.'

'Too easy, star. Need to sharpen that shit out.' Jake chucks him a packet of Rizla tutting and mocking.

Carlos smiles back, shaking his head. He opens his bomber jacket like he's going for a gun and draws out a small, tightly wrapped cellophane bag and begins the ritual of rolling a twelve-skin.

'Hydroponic god-head baby.' Carlos keeps his eyes on the joint. 'Sensomelia of the sweetest order. This shit'll give you visions. Smoke enough an' you'll see monsters, blood.' Carlos chucks the bag over to Jake.

'Fuckoff. Probably some of your brother's homegrown shit.' Jake opens it up and smells it.

'My dad's life.' Carlos marks the sign of the cross on his chest.

'Your dad's dead, bro.'

'Mum then.'

'Hate her much as you did your dad.' Jake brings the bag close to his face, taking a deep breath. 'Fuck. Smells like the bomb!'

'What I say to you? You got to truss your mandem.' Carlos kisses his teeth, concentrating hard on the joint.

Jake takes out two cans of Carlsberg from his jacket, cracks one for Carlos and hands it over. He takes it, nodding respectfully.

'Need some music.' Jake opens his can and drinks. 'Fucking hate getting stoned in silence. Too damn cold in here.'

Carlos completes the joint, rolls it between his fingers, brings it to his ear listening to the crunch of tobacco against bud. Jake flicks the flint of his lighter, bringing the flame to the neatly tapered joint.

Blue smoke rises above Carlos's head, drifting over to Jake. He draws it in, eyes closed, lips grinning.

They smoke, finish the lagers and sit back. Silence fills the room. Jake lets the THC and alcohol creep into his limbs. He worships this feeling. The hassle of homelife and school recede leaving him where he is, on the sofa, staring into space with his oldest, best mate. The smell of the long-gone cooking downstairs grows in his memory. Along with his hunger builds the familiar burn of anger. His busted family. His dad and the fucked-up way he makes money.

Jake lies to everyone except Carlos about what his father does for a living.

Jake stands. 'Let's smash the fucking place up.'

'Fuck you on about, blood?' Carlos's eyes remain shut.

Jake picks up a wooden chair and smashes it against the wall opposite. Carlos snaps his eyes open and jumps up. Splinters rain down.

'You're fucking nuts, bro!'

'Don't talk to me about food. Coming?' Jake heads downstairs. Carlos follows, mumbling, cursing and limping.

They walk back into the restaurant. Jake looks round.

'Come on bro.' Jake points to a pile of chairs at the far end. Carlos walks over, picks one up and chucks it at a mirror. Shards of glass fly out.

'Now that's what I'm talking about.' Jake holds out his palm, Carlos walks back over and slaps it.

'Been wanting to do this for years.' Carlos grins insanely.

They go berserk, hurling chairs and tables round the room. Carlos systematically smashes every remaining wall mirror and light, sending glass three hundred and sixty degrees around the room.

Jake takes out a small can of lighter fluid and pours it on to the pile of broken wood.

'You planned this you fucking psycho,' Carlos stammers, out of breath.

'Like to be prepared innit.'

'Dib fucking dib. Burn it scout boy.' Carlos tears a strip of material from his shirt, flicks the flint, lights it and drops it on to the fuel.

The wood burns quickly.

The two of them stand close, staring wide-eyed into the flames, faces lit orange. They hold the palms of their hands to the rising fire in triumph.

Jake smiles and nods at his friend across the flames. No words needed; feeling happy for the first time in months.

Four

Warren sits smoking a small joint, can of lager in hand. Pleasure seeps through his body. The television flickers in front of him broadcasting a programme he's not taking in. The room is a mess, same as usual. Takeaway cartons and empty beer cans strewn across table and floor. He tidies the small flat once a week for the weekend visits from his kids. He loves them but the rest of the week he sees as *his* time. Time to let go and properly relax. He works nights either with Nick or alone, sleeps most of the day, reads in bed, watches television or listens to the radio.

He and Nick agreed to stash the bulk of the cash for the standard two months before they spend it. The size of the haul was a welcome shock. But it's made him nervous. The death of the dog clinched it. If anything was going to send someone after them, it would be the dog.

Warren flicks the channel making himself more comfortable. *Later With Jools* is as good as anything to help him relax. His head slumps back against the sofa. He lets out a long sigh as Alison Goldfrapp begins to sing. He taps his foot.

The sound is slight at first, like kids whispering, then movement out in the communal stairwell. He tells himself the spliff is heightening his sensitivity, making him paranoid, just the neighbours. He isn't about to move from his newly found comfort and pleasure.

Then creaking against the door. He puts the TV on mute, rests his hands on the skin of his thighs and holds his breath. Just as his mind is telling him he needs to get up and chuck the drugs out of the window a heavy metal object makes impact with the front door; three times in quick succession. The biting sensation around Warren's cock forces him up off the sofa. Panicking, he inspects the damage. The prostitute on her knees on the floor in white suspenders, naked from the waist up, looks at him in surprise and abject apology.

'Shit. You all right, luv? That's never 'appened before. Gave me the shock of my life!'

Warren looks down at the quickly reddening teeth marks, no blood, skin unbroken.

'Get your clothes on.' He picks up the drugs off the table and blows the cocaine on the mirror into thin white dust.

The reinforced front door takes two final blows from the ram before it finally gives, exploding into the hallway rapidly followed by over-the-top, excited male voices barking commands at an army of imagined crooks.

Warren darts around the mess in the room, snatching any traces of drugs he can find, while still cradling his cock in his oversized hand.

Within a few short seconds the room is full of uniformed and plain-clothes police. The only woman out of the eight officers stands in the doorway, hand over mouth, stifling laughter. Warren's cheeks flush in humiliation; drugs in one hand, cock cupped gently in the other.

Jake turns the corner into his street. The pavement is covered in a layer of ice. The weed and beer spin his vision in and out of focus. He does his best to straighten himself out. He's got a lot less strength in his legs than he needs to walk in a straight line. If Nick sees him like this he'll give him another lecture. Jake knows Nick prefers his eldest son indoors, at home where he can keep an eye on him. Cigarettes are a 'no'. Although joints get the green light, Jake would never smoke spliff in front of his father.

He stops and steadies himself, one hand on the black iron railing. The cold metal on his palm sobers him. He looks down through the cast-iron spikes to the basement. His stomach lurches. He breathes fast and shallow, just managing to stop throwing up. He crouches down, sweat beading on his face. The spinning eases.

The slap of trainers comes towards him. He knows the sprint of his younger brother anywhere. Jake rises too quick. Blood rushes to his head. He loses his vision for a second.

'Hey, bro.' Zeb skids on the ice and slides to a controlled stop two feet in front of him. 'Wassamatter, bro? You look like shit.'

'Bad kebab.' Jake wipes the sweat from his forehead.

Zeb gives him a disbelieving look then takes a pull on his inhaler.

'Dad's mashed up his nose he's got a big bandage on it and everything it smells weird like a hospital.'

'Slow down.' Jake lights a cigarette.

'Said he slipped on ice.' Zeb copies Jake's exhale with the cold condensation of his breath.

'Sounds like more bollocks.' Jake blows smoke up into the sky.

'He did!' Zeb protests.

'You see it?'

'I nearly fell over earlier, on the ice. Dad was probably pissed.'

'Where you going?' Jake asks.

'Shops. Dad says he wants two hundred fags, Lucozade and crisps, lots of crisps.'

'It's the weekend, stupid.'

Jake knows Nick only gets the Lucozade and crisps when he's in a good mood. Zeb hops from left to right. 'Need to piss, bro?'

'When I get back. Dad said I could get some chocolate.' Zeb unzips his trousers and starts pissing into the basement.

'Fuck sake, Zeb, I thought you said you could wait.' Jake walks towards the house. The slap of Zeb's trainers fade in the direction of the corner shop.

Nick comes out with the rubbish. Jake drops his half-smoked cigarette into the gutter. He's shocked by the bandage on Nick's face but doesn't show it.

Nick looks at Jake and nods.

'Hey kid. Where you been?'

'With Carlos.'

'You look stoned.'

'Bad kebab.' Jake heads up the steps.

'You can smoke in the house with me – not outside. You don't know what they're fucking lacing it with.'

'And *you* do. Sons don't smoke weed in front of their dads.'

'Stuff I got won't make you look like that.'

'Like what?' Jake curses himself for taking the bait.

'Snow fucking white.' Nick chuckles to himself and walks back in the house, draping his arm across his son's broad shoulders.

Nick parks the car further away than he would like from Warren's. He gets out and heads towards the block. He knows something is wrong. He puts it down to too much weed. The doors to Warren's block are open. He hears footsteps and voices. He carries on walking. As he turns left at the corner he glances back and sees Warren being led by two plain-clothes officers to a waiting car.

Nick keeps walking.

Zeb and Jake are in bed upstairs. Nick sits down at the kitchen table and begins to write. He knows he should just go but he takes his time.

> *Hey kid,*
> *I had to go and see a mate out of London, some urgent business. Take Zeb back to Mum's when you get up. Sorry to mess you about. I'll call you next week. Look after Zeb.*
> *Love you,*
> *Dad*

He folds the note and stands it up against a cup. He walks quietly upstairs to get his bag. He stops and looks at Zeb's door. He opens it carefully and stands in the doorway looking in at the outline of his son under the duvet. His head tells him to turn round and leave.

He slowly pulls the door to.

'Dad?'

Nick stops, hoping he isn't properly awake. He waits a moment then clicks the door shut.

'Dad?'

Nick reluctantly opens the door again. 'It's late, go to sleep kid.'

'What time is it?'

'About two o'clock. Go back to sleep.'

'Why aren't you asleep?'

'I'm going to bed now.'

'Dad?'

'Yes, kid.'

'Where are you going?'

'To bed.'

'No, where are you going really?'

Nick exhales and walks into the bedroom. He sits on the bed. 'You ask too many questions.'

Zeb sits up. 'You said asking questions was good.'

'I know.'

'When will you be back?'

'Soon.'

'I know you're fibbing.'

Nick strokes Zeb's hair, figuring out what to do. Raids are done at dawn. He has to leave.

'I have to go and see a mate out of town. Jake's taking you to Mum's in the morning. I'll call you when I get there.'

'I want to come with you.'

'You can't, kid. It's business. You'll get bored.'

'I won't. I can read my book and stuff.'

'Sorry, kid. I'd like you to, you know that, but I have to see him on my own.'

Nick sees tears welling up in Zeb's eyes.

'Come on, kid. I'll be back soon . . . I'll take you to the Imax.'

'Don't wanna go to the shitting Imax. Wanna go with you.'

Nick runs through the options. How long he will be gone. Where he will go. He has no idea. He could take Zeb for a few days then put him on a train back to London. Stupid idea. Maybe get Jake to come pick him up. Forget it. Leaving him and Jake is the last thing he wants to do right now. He sits looking at Zeb for a long moment. Zeb moves forward and hugs him. He starts crying into Nick's chest. Nick knows he cannot take him. And he knows he can't leave him. He's fucked if he does and fucked if he doesn't.

'Get dressed, pack some clean clothes. You can come for a few days.'

'Yes!' Zeb punches the air, flings the duvet aside and jumps off the bed.

Nick knows he's being insane. *Fuck it*. It'll blow over before he knows it.

'Keep it quiet. Don't wake Jake.'

'Can't he come?' Zeb asks, surprised.

'Maybe when we get there he can come up on the train. Don't wake him up.'

Zeb and Nick head out on to the landing. Nick heads down the stairs first. Zeb follows quietly behind.

'I have to get my book!' Zeb whispers. Nick stops and waits on the stairs.

Zeb heads back in and slams his bedroom door shut on his way back out. He looks at Nick in an alarmed apology.

Nick waves him down the stairs.

As they reach the bottom, Jake's bedroom door opens. Nick and Zeb look up.

'Fuck's going on?' Jake scratches his arse. His eyes widen as he spots Zeb and Nick fully dressed, bags in hand. 'Where the fuck are you two going?'

'Dad's taking me with him to see his mate. We'll be back in a few days. Wanna come?'

Jake looks dumbfounded at Nick. 'Serious?'

'I was going alone. I left you a note but Zeb woke up . . .'

'You can't just get him out of bed in the middle of the bloody night, Dad.' Jake slides down the wall, angry, half asleep. 'This is fucked up.'

'I was going to write you another note.'

'Dad didn't take me out of bed, I want to come.' Zeb stands in the hall holding his bag.

Jake scowls down at Nick. 'Mum won't have it.'

'It's a few days. She'll be cool . . .'

'No she won't, you know she won't.'

'Come with us!' Zeb shouts up.

'No chance.' Jake shakes his head.

Nick knows this is a bad idea. He also knows Jake will be able to keep an eye on Zeb. And he in turn will be able to keep an eye on Jake. Win–win. His mind is made up.

'Come?' he asks Jake.

Jake looks straight at him. 'You're mental.'

'We can go to the seaside. It'll only be a few days.'

Jake doesn't reply.

Nick continues, 'I'll put on a brew, give you a few minutes to think about it. We need to get moving.'

Zeb lies asleep on the back seat. Jake sits in the passenger seat blowing breath on the side window, writing his name in the white mist. Nick tunes the stereo to 6 *Music*. John Martyn's soft voice fills the car.

Jake shakes his head in despair. 'Can I put a CD on?'

Nick ignores him, humming to himself.

The motorway ahead is clear of snow. The countryside left and right stark white.

'Where are we going exactly?' Jake asks without looking at him, writing more words into the mist.

'Told you, Brecon Beacons, Wales.' Nick turns the radio up.

'Must be serious.'

'Someone's in trouble.' Nick knows Jake can tell when he's lying.

'Why's it gonna take two days?'

'We'll stay in a B and B.'

'You're in trouble aren't you?' Jake stares out of the window, bored.

'I will be if we don't get there by lunchtime.'

'Not buying it.'

'Don't have to, kid.' Nick doesn't hide his irritation. He presses down a little harder on the accelerator.

'Police after you? Rob the wrong nutter?'

'Don't get cocky. Pass me a fag, will you?'

Jake reaches into the glove compartment, takes the

cigarettes out, lights up, taking a long drag for himself before passing it to Nick.

'Want one?' Nick rarely offers Jake a smoke.

Jake pretends not to be surprised, happy even. He lights up and sits back in his seat.

'Why can't you get a proper job like all the other dads?'

'We ain't made that way, you know that.'

'You're not made that way. I'm going to college, get myself a real job. Get a house.' Jake takes a slow drag from his cigarette.

'I'm proud of you, kid but don't ever mistake me for one of those muppet middle-class wankers who push their kids into university. Not many dads like me, you should make the most of it.'

'You didn't answer the question.'

'Few days out of the smoke, help out a mate then we can head into the mountains for some walking. It'll be good, clean air in our lungs.' Nick blows smoke into the windscreen.

'I'm not an idiot. Why do you lie to us all the time?' Jake opens his window and flicks ash into the night. 'What happened to your face?'

Nick knows Jake won't buy the ice story he sold Zeb.

'Some wanker cut me up on North End Road. Took on more than I could handle. Fucker came at me with a potato peeler.'

'What happened to him?'

'Left three of his front teeth stuck in the tarmac. Don't tell Zeb. It'll give him nightmares.'

He sees Jake out of the corner of his eye nodding in belief and a little approval. Zeb stirs in the back.

'Shut the window, bro! Bloody freezing!' Zeb pulls himself up and leans into the space between the two front seats. 'We there yet?'

'Bout another two hours,' Nick replies, squinting at the road signs.

'I need a piss.' Zeb looks at Jake. 'How come he's smoking a shitting cigarette, you said fags will kill us?'

'He's old enough now.' Nick leans across and ruffles Zeb's hair.

'Can we stop for a piss, Dad?'

'Never known anyone piss so much.' Nick feels a judder on the steering wheel. 'We'll stop at the next services, have a cuppa and a sandwich.'

The judder intensifies.

Jake tuts. 'Is this heap of shit gonna break down?'

'Treat her with respect, kid, no cussing, she's sensitive.'

'I really need a piss,' Zeb whines.

The judder becomes a shudder, starting at the bonnet and working its way to the roof.

'Maybe you need to slow down,' Jake mocks.

'It's not the speed it's the cold. Engine's freezing.'

'Maybe we should pull over, Dad, then I can have a piss,' Zeb chips in. 'I'm hungry.'

'We'll have a look when we get to the services.' Nick takes his foot off the gas. The car shudders harder, followed by a loud banging then it begins to slow down of its own accord. Nick is forced to pull into the hard shoulder. As the car comes to a stop, Zeb clambers manically over the seats, tumbling over a grumbling Jake and out of the passenger door. He slips and skids as he heads for the verge, straightens up and unzips.

'Ahhhhh! Now that's what I'm talking about, star!! Nearly pissed my pants.' Zeb looks over his shoulder and winks at Jake. Jake gets out of the car, takes a last drag on his fag and flicks it into the passing traffic.

'Bloody taters out here!' Zeb shouts over the roaring cars. Jake joins Zeb, pissing spirals into the snow. 'I want at least two sandwiches, cheese ham and tuna and three cups of tea.' Jake shoulder shunts Zeb. Zeb staggers and falls over, still pissing.

'Dad! Jake made me piss on my trainers!'

'Grasses don't last five minutes on the street, dufus,' Jake hisses.

'So I'll stay out here in the snow and I'll shit in your shoes when you're asleep.'

'Kill you dead before your trousers down.'

Zeb pisses his last two squirts on to Jake's legs and shoes.

'You little FUCKER!! COME 'ERE!'

Zeb flips his flies up and runs along the verge for a few yards then high jumps over the wooden fence into the field. Jake follows, slower, vaults the fence and tumbles over the other side into a two-foot snow drift. He struggles to his feet. Zeb is already almost out of sight sprinting into the darkness screaming and laughing, arm raised, 'wanker' gesticulating at Jake who trudges after him shouting obscenities.

Nick remains in the car, looking ahead. He wonders if Warren's talked. Dumb thought. He never talks.

This is it then. You did it. And you got the kids. You stupid, useless prick.

He sees the image of the croft in Wester Ross in his mind

and sits back. It's a long way. Jake will kick off, he knows that. Whatever he does he has to keep everything calm. Zeb will be easy to handle. Jake won't.

He beeps the horn three times.

Zeb runs in a wide arc, taunting Jake as he heads back to the car. Jake lumbers, out of breath, a few yards behind.

Five

Warren sits in the small, airless room looking at the door. He has no idea how long he's been sitting here. Cell boredom kills him. He regrets not enjoying the hooker more.

After what feels like an hour, keys stumble in the lock. The door swings open. Pale strip-lighting floods in. Warren shields his eyes to protect the rising hangover. Two men walk in. One has a tray with tea and biscuits. He doesn't know which one is going to be the arsehole. He looks at them and concludes probably both.

'Good to see you again, Warren. Always nice when the punter makes the job easy.'

Warren doesn't respond.

They sit down. The younger one pushes a polystyrene cup of tea across the table towards Warren.

The bigger of the two takes charge and speaks.

'My name's Detective Sergeant Stringer. Cigarette?'

'Cheers.' Warren looks straight at him.

'Slightly embarrassing situation . . . in your flat. For you anyway, made my fucking week.' Stringer laughs to himself. He lights a cigarette. The younger officer stays quiet.

'You gonna charge me?' Warren asks flatly.

'We can do that, sure. Just a matter of what we're charging you with.' Stringer takes a thoughtful toke on his cigarette then continues. 'Seen Nick lately?'

'Last week. We're not working together if that's the next question.'

'Would've thought it would be part of your pre-release agreement . . . to stay away from each other.' Stringer shrugs and takes a sip on his tea.

'Neither of us are stupid enough to start working again.' Warren sits back in his chair.

'No . . . course not, that would be stupid. But – you see, we had a lead telling us different.'

The alcohol and coke have worn off. Warren does his best not to look disturbed. He's now feeling properly hungover.

'See, thing is you were seen leaving Cracknel's place. And there's something about a dog. Not good.' Stringer shakes his head.

'No idea what you're talking about.' Warren wonders if they already have Nick.

'Where is it then?' Stringer asks.

'What?' Warren knows they will have enough to keep him locked up.

'The money. It's not in your flat. It's not at Nick's, nor is he for that matter.'

'Do what you want, mate. Can't help you.'

'But you wouldn't, would you?' Stringer continues. 'Fucked off the wrong people with this one. Cracknel's a known nutter. I'd hate to get on the wrong side of him. Used to be a boxer. Done twelve years for ABH already.

Inside's probably the best place for you.' Stringer sits back.

Warren sips his tea and thinks. Whatever happens it'll be six months. He'll keep his mouth shut for now; see how this unfolds.

The two officers stand, finish their tea and head out. Just before he closes the door Stringer turns.

'They got Narcotics Anonymous meetings in there now . . . and help with sex problems. Keep you busy.' He winks at Warren. 'With any luck you'll come out a changed man.'

The door clicks shut and is locked.

Warren tries to relax his muscles. He rests his head in his hands and lets out a despairing breath.

Nick lifts the bonnet and looks in; too dark to see properly. He flicks his lighter into flame. The engine is no more than a mass of metal to him. Jake stands beside him. Zeb jumps in the car, covered head to toe in duvet.

'What is it?' Jake asks, genuinely interested.

'An engine.' Nick scratches his chin.

'I know it's a fucking engine, what's up with it?'

'No idea. Think it's fucked.'

'I'll walk down and call the AA?'

'Too far and too cold.' Nick shuts the bonnet.

'Can't stay here all night.' Jake walks back to the car. Nick follows.

They sit drinking cold tea from the flask.

Eventually Jake and Zeb fall asleep. Nick keeps his eyes on the road, exhausted, unable to sleep.

* * *

Two hours pass.

An LDV van pulls into the hard shoulder a hundred yards ahead of them. It reverses up to the car. A large, bearded man climbs out and walks towards them, zipping up his jacket against the wind.

Nick winds the window down and leans out.

'Know anything about engines?' Nick asks.

'I'll have a look. Worst comes to worst I'll tow you.'

It takes LDV man twenty minutes to get the engine going. Nick offers him a fifty. He refuses.

'Best get yourself a new car. This one's close to dead as you get.'

Nick nods and thanks him.

They head into the breaking dawn, Jake awake, Zeb asleep in the back and Nick doing his best to keep his eyes open.

Emily struggles into her flat loaded with bags of shopping, kicks the door shut and walks into the kitchen.

She hopes she hasn't woken Frank.

She takes her time unloading, keeping quiet.

Cupboards half full, the phone rings. Her sister always calls same time, every day.

'Hey.' Emily sits on the stairs, grateful for the rest.

'How's it going, you OK?' Sally asks.

'Knackered.' Emily is comforted by her voice.

'Food for the five thousand?'

'Just loading the freezer. They'll be back tonight.' Emily puts the kettle on. 'Need more money from Nick to keep up with the food they put away.' She continues unloading the shopping.

Sally's tone drops. 'Still messing you around then?'

'A lot less than when he was here. I can handle him. He's back on the weed though. Bloody knew that wouldn't last.' Emily makes the tea.

'I never liked him.'

'Rubbish. You flirted with him any chance you got.'

Silence.

Emily continues. 'Feel a bit sorry for him actually.'

The doorbell buzzes twice.

'Hang on, Sal.' Emily puts the phone down, walks into the hall and opens the door. The man standing in front of her is well dressed, polo neck, blazer, smart trousers, shined shoes. She dislikes him and fears him immediately.

'Emily Peters?' Milton smiles warmly.

'Can I help you? I'm in the middle of something.' She does little to hide her dislike, hoping he'll pick up on it and leave.

'Won't take a minute, it's about Jake.'

Her stomach lurches.

'What about him?' She knows the news must be bad.

'He's got himself into a spot of trouble.'

'Are you a policeman?'

'Not exactly, but I am here to help sort things out.' He extends his hand. 'Trevor Williams. Mind if I come in for a sec, bit cold out here?'

'I'm not letting a complete stranger into my house, can we do this here?'

'I'm a friend of Nick's. He said you would want to know.'

Everything in her body tells her not to trust the man in front of her. She stands looking at him and he looks back, smiling inanely. It would be very easy to slam the door in his face. *What about Jake?* she asks herself. She opens the door wider.

'Have a seat in the lounge. Through there.' She heads back into the kitchen and picks up the phone. 'Sally, it's Jake, I'll call you back.'

'What is it?' Sally asks. 'You sound stressed.'

'Probably been setting fire to things again. I'll call you later.'

Emily hangs up and heads into the sitting room. Milton has made himself comfortable on the sofa, legs crossed, hands resting on knees. He looks up at her expectantly.

'So what is this, is he in trouble? I'm sorry but who are you, Nick never mentioned you?'

'Any chance of a cup of tea, cold's got into my bones?' She wants to refuse, just find out what's happened to Jake and get him out as quickly as possible.

'Kettle's just boiled. Milk and sugar?'

'White and one please, love.' The word 'love' completes her judgment. She turns, feeling his eyes on her back. Goosebumps rise on her arms. She hums like it's OK, knowing it isn't. She goes into the kitchen to make the tea.

She heads back in with two cups.

'Mind if I smoke?' Milton asks, reaching into his pocket.

'Prefer if you didn't . . . but if you must.' She hands him the tea and gets an ashtray. She watches him handle the silver cigarette case methodically, taking his time.

'Look, I don't mean to be rude but can you tell me what this is about? I've got a lot on.'

'We're all busy, love. Bit of patience wouldn't go amiss.'

'I beg your . . . sorry?' The atmosphere in the room shifts. The power Emily should feel in her own home now belongs to the stranger sitting opposite. She is finding it harder and harder to speak, to be clear. She steels herself.

'Who are you and what the hell's going on with my son?'

'So many questions.' Milton lights his cigarette, looking at her through the rising smoke. 'It's actually less about Jake, more about Nick.'

'What?' Momentarily confused, definitely pissed off, now spurred by anger. 'For fuck sake what is this? Is this what it's all about? Does he owe you money? He owes a lot of people money, including me. I can't help you . . . Christ . . . I really don't appreciate you coming to my house asking me for money Nick owes you.'

'I didn't say anything about money.'

'Well whatever it is I want you to leave . . . now.' Emily stands, hoping he'll follow her lead. He stays seated. She begins to panic. 'Has any of this actually got anything to do with Jake? Is he in trouble or not?'

'Your husband is, no doubt.'

'He's not my husband. Look . . . please, will you leave.'

'When I've got what I've come for, sure.'

Sweat trickles down Emily's back.

'My boyfriend's upstairs, he does . . . he does judo. He won't be happy to see you I promise you that.'

'I don't give a fuck what he does.'

Milton stands and walks over to her. She is immobilised by fear.

He brings his lips to her ear. 'Your cunt of an ex killed my boss's dog.'

'What?' Tears begin to roll down her cheeks. If she could raise her hands to push him back, she would.

'He loved that dog . . . like family.'

'Please . . . go.' Her body trembles uncontrollably.

'Where is he?'

'Who?'

'Please don't fuck me about.'

'N . . . Nick?' Emily tries to take a deeper breath.

'Yes, Nick.'

'He's got the kids . . . for the weekend.' *Jake must be OK. He has to be.*

'He's not at home.'

'He must be out . . . with the kids.'

Milton steps back. 'I wish I had more time to talk but I have to be getting on. You really shouldn't let them loose with him, he's reckless.'

His shift from anger to calm in a heartbeat scares her even more. She doesn't speak.

'I've no interest in the kids. That would be wrong,' he continues. 'If you can help, it would be a good idea. It's far better I get to Nick before my boss does, he's far less discriminating . . . and patient.' Milton takes out a piece of paper. He writes his number down and leaves it on the side.

'Call me if you have any thoughts, anything at all.' He walks into the hall, towards the front door.

The upstairs bedroom door opens. Frank walks down

the stairs, bleary-eyed. Emily stands in the doorway, mascara running down her cheeks. Frank looks at her then Milton.

'Fuck's going on, Em? Who's this?'

'It's OK, sweets. Friend of Nick's. He's leaving.' Emily tries to hide her eyes with her hand.

'He touched you?' Frank straightens up and jogs down towards Milton. 'This prick hurt you?' He reaches punching distance when Milton jerks forward and head-butts him once on the bridge of the nose. Frank drops to his knees. Blood seeps through his clenched fingers.

Milton smoothes his hair, takes one final look at Emily and closes the door quietly behind him.

Jake sits on the bed staring out of the window. Zeb is on the floor reading his battered copy of *The Hobbit*. Nick walks out from the bathroom, drying his hair.

Jake looks at him and shakes his head. 'Been raining two days, Dad. Where's the man you were gonna meet?'

'His plans changed.' Nick doesn't look Jake in the eye. 'Now we're here we can hang out. Go for a walk.'

'When we heading back?' Jake asks impatiently.

'Not just yet.' Nick starts to get dressed. Zeb stops reading and scrutinises him.

Jake snaps. 'Don't fuck about, Dad. When are we heading back?'

'We're heading up North for a while.'

Zeb sits up. 'I've got school in the morning, cookery, we're making apple cake.'

'Fuck sake. I knew this would happen.' Jake stands up.

'You have to take us back to Mum's tonight. She'll call the police.'

'No she won't.'

'Why not?'

'Spoken to her. Told her we're gonna stay here a few more days. Said I'll call the school.'

'You are such a fucking bullshitter!' Jake glares at him.

'Cool!' Zeb jumps up and heads over to the window. 'I want to walk up *that* mountain tomorrow, even if it's pissing it.'

'It's not a mountain, Zeb, it's a hill and I'm not going up on it.' Jake looks at Nick and shakes his head again in disgust. 'I don't want to be here. We've been stuck in this shit heap for two days. Fuck sake, Dad, you can't do this shit.'

Nick knows Jake is making perfect sense. A familiar guilt builds in his gut. He does his best to ignore it. He can't afford to listen to sense right now. He has to get further up North; as far away from London as possible. There's enough money to make it good. *They'll get used to it*. He's sure of it, prays for it. Maybe one day Jake will see this was the best he could do in a fucked-up situation. He needs Jake to keep an eye on Zeb.

'We'll find somewhere better,' Nick replies.

The last time his eldest son looked at him the way he is now he took a swing at Nick. Jake won't be doing it again, not for a while. Not until he's grown eye level at least.

'You're gonna have to loosen up, kid. Nothing's as bad as you think it is. I'll roll us a joint.' Zeb will be convinced by the ease and calm front he's putting on but he knows Jake no longer believes it.

'Not interested.' Jake ruffles Zeb's hair. Zeb smiles up at him. 'You're smoking too much weed.' Jake doesn't look at Nick. 'Probably half the reason we're up here. Paranoid to fuck.' He gets up and brushes Nick's shoulder as he walks out of the room. Nick doesn't react.

Zeb wipes the condensation off the window and squints out across the garden to the fields and hill beyond.

The landlady of the guest house glares at Nick and Zeb, waiting angrily for Nick to reply. Nick carries on smoking.

'I'm afraid you can't smoke here, Mr Harris.'

Jake stands by the fence fifty yards back.

Zeb tugs on Nick's jacket and whispers in his ear, 'Why's she calling you Mr Harris? That's not your name.'

'We're in the garden,' Nick replies. 'Can't be a problem smoking out here can it?'

'Dad, just put it out,' Jake calls across. 'Let's go to the pub, I'm starving.'

'If you don't put it out I'll have to get my husband,' she continues.

Nick looks at her, takes a final toke on the joint and gestures to Jake to take it. Jake ignores him.

The landlady sniffs the air. Her stern expression drops in shock.

'Are you smoking drugs, Mr Harris?' Nick shrugs. 'Right, I'm calling the police.' She turns back towards the house.

Nick stubs the joint. He and the boys head silently back to the house.

Nick packs the bags.

'We should go. I can eat later.' Jake takes hold of Zeb's

hand. Zeb pulls away and runs ahead.

Nick wants to go to the pub to make a point. He doesn't want to be seen to be running. Which is ridiculous because that's exactly what he's doing.

'You're right, kid. Go get Zeb. I'll get the car.'

Six

Zeb hops from boulder to boulder. Old trees lie broken across the path.

'Watch yourself on the ice, we don't want you smashing your head open, ey.' Jake grimaces looking like a ghoul.

'Shut up! How far is it?' Zeb looks ahead.

'Not far, two more fields. This is gonna blow your pea-sized mind.'

'Don't believe you. You're winding me up. You're always winding me up.'

'You'll see.' Jake walks ahead.

'Is it properly dead and rotting and shit?'

'It's definitely dead, blood.'

'Dad says we're going to be crying jellic freezed and live forever, that's why he has to nick so much money, to put it in a bank for when we're old.'

'That's bollocks and you know it. What the fuck's crying jellic freezed?' Jake walks in the spaces between the boulders, cigarette in mouth, can of beer in hand. The sun still has a good hour of light left.

'Crying jellic. With all smoke and ice and stuff.'

'You mean cryogenic.' Jake laughs. 'Don't be fucking silly. Only person who can afford that shit is Walt Disney. His head's in a freeze tank waiting for the time when they got the technology to wake him up, bring him back to life. That's some sick shit.'

'I know, Dad told me. Crying jellic.'

They climb through the crumbled opening of a dry stone wall. Jake continues to lead the way. Zeb kicks the lowest part of the wall deliberately trying to break it apart. Jake watches, amused, as Zeb tries to tone down the shiny white of his new trainers.

'Come on, plonker, be dark soon.' Jake continues to lead the way.

'Where is it then? This is bloody boring.' Zeb stops kicking the wall. Jake beckons him on.

They climb over two more walls, across a field and over a locked gate. The next field is rougher, covered in frost. Jake walks on while Zeb clambers over the gate.

'Oi, bastard head, wait!' Zeb sees Jake stop a hundred yards ahead, squatting over a large black and white object. He pokes it with a long stick. Jake's left hand covers his mouth and nose. Zeb runs up to him. He gets halfway, stops dead in his tracks and stares dumbstruck.

The bleeding eyes of the dead Friesian cow look up at him, milky and calm.

'Come on, scaredy cat, it ain't gonna do anything.' Jake's voice is muffled by his cupped hand. 'Fucker's dead!' He stands up. 'Got something else to show you.' He chuckles, continuing to poke and prod the cow as he walks to her rear end.

Zeb sees two frozen tears of blood on black fur. He looks

over to his brother, amazed at his ability to mess about with it so easily.

Jake starts to speak to the cow. He pokes the stick into its rump, twisting it to the rhythm of his chant.

'Dead, dead, dead. Dead as a fucking dead and long-gone dodo. Ain't going milking no more, are you, mate.'

Having stared transfixed for a full minute, Zeb finally manages a single dry blink, then whispers, 'How long's it been dead?'

'She can't hear you, you plonker. Found her this morning when you and Dad went to the shops. Scared the shit out of me at first . . . you get used to it.'

'How'd you know it's a her?' Zeb feels his fear ease a little.

'Show you . . . come round here. Best bit.'

Zeb walks tentatively down from the head and stands next to Jake. The stench is almost too much to bear. Zeb copies Jake, covering nose and mouth.

Jake looks down in mock-penitent silence. Zeb opens his mouth. No sound comes out. He starts to breathe faster, trying to catch his breath. He trips back over a log and lands hard on the ice. Jake squats down bringing his face close and prods. Zeb takes out his inhaler and takes three quick hits. He looks through the gap between Jake's skinny legs. He makes out the head and shoulders of a surprised-looking calf, half in half out of its dead mother, still covered in the opaque skin of afterbirth. A fat purple tongue pokes out rigid. Zeb is quiet, continuing to stare. Jake continues to prod and inspect.

'Never seen nothin' like that before ey, bro?' Jake shouts excitedly.

Zeb doesn't answer. He gets up and crouches behind Jake's protective back, arm over nose and mouth. Jake bends down and smells its head.

After a few silent minutes they get up and back away. They walk slowly back to the gate.

Jake speaks first.

'If you could die – any way you wanted, bro, how would you go?'

'I don't want to die.'

'You said you were going to have your head frozen like that freak Walt.'

'Don't want to die.' Zeb's lips quiver. Jake puts his arm round his shoulder. Zeb is reassured by his brother's affection.

'What did it smell of?' Zeb asks.

'Chocolate . . . chocolate and dead, rank fish.' He pauses for thought. 'Funny?'

'It's not funny, it's shitting nasty.'

'Funny dying before you're born.'

Zeb is terrified of dying. It keeps him awake at night. He holds back his tears.

'Jake?'

'Yes.'

'How would you like to die?'

'Wouldn't. But if I could choose, I'd be wrapped up in bandages, like a mummy.'

Zeb looks back to the cow and stops.

'Do you really want to go home?' he asks Jake.

'Soon.'

'I want to go with Dad. We can get a goat.'

'Dad hasn't got a fucking clue what he's doing.'

'We can camp. You're good at camping and stuff.'

'I'll keep an eye on you, bro. Know that.'

They head back through the fields, Jake's arm round Zeb's shoulders, easy in each other's silence. Zeb does his best to shut the image of the calf and her mother from his mind.

Vincent Cracknel grips the phone gently, talking quietly.

'You'll get paid when you get me what I need, Stringer.'

'We've given you their addresses. Warren's inside, that's all we know.'

'You gave me an empty house and a connection to an ex-girlfriend. Neither were value for money.' Vincent takes a sip of the warm whisky.

'You saw her?' the voice continues.

'Waste of time.'

'Not sure what else I can get you. Hard enough getting her address.'

'Find out where he is and I'll chuck you a bonus.'

'There is some good news.'

Vincent's voice is flat and calm. 'Fill me with joy.'

'Warren's in Pentonville. I'm sure he'll help out.'

'Get me a visiting order. I'll come myself.'

'I'll see what I can do.'

Vincent puts the phone down and gets stiffly up.

He looks at himself in the sitting-room mirror, at his greying hair and sagging pale skin. He grimaces at his reflection, turns the table light off and heads out into the hall. The photographs on the side table come into view.

He picks them up in the same order every time. The ritual calms him, reminds him of his roots; keeps him going. He looks at the side-on shot of his young black and white body, hands dressed in oversized boxing gloves, a forced angry glint in his eye. He opens the back of the frame and takes out the faded newspaper clipping with his picture on it. He opens up the folded edges and reads the 1980 tabloid headline.

BLACK THUNDER FROM DOWN UNDER BEATS
GREAT WHITE HOPE VINCE CRACKNEL TO A PULP.

He reads to remind him of what he was. Same thing every week for the last thirty years. He looks back at himself in the mirror and sees what he's become. The resentment and regret give him all the energy he needs.

Further along the table are trophies, signed photos, boxing shorts and gloves in glass cases. Objects of desire. This kind of iconography has made an exceptionally good living for him over the years. He never thought dealing in the sports memorabilia of the dead would make so much so soon after his dream to be a middleweight champion evaporated in front of his bloodied eyes. His aspirations of making glory money hammering heads was replaced by dealing and stealing the highly prized chattels of certified, bona fide, sports stars. The objects on the table all reminders of what paid for the house, the car, the wife. Keeps his feet on the ground.

His initially bitter slide into working for the seedier side of London's underworld was slow. Over the last three decades he has grown to love the work, respect it, even if outlawed. The punter's hunger for the connection to sporting greats never satisfied. An addictive religious fervour Vincent can easily understand. You have to identify with your customer, with the product. Much like any other religion, this trade sees vast sums of money exchanged for objects whose origins can never be verified, least of all by the dead. The icons are as close as he will ever get to genuine greatness and he knows it. He has risen to the top of his game through savvy and violence. He is respected throughout London.

He notices the empty space where his Sugar Ray trophy should be.

He puts his palm down flat where it was and closes his eyes.

Money. Dog. Sugar Ray. All gone at the hand of an amateur. Nick Geneva was going to be a rewarding experience.

He puts the newspaper clipping back in its frame and returns it to its place on the table.

He walks out of the patio doors into his garden. The house behind him now empty. He likes the garden the best. He's proud how he's shaped it over the years. The colour, the care, the detail. The daffodils will be in flower before he knows it. He takes a deep breath, steps off the veranda and walks slowly across the lawn.

As he reaches the end, cold rain begins to fall. He ignores it, stepping on to the gravel path, walking towards the compost heap. He stops and looks down, prodding the freshly dug mound of earth with his shoe. He walks over to the fence and picks up the shovel and looks at it, wondering how big Nick Geneva's hands would be. *Did the digging wear him out?* Why would he come into this house, turn it upside down, take his money, kill his dog and then take the time to bury him?

The edges of the hole are neatly cut into the earth; the mound flattened down and levelled out. Vincent can see the thief felt guilt, remorse, trying to show some respect with the burial.

Too late for that.

He takes the spade in his gloved hands and begins to dig, trying to jam the blade in the hard ground with his boot. The frozen crust of earth doesn't break. He leans his body weight down until the spade sinks in up to the hilt. He lifts the first chunk of earth away. He continues for five exhausting minutes. Finally the spade reaches the definable softness of what he knows is Jasper. He stops a moment then clears the earth away carefully. He takes a trowel out of his pocket, kneels down and scrapes the damp earth away from the tidy bundle. He reaches down and lifts it out of the ground. The smell of decomposition fills his nose. He dry retches, forcing tears into his eyes.

He feels something moving in the palms of both hands. Split-second thoughts fly.

He drops the bundle on to the path and steps back. He looks down filled with grief and rage. He rattles out a cracked cough, covering his mouth. As he moves the blanket with his foot, he sees a mass of half-inch white maggots heaving across the ground, over the blanket and the exposed flesh and fur of the dead animal. The retch reaches the top of his throat. He turns away, gagging.

'For fuck sake.' He walks over to the wheelbarrow and brings it to the corpse, slides the spade underneath, staggers for a second then lifts it up, dumping the dog into the wheelbarrow. He heads just to the left of the veranda and begins to dig a fresh grave into the neatly cut grass; just next to where the daffodils will rise.

Zeb picks up the stick and looks at it. A bluebottle is stuck to one end. Something soft and brown holds its legs down. Its wings buzz frantically. He turns stick and fly upside down and brings it to his nose. No smell. He wants to pull the fly's wings off its body but something stops him. He enjoys watching it trying to get free. The air around his face is cold. His bare feet numb. He walked out here alone, through the wood, the broken wall and two fields. He felt like he was being followed and thought Jake was sneaking up, trying to freak him out. Every time he looked back he was met with nothing but the sound of the wind in the trees. The cold on his feet forced him to keep moving.

He sits on the log, looking down at the dead cow, her calf strategically out of sight. He stares at her bulging eyes. He thinks she doesn't look like she died giving birth but straining to take an enormous shit. He tries to forget the calf, but keeps seeing its half-out body in his mind. His eyes follow the dark line of dried blood from the corner of the mother's eye socket to the nose and the blue tongue jutting through grey/brown teeth. He scans the empty field. He no longer feels the cold. If Jake is hiding he wishes he'd come out and come sit next to him.

He looks down at the fly. He lays the stick down by his feet. He leans down, pulls off one wing, then the next. The fly's movement is slowed to a pointless wriggle. Zeb smiles. He stands up and walks to the back of the cow, eyes closed. He stops, listening to his breath, counts, one, two, three and opens his eyes. It's still there. He stares down, transfixed, unable to breathe. The milky afterbirth covering its unborn body is shrivelled, revealing more of the black fur of the young animal beneath. He stares at its dark dead eyes for a long time.

The calf blinks.

Zeb stands up and staggers back. He tries to scream. No sound comes out.

The calf speaks. 'Please get me out of her.'

Zeb tries to turn and run but his feet are stuck, sinking into the mud. Panic sets in. His shoulders shake. He bursts into tears, jamming his eyes shut, counting one, two, three.

When he opens his eyes again, Jake is leaning over him.

'Fuck sake, Zeb. Moaning and whining like a little girl, thought you were having a fit!' Jake sits on the camping bed next to him. 'Do you need your inhaler?'

Zeb turns over to face the canvas and buries his face in his pillow. He does his best to get rid of the image of the calf and not stay awake.

Jake ruffles Zeb's hair. 'Nutter.' He gets back into his own bed and soon starts snoring.

Zeb lies looking up at the canvas ceiling awake and scared. The wind pushes in the sides of the small yurt. He touches the canvas and pushes it back. The wind blows harder. He brings his hand back under the duvet.

After a few minutes he gets out of bed and crawls over to Nick.

'Dad.'

No response.

'Dad.'

Nick turns over. 'Wass up, kid?'

'I want to go home.'

'Go back to bed. We'll talk in the morning.' Nick rolls over.

'I don't want to die.' Zeb is doing his best to hold back his tears.

Nick sits up. 'Jake been winding you up?'

'I had a bad dream.'

'Come here.' Nick puts his arm out.

Zeb stands there looking at him. 'Can we go for a walk?'

Nick looks at his watch. 'It's three in the morning, kid. We'll go when it's light.'

'I want to go now.'

'Crazy little fucker. Hang on . . . get yourself dressed.'

Nick and Zeb walk through the mostly sleeping site of Tipi Village. Most of the tents, tipis and yurts are quiet. Three huddled figures sit by a dying fire talking quietly, smoking, drinking tea. Nick and Zeb walk past. The firesiders look up and nod. One of them, clearly wrecked, lifts a bottle of vodka in salute. Zeb eyeballs him nervously.

Nick rests his hand on Zeb's shoulders. 'Warm enough?' Zeb nods.

'Can we go up into the hills?'

'Sure. We'll go where you like.' Nick takes out a half-smoked joint and lights it. 'What's all this about dying?'

'Me and Jake saw a dead cow . . . and a calf half out of her vagina.'

'When?'

75

'The other day when we were out walking. It's been giving me shitting nightmares.'

Nick walks close to him in silence.

'I want Mum.' Zeb's voice is clear.

'We'll call her tomorrow, it's too late now.' Nick is unable to look Zeb and Jake in the eye when he lies. He knows Zeb should be at home in his own bed. He curses the decision to bring them with him.

'You're not looking at me. I know you're fibbing when you don't look at me. I want to see her.'

'You will, soon. We'll give her a call.' Nick does his best to mean it. 'Things are always worse at night. You'll feel better in the morning, I promise.'

They head on through an opening into a field and walk up towards the hill Zeb has chosen. Nick finishes his joint and looks up at the stars. He wonders how Warren is and if he knows he's left London. Warren will be in a cell by now. No doubt.

'Mazing night ey, kid. Don't get stars like that back in London.' Zeb follows his line of sight.

They stop and look up.

A meteor flashes across the sky and vanishes.

Zeb lights up. 'See that?'

'Make a wish.' Nick closes his eyes and wishes for a hassle-free journey. No police. Just keep going. No turning back.

Zeb looks at Nick then closes his own eyes.

'Don't tell me what it is,' Nick tells him.

Zeb shakes his head in agreement.

They both open their eyes, still looking up.

'Why can't you and Mum live together?' Zeb asks.

Nick keeps looking up.

Zeb continues, 'Wish you could live together again; wish all of us could.'

'Not sure that's possible, kid. Not now.' Nick puts his arm back across Zeb's shoulders.

Zeb steps away and takes hold of Nick's hand. They head through the final gate and up into the darkness of the hill.

Seven

The high Victorian walls of Pentonville prison look beautiful to Vincent. The early-morning sunshine forces him to squint. Detective Sergeant Stringer walks by his side, a comfortable distance apart. This would normally be Milton's territory, the search for information, the shit work. Vincent wants to look at the man responsible for the death of his dog. See the whites of his eyes. They head through the main gates along with a mix of visiting mothers, girlfriends, friends and children. One by one they filter into the first of the electric doors. Stringer shows his warrant card at reception. Vincent is asked for his ID. The two of them are waved through.

As they get through the second electronic door Vincent quietly asks Stringer who he put him down on the visitor list as.

'Expert witness. I'll only do this the once. Don't ask me again.'

'You'll only need to do it the once. Think of the beach you'll get to lie on.'

They continue walking through the maze of doors and corridors to the main holding area for the massing visitors.

After a further fifteen minutes they're led to the main visiting hall.

They find an empty table and sit.

'I'd've preferred it if you'd got someone else to do this.' Stringer lights a cigarette.

'You need to relax.' Vincent looks around the hall. He remembers this place. Three months while waiting for trial. He remembers the sickening smell. The lack of air. The mindless, cathartic violence.

A child runs between their table and the next, arms outstretched screaming out a machine-gun attack.

The room fills up. Tables are taken and the queue for the canteen at the end of the room builds.

'Tea?' Stringer asks.

'White and one, cheers.'

He heads to the canteen. Vincent waits.

He scans the room for familiar faces. He finds none. He coughs loudly. Leaning forward, he takes out his handkerchief and covers his mouth.

'Nasty cold you got there. Lot of it about.' Stringer puts down the tray of teas.

'Cancer?'

Stringer looks at him apologetically. 'Sorry. I didn't realise.'

'Why would you?'

Vincent sees a group of prisoners walk in. One of the bigger men at the back looks over at Stringer who waves him over. He walks slowly, exaggerating his stride, pulls out a chair and sits.

'You'll be Warren then.' Vincent extends his hand. Warren keeps his palms on the table.

'You're not from the Yard.' Warren looks around the room, disinterested.

'No, not exactly, but I am involved in your case.'

Stringer pushes a cup over to Warren. 'How's it going, Warren?' Warren nods. 'Took the liberty of getting you some tea, no sugar, right?'

The three of them drink their first sips in silence.

'Warren, this is Vincent Cracknel, friend of mine.'

Warren burns his lips on his tea. He looks at Vincent then back to Stringer.

'What the fuck's he doing here?' Warren puts his tea down.

'You wouldn't have come, would you?' Stringer sips his tea, unfazed.

Vincent leans forward, tea in hand, looking straight at Warren.

Warren leans back defiantly. 'I don't have to sit here with you two pricks.'

Stringer smiles. 'No, you don't, but we all know how badly you want to get out of here.'

Vincent looks Warren straight in the eye. 'Which one of you thieving cunts killed my dog?'

'Don't know what you're talking about, mate.' Warren looks away.

Vincent continues, 'You turned my place over, killed my dog and cleaned me out . . . took my Sugar Ray. Now that you're safely locked up in here it's in your best interest to tell me where my money, the Sugar Ray and your mate are.'

'That some kind of a threat?' Warren holds Vincent's gaze.

Vincent leans further forward. 'The money can be replaced, Sugar Ray and Jasper can't. You'd be advised to stop acting the gangster and tell me what I need to know. Or, you can be tortured in your cell.'

Warren does little to hide his anger. 'Who the fuck's Sugar Ray? Jasper? You're fucking cracked, mate.'

'The animal you buried in my garden and the trophy that took me twenty years to get hold of.' Vincent pauses. 'Let's just say both meant a lot to me.'

' 'Scuse me if I don't sympathise. I didn't kill your cunting dog or take your fucking Sugar Ray.'

Stringer interrupts. 'You were seen coming out of Vincent's house with a man fitting Geneva's description. You can take this on your own or help us out. You know how this goes. We're all sensible grown-ups here. Like Mr Cracknel said, it's in your best interest, save us all a load of unnecessary fucking around.'

'Last time I saw him was three days before I was nicked,' Warren concedes.

Vincent rests his hand on Warren's. 'I hate having my time wasted. I know where your mum lives, your sister and your nephew. Don't force me.'

Warren pulls his hand away and scrapes his chair backwards. Stringer looks over to the nearest guard who starts walking over. Stringer gives him a reassuring nod and beckons Warren to pull his chair back in.

'Come on, we can do this. Warren, tell Mr Cracknel where Nick and his stuff is.'

'What is it about ignorance you arseholes don't get?' Warren looks over to Stringer. 'You can't let this cunt threaten my family.'

'Mr Cracknel's a friend of mine, we both want the same thing. Far as I'm concerned he can say what he likes. You're not in a strong position here.'

The three of them fall silent.

After a few moments Warren exhales and shakes his head.

'No idea about the fucking trophy.' Pause. 'I get the money to you and you reduce my sentence to a minimum?'

'Do our best,' Stringer replies, smiling.

'And tell us where this mate of yours, Nick, is,' Vincent urges.

Warren stares at the wall behind them, counts to thirty in his head. He thinks about his family. He doesn't have much time for any of them, but he wouldn't wish harm on any of them.

He keeps looking at the wall. 'Got a pen?' Stringer hands Warren a pen and paper. He begins to write.

'This is where it goes after each job.'

'And it'll be there?' Vincent asks as he reads the address.

Warren nods and sits back. 'What do I get for that?'

'Not much, but Mr Cracknel here gets his money back. We still need to know where Geneva is.'

'What the fuck you mean "not much"?' Warren's voice can be heard across the visiting hall.

Vincent smiles thinly. 'Never trust a copper on the kind of salary they pay these days. If you're fucking us about . . . I have mates in here who are far less patient. Think yourself lucky I didn't set one of them on you earlier.' Warren stands up abruptly. Stringer commands him to sit back down. Warren pushes Vincent back into the empty table behind them. Two prison guards are on Warren's back before he has a chance to take the first swing. Stringer stands up calmly and finishes his tea as Vincent straightens out his shirt and jacket.

The two men start to head for the exit. Warren struggles to get free of the guards, shouting after Vincent.

'Your cripple of a dog had a fucking heart attack, mate. Should've put the poor cunt down years ago.'

Everyone in the room turns to look at Warren as he's led out of the visiting hall; a few of the prisoners laugh. Vincent keeps walking without looking back.

The way is clear. Vincent and Stringer head through the visiting-hall door.

The murmur of visitor conversation and manic kids resumes.

Nick sits by last night's fire, stoking the embers, trying to get it going. Kids slowly emerge from tents, tipis and caravans. Jake and Zeb are still asleep. A skinny hippie with skanky dreads sits down opposite him.

'Morning . . . Nick, right?' Nick looks up and nods. 'How's the ol' yurt? Bit fucking leaky but it keeps the wind out, ey?'

'Slept well until Zeb woke me up.'

'He the young one?' Nick nods. 'So where you headed? Bastard!'

'You all right?' Nick shifts on his log.

'Sorry, mate. Tourette's.' The dread scratches his head, confused, like he's forgotten what they were talking about.

'That's a tough one to carry,' Nick sympathises.

'Got me into more punch-ups than I can count . . . and

I do love a ruck. Had my nose broken three times for shouting "cunt" to the wrong people. Where you headed?'

'North.'

He looks over to Nick's car. 'Not in that you aren't.'

'Fucking thing died on me on the motorway. Got towed to a service station. I need something new.'

'What you looking at?'

'Something big enough for us to sleep in that won't die in the middle of nowhere.'

'How much you wanna spend?'

'Got something in mind?' Nick looks over to a cluster of rusting cars and vans.

'Always something for sale here, mate.' The dread rolls a thin cigarette, lights it and hands the pouch to Nick. 'Where 'bouts north?'

'Far as we can get. Maybe Scotland.' Nick rolls himself a cigarette. He looks around the site. Most of the kids and their parents are preparing breakfast. Most look like they've walked out the tail end of a festival. Nick smiles to himself. Not unlike the crowds he hung out with in his twenties. He's glad to see some things clearly don't change.

The dread continues, 'You don't look the travelling type.'

'What do they look like these days then?'

'A little more worn in.'

'Feels good here, safe. Brings back some memories.'

'Wouldn't live anywhere else.' The dread stands. 'Come look at some wheels.'

'You do part exchange?' Nick smiles, knowing the answer.

'For that old banger? We could give it to the kids to play in.'

Nick stands. He feels stiff, tired. He follows the dread round to the back of the site.

Nick and the dread stand talking to each other, looking at three different vans. Zeb walks up behind Nick and wraps his arms round his waist.

'Hey, kid, nuff sleep?'

'I'm hungry.'

'Sure we can find something for you.' The dread smiles down at Zeb and puts his palm out. Zeb gives him five.

Zeb makes his request clear. 'Bacon . . . and eggs.'

Nick kisses the top of his head and draws him close.

'Bacon and hugs it is then. Where's Jake?'

'Snoring.'

Nick doesn't hear the cars pulling in. It's the dread's shift in attention that alerts him. He can see by the look on the skinny man's aging face that something's wrong.

'Hang on here a sec. We're not expecting guests, not this time of day.' The dread leaves Nick and Zeb by the vans. Nick crouches down and looks through a gap between the vehicles. One after another police cars pull into the main yard. Nick watches the dread boldly approach the first car; the skinny hippie looks like he's in charge. Adrenalin runs through Nick's body. He knows they couldn't have come for him but he can't help the panic in his chest. He pulls Zeb close. He wants Jake with him. He watches a uniformed officer get out of the first car and walk up to the dread. They start talking. The dread becomes more animated. Nick is unable to make out what they're saying until he hears the word 'CUNT' loud and clear from the dread's mouth. The officer steps back, clearly pissed off. The dread raises his hand in supplication, obviously explaining his condition. The officer looks placated. Two other uniformed officers join the first. A small crowd of travellers gather behind the skinny dread. The first officer takes out a sheet of paper and hands it to the dread.

'What they doing, Dad?' Zeb asks.

'Looks like they're here to nick someone.' Nick's breathing becomes shallow.

'Are they here to nick you?'

'Stay down and don't make a sound, like I showed you.'

Zeb moves closer to Nick's side, crouching down, out of sight. Nick wants to run but knows he has to stay put. He feels Zeb's heart beating against his body. He knows Zeb's scared. He pulls him round to his front and puts his arms round him.

They watch the scene unfold, still unable to hear what's being said save the peppering of obscenities from the dread. The exchange slowly becomes more animated. The first officer attempts to move past the dread but is blocked by the crowd behind. The travellers and their grimacing, jeering kids bunch closer together. Six more uniformed officers get out of the last two cars, clearly agitating the travellers. The main officer tries to head for one of the bigger yurts. His way is blocked. The six newly emerged officers take out their batons and move in, hitting the dread on the back of the legs then cracking one of the bigger travellers over the head. Zeb slides up to the gap and looks through.

'Why are they bashing them?' Zeb is jittering. 'Shall we help them?'

'Love to kid, but we need to stay here.'

'Come on, you're good at bashing.'

'These hippies look like they can take care of themselves.' He does his best to force calm, keep hold of himself. He hopes Zeb won't sense his anxiety.

Zeb grips him tighter.

The travellers quickly get the upper hand, forcing the police back into their cars. A white, unmarked van drives erratically into the yard, skidding to a muddy halt. Another load of police clamber out. Within a few minutes they gain control. The main officer orders two of his men into the bigger yurt. They come out a few moments later with a young woman and an older man. They lead them to the white van amid jeering and screaming from the physically restrained travellers. Three other travellers are forced into the back of the van. Within a minute the campsite returns to its previous quiet. Nick watches the dread head back over, only a slight limp giving away anything of what just happened.

'You hiding down there, mate? Thought you might give us a hand, bit of vocal support at least.'

'You looked like you were doing OK, until the second van rocked up.'

'My dad's good at bashing.' Zeb punches the air twice to demonstrate.

The dread nods with a wry smile on his face. He looks at Nick. 'Starting to get a better idea why you're heading north, mate.'

'Best I keep out of the way for now.'

'Why, Dad? Why didn't you bash the police?'

Nick looks over to the last of the police cars leaving the

site. 'Fuck was that all about?' He feels his breathing slow.

'Ruby and her old man were due in court yesterday. They never turned up. Nothing too heavy.'

'Looked pretty heavy to me.'

'You get used to it. So . . . decided?' The dread leads Nick back to the cars and vans. Zeb follows behind, punching imaginary foes.

Nick's stopped in his tracks by a wiry mongrel biting his ankle. He tries to shake it off while pointing at the VW Camper. 'How much is that one?'

Eight

Milton walks down the cul de sac, past the lock-ups to the gate at the end. He lifts the catch and climbs through. Walking a further twenty yards he reaches a locked door with a white plastic number 12 nailed to the wood. He pushes the door. Locked. He shoves it twice with his shoulder, unsuccessfully. He shrugs and puts his foot through it. He pauses to check around him then enters. The room is dark save three shafts of light coming through a jagged hole in the roof. The space smells of dirty engine oil. He clicks his torch on, directing the beam into the corners. The white light finds a large pile of metallic and wooden clutter in the two farthest corners then the remains of a crushed car against a wall. A siren wails past in the distance.

The torch lights up a box underneath a long wooden table against the farthest wall. It fits the description in Warren's note. He takes out a small crowbar and walks over, drags it out, lifts it up and drops it on the table. He sticks the torch in his mouth.

The metal box is easy to open . . . and empty.

He tuts, puts his hands in his pockets and thinks.

He picks the torch back up and shines the light around the room, walking over to the pile of metal and wood in the top left-hand corner. He starts pulling pieces away. After a couple of minutes he finds two plastic containers. He opens one up and smells petrol. He takes them to the centre of the room and pours the fuel across the floor, wood, car, and repeats the dousing with the second container. He walks to the door, trailing the last of the fuel, takes out his lighter, crouches down and ignites the liquid fuse. He watches it snake its way to the centre of the room, stands up, heads through the door and slams it shut. The rush of flame hits the other side of the door with a thump. He leans against the door, looking up at the starless sky. He takes out his mobile and calls Vincent.

'Nothing here.'

'You find the box?' Vincent asks flatly.

'Empty. Looked around, fuck all here.'

Milton looks up. He just makes out the blur of the North Star, the only visible sign of anything natural beyond the city skyline.

'Go to Pentonville, speak to the boys. Crank this up. I want it back and I want the apology, some kind of remorse, even if we have to tear it out of him.'

'No problem.' Milton hangs up. He enjoys the warmth of the door on his back for a few moments then heads back down the lane to the main road.

The sound of the ancient VW engine rattles through the inside of the blue and white van. Jake fiddles around with the radio looking for a station.

'Piece of shit hasn't even got a CD player.'

Nick doesn't react, but he wants to. He knows his patience has to double to make up for the decision to head further north. A lot further than he planned. But then he had no real plan in the first place. Only to get out.

Zeb sits at the back staring at the road as it rushes behind them. A mongrel dog sits close to him.

'Where are we going?' Jake asks looking straight ahead, bored.

'Snowdonia. Haven't been there since I was a kid.'

'Sounds cold and boring. You spoken to Mum?'

Nick ignores the question. 'Snow on it most of the year; stunning place. Take you half a day to walk up it.' Nick steers the van along the empty, narrow lanes. The glare of mid-afternoon sunshine forces him to drive slower than he'd like.

'Well?' Jake asks, agitating.

'What?'

Jake finds Radio 1. Dizzee Rascal crackles out in monotone. 'Mum. Zeb wants to speak to her. My mobile's battery's gone. He needs to use yours.'

'Next stop. He can call her at the next stop.'

It takes Nick a few minutes sitting in the awkward silence before he finally manages to say it.

'I'm sorry, kid.'

Jake looks at Nick, confused. 'What you on about?'

'Sorry I fucked it all up. Last few years've been shit.'

'Know that,' Jake replies without emotion.

'It's not like she's easy to live with.'

Jake crosses his arms and looks out across the fields into the woods beyond the river running parallel to the road. 'If you're trying to "bond", it ain't working.'

'I think Gandalf needs a shit.' Zeb looks down at the dog and strokes him.

'How do you know he needs a shit?' Nick asks, smiling.

'Just do, and I need a piss.'

'I get it. Soon as I see a lay-by. Need a piss myself.'

'Why did you let him have the dog? He can hardly look after himself,' Jake complains.

'Told you, came with the wheels. Anyway, Zeb's good with animals, keep him out of trouble.'

'Don't expect me to have anything to do with it.' Jake keeps his gaze on the leafless treeline.

Nick follows Jake's line of sight. 'Zeb said you saw a dead cow the other day.' Jake nods. 'How come you didn't tell me?'

'Didn't think you'd be interested.'

'Do you do this cos your mates do it?'

'What?'

'The too cool for school bollocks.'

'Don't know what you're on about.'

Nick grips the wheel a little tighter. 'You don't have to hate me just cos you turned fifteen . . . cos you think you're meant to.' He pauses a moment, concentrating on the sharpening bends. 'We used to have a laugh. I miss the hugs.'

Jake falls silent. Nick can see he's uncomfortable.

'Jakey's too big for hugging now . . .' Zeb chips in. 'It's not gay you know . . . Dad's not gay.'

Nick continues, 'We can have a shit time or a good time, up to you.'

'Wanna be back home with Carlos,' Jake monotones.

Nick loosens his grip on the wheel.

Silence ensues.

Nick finally spots a lay-by. Zeb jumps up. Gandalf jumps on to his lap looking out the window. Nick pulls over. All three get out. Zeb leads Gandalf on the dirty string the dread gave them.

The three of them line up, unzip and piss. Gandalf stares expectantly up at Zeb.

Zeb finishes pissing first and jumps back in the van with the dog.

Jake looks out across the fields, continuing to piss. I don't hate you, Dad. Just hate what you do for money and all the stupid fucking lies. He zips up and sticks his hands in his pockets, continuing to look across the field. Nick finishes. He rubs his hands together for warmth.

'Why are we here?' Jake asks.

'Spend some time together . . . so I can make up for being so fucking useless over the last few months.'

'Months?' Jake kisses his teeth. 'Seriously, why are we here?'

'Zeb wants you here, so do I.' Nick hates that Jake knows how to pick him apart and he hates the guilt. 'I don't think you get how tricky it is being around you sometimes, sulking around with a face like a slapped arse.' Nick turns and walks back to the van. 'We'll walk up Snowdon tomorrow. The view is incredible.'

Jake follows a deliberate three paces behind.

'Don't know why you expect me to join in the happy families when you keep lying all the chuffing time.'

Nick snaps. He couldn't stop if he wanted to. He grabs Jake's arm, speaking in a repressed whisper.

'Getting a bit fucking tired of this, kid.'

'So am I,' Jake snaps back. He tries to pull away. Nick's grip tightens. 'Let go my fucking arm!' Zeb peers through the van window.

'How many fucking times have I told you not to speak to me like that?' Nick barks into his face.

'Leggo of my fucking arm!'

'When you're eighteen you can do what the fuck you like. 'Til then you'll do as I fucking say.'

'What, so you're going to force me to stay with you while you drive into the middle of fucking nowhere?'

Nick releases the grip on his arm. Jake pulls away and gets back into the van.

Zeb watches as Nick walks out into the field.

Snowdon looms through a gap in the valley ahead. He crunches across the frosted grass to the middle of the field and lights a cigarette. He squats down and runs his fingers through his hair. He looks around, takes in the view of the mountain and surrounding hills, draws in a cold breath and closes his eyes.

1970 Snowdon

Eight-year-old Nick looks up ahead at his father, John, who is in full rambling uniform: plus-fours, walking boots, stick, rucksack, chequered shirt and red woollen hat with a limp bobble. He wonders why his dad's legs are so hairy. He hopes his don't look like that when he grows up. Nick is hot and tired but determined not to show it. He's well accustomed to the consequences. Early May weather brings short bursts of sunshine quickly broken by showers of torrential rain. They've been soaked several times in the last two hours. Nick knows if he stops for too long the wind will chill his wet clothes along with the sweat on his body. His dad has tried to teach him about walking in the wilderness; the rules. How to stay warm, deal with an emergency, sleep rough, make a shelter, eat wild food. Nick doesn't remember everything his dad tells him, but he tries.

The summit of Snowdon lies just over a mile ahead. John Geneva has taken them on one of the tougher routes. He stops by a cairn and sits down heavily on a slab of rock. Nick stops a few yards behind, nervously waiting for the signal.

'Over here, son. Pit stop, sit yourself down.' Nick sits down at a safe distance. John takes out a silver flask and glugs back three large mouthfuls of his favourite brandy. He drinks when he wakes and tops himself up throughout the day. When the clock hits six he hits the bottle harder and Nick soon after, usually for no reason that Nick can make out. On the outside Nick looks like a tough eight-year-old. He can take care of himself in the playground. Not many kids mess with him and this makes his dad proud. At home, however, it's hard to hide the shaking knees and stuttering that instinctively precede the daily beatings his father also takes pride in.

'Here.' John holds the flask out to Nick.

'No thanks, Dad.'

'Take it, you're soaking wet, keep you warm.'

'Can I have it in some tea?'

'Sure.' John takes out the flask, pours Nick a cup and tops it up with brandy. He hands it to his son. Nick has never liked the taste of spirits and can't understand why his dad does, but he drinks without objection.

'About another mile. We'll have our sandwiches when we get to the top, I've got us some chocolate as well.' Nick forces a smile, finishes his drink and hands back the cup. John takes out a worn map and carefully opens it up. He always does this, it's a habit, he knows the route off by heart but likes to study the contours of the land, running his finger along the thin lines, like he's reading a complicated, precious book. Nick looks down the path they just walked up. The clouds have cleared, leaving a sharp blue sky in their wake. Nick lets the heat of the sun warm his face as the brandy warms his insides. He soon forgets about his wet clothes. He closes his eyes, listening to the wind rattle their thin nylon windbreakers.

'Right then, soldier, time for the last march. Ready?'

Nick nods. He isn't. He puts on his pack. His dad heads off, breaking into a fast pace. Nick does his best to keep up.

Sometimes Nick wishes his dad were dead. Walks like this usually do it. He imagines a mythical mountain beast rearing up from nowhere, picking him up with a giant hand and crunching his head in a single bite. Or a plane crashing into the mountain engulfing him in a slow aviation-fuelled death, watching his arms and legs explode into flames. Or just a simple stopping dead in his tracks while he endures the pain of a fatal heart attack. None of this ever happens of course. But on days like this he prays hard.

Despite this, being outdoors is the best time to be around his father, the safest. John is happiest on the side of a mountain or stomping across moorland. As long as there is light in the sky, drinking and violence are kept to a minimum.

Nick's mum never comes on the walks.

But Nick still can't help loving his dad. He idolises him and nags him for stories of the war. Of all the Germans and Italians he killed and exactly how he did it.

They continue on. The ridge ahead gets steeper, the rocks more jagged and harder to climb. John continues the pace. Nick falls further behind.

'Dad, wait!'

'Come on, son, got more in you than that, remember what I told you . . . keep up the pace and you'll be rewarded like a king at the top.'

Nick's anger rises as do his silent prayers. He looks down the sharp fall to his left, gets scared and loses concentration. He slips and slides on a hidden scree. He tries to right himself but falls, hitting the jagged ground hard, cutting and grazing his knees. He grabs his leg and holds it tight. He looks down and waits for the blood to come. Tears well up in his eyes. He looks up at the fading figure of his father.

'Bastard.'

As if hearing him, John turns back and sees Nick squatting, nursing his knee.

'Come on, Nicholas, sandwiches at the top!'

Nick curses under his breath. 'Don't want bloody lunch. Wish you were dead.'

As John turns back to continue walking he trips and falls forward. He disappears out of sight. Nick holds his breath. He has no way of working out how far the drop is. He blurts out a breath, shouts and runs ahead to the ridge.

He looks down and sees his dad, thirty feet below, lying face down, unconscious or dead.

'Oh god I'm sorry, I'm sorry, I'm sorry I didn't mean it . . . please don't kill my dad . . . please don't kill my dad . . . not yet, please, please, PLEASE!'

He scrambles down the steep escarpment. It takes him almost ten minutes to get down. He walks tentatively up to his dad's still body and waits. After a few minutes he squats down. With all his strength he rolls him over. He sees a deep cut along the side of his head. Nick looks around him, tear-filled eyes searching for help. He finds nothing except three wet sheep further down the ridge, looking up at him as if waiting for something to happen.

Snapped back to the present, Nick opens his eyes, focusing ahead at the unmoving mountain. He rubs his forehead, steadying himself with a hand on the grass. The chill stings his palm. He holds it there. He touches the edge of the dog bite, feeling the damp dressing barely covering it. It feels like it's healing.

After a few minutes he stands, turns and walks back to the van.

The windows of the VW are whited out, the scene inside made invisible by the breath of Jake, Zeb and Gandalf. Nick knows instantly that they're up to something.

He walks quietly round to the driver's door and opens it. The two boys and dog look up at Nick simultaneously, equally surprised, equally guilty. On the seat between Jake and Zeb is a pile of ten- and five-pound notes.

'Fuck's going on here?' Nick demands.

'Hi, Dad.' Zeb smiles broadly.

'Don't hi Dad me, what are you up to?'

'Counting,' Jake replies, looking at the money triumphantly.

'I told you both to stay out of my fucking stuff.' Nick climbs in. Jake starts to arrange the money into neater piles. 'Gandalf found it when he was looking for that toy Zeb keeps fucking chucking.' Gandalf is lapping up beer from the Sugar Ray Leonard trophy.

'You expect me to believe that?' Nick looks at Jake waiting for an answer. He takes the trophy and empties the beer out the window. Gandalf barks in complaint.

Jake carefully puts the bundles of notes into the open box. 'How long we going away for, Dad?'

'What's that got to do with you nosing around in my shit?'

'You wouldn't bring this much cash unless you needed it.'

Zeb strokes Gandalf. 'You always say only take what you need when you go out, in case someone wants to bash you and nick it off you.'

Jake puts the last bundle into the box and hands it to Nick.

Nick finally answers, 'A few weeks.'

Jake looks at him hard and confident. 'There's enough in there to last us six months. When are we going home?'

Rain starts to rattle on to the thin metal roof.

'Few weeks, that's all,' Nick continues. 'It'll be good for us, you don't have to go to school.'

'Why lie, Dad?' Jake asks. 'We know when you're lying just like you know when we are.'

'Jake knows when I'm shitting fibbing too, bastard.' Zeb shoves Jake against the cooker. Jake shoves him back.

'All you need to know is that we're going north. I'd like to go to Scotland, show you where me and your mum used to live, we'll take it a week at a time, see how we get on. Have a look at the map and tell me where you want to go along the way, you decide.' He looks at Jake. 'We can go anywhere . . . on the north-west coast, not back to London, not yet.'

Nick shows confidence, sincerity. He does well to hide the rising dread that this is all a mistake.

He turns around, starts the van and drives north in the pissing rain towards the village of Betws-y-Coed.

Warren sits on his bunk reading the paper. The sounds of the prisoners on the landing outside fill the cell. He's good at doing time. This is the worst part; remand. He knows he won't get more than six months – he could get lucky and be out before the end of the summer. Everything he takes for granted always comes back to make his time inside that much harder. He wonders why he's unable to appreciate anything outside a cell door or prison yard when he gets it back. Beer, tailor-mades, spliff, his sofa, bed, food, even the homely hooker he hates the sight of the moment he shoots his load. But it's easier inside, no bills, no stress, no push to earn. Warren hasn't gone over the line. It'd take a lot longer than a few months to institutionalise him. He does the crime, the time and is always prepared to pay the price for a line of work that pays well. Danger money, well worth the risk.

This is a rare moment of peace. His farting, wanking cellmate hardly speaks but always manages to take up every available inch of space. Warren would never wank in the same room as another man; standard cell etiquette. If he thought he could get away from him he would've given the overweight, grunting cunt a dig weeks ago. Instead he works off the anger, lack of space and testosterone with circuit training and, much to the amusement of at least half the prisoner population, yoga. Nick got him into it three years ago then swiftly dropped the idea and got into walking.

Nick is normally in touch by now, if not a visit then a letter. No contact is bad news. In his gut he knows what must've happened. He buries the thought, alongside the growing fear of a wanker of a judge giving him an over-the-top sentence for a low-level crime. He prays the money's still in the lock-up.

The light in the room dims. A shadow casts itself across the tits of the seventeen-year-old 2D glamour model in Warren's lap. He looks up and sees a large Asian man with a fat moustache standing in the doorway, another smaller man stands behind him, trying to look in over the Asian man's shoulders. Warren knows in the time it takes to blink that the next few minutes will leave him in one of two states: unscathed on the outside but battered inside, burnt up with the shame of the grass; or a beating, meaning he may end up in hospital but able to feel pride in keeping his mouth shut to any demands, however violent.

'Good afternoon, sir. Warren, yes?' The Asian man is well spoken, polite, perfect English. Warren carefully folds his glamour model up and lays the paper down on the bed. 'I have a message from a good friend of mine,' the man continues.

'Who's that then?' Warren asks blankly.

The man steps into the cell, his second following closely behind. The cell door is pushed to. Warren leans back against the cold wall. The Asian sits down in a chair too small for his oversized arse.

He stares at Warren, waiting for a reply. Warren raises a questioning eyebrow. 'Mr Cracknel has engaged me, employed me, to give you a message and ask you a question.'

Warren knows the message is the beating he was hoping to avoid, whether he has a good answer or not.

'Why don't the pair of you fuckoff back to the shower and wash that rank sweat off your backs.'

'We have just one question for you. Shouldn't be too difficult to answer.'

The second man reaches into his sock and pulls out a toothbrush. Its bristles removed and replaced with three disposable shaving blades. He hands it to the Asian. Warren looks at the weapon and chuckles to himself. Hoping it will look like he isn't fazed. He is. The second man walks quickly over. Warren jerks forward trying to pre-empt him but the man grabs hold of his feet and with a single, violent grunt, pulls him off the bunk, cracking the back of Warren's head on the edge of the bed. Warren loses vision for a second. His body hits the floor hard. That in itself would've been enough he thinks. The Asian man rises from the chair and lumbers over to him. The second man holds Warren's shoulders to the floor. The hot garlic breath of the Asian leans close to Warren's face.

'Now then, my friend. Before we begin, *this* is for wasting my employer's valuable time.' He lifts the three blades to the corner of Warren's mouth, holding his head steady, a barber preparing for the first pass. His second puts his knees on Warren's shoulders, pinning him down hard, freeing up his hands to cover his eyes. The Asian twists the blades in, finds the right depth and drags the thin strips of silver back towards Warren's ear. Warren's body bucks up and to the side, forcing the blade to change direction and sink in deeper. His scream doesn't reach the door. The chatting and shouting on the landings outside continues unaware. 'And this . . . is for his beloved dog, Jasper.' The second incision cuts into the bridge of Warren's nose. The skin opens up, revealing the white of the bone beneath. Blood rises smoothly to the slit, runs on to Warren's face then to the floor.

'And the single question is, where is this good friend of yours, Nick Geneva?' The second removes his hand from Warren's eyes. Warren looks up at the now sweating Asian face smiling down at him, loving his work. 'Now.' He brings the blade to the underside of Warren's eye. 'No unnecessary noise or complaining, no.' Warren's eyes widen with rage and fear. Warren sneers at the Asian, blood pouring steadily out of the corner of his mouth and nose. 'You pair of cunts, you expect me to tell you . . .' The hand slides back over his mouth.

'Ah ah.' The Asian shakes the blade at Warren. 'This has only just started. It is a simple question with a brief answer. You tell us where this friend of yours is and we will leave you in peace.' The hand is drawn away again.

'I fucking told him where the money was, I have no

fucking idea where he is.' The Asian brings the blade to the skin beneath his eye. 'Jesus fucking Christ, you need to find another line of work you sick . . . cunt.'

'I have a flair for this one.' The Asian looks at his second for a reply, he smiles and nods. 'Last chance.' The Asian smiles. He signals to the second man to hold him down harder then swipes the three blades across Warren's retina. He stands up, looking with pride at his work writhing on the floor, bleeding and roaring with pain.

'I know you'll want to keep the other one. Give me something we can work with. Something to justify my fee. Please.'

Warren's body shakes from head to toe. He tries to cover his eye. He runs through a dozen conversations he had with Nick over the last few weeks. Scotland. He wouldn't, not that far. Then he remembers the stuff about Nick's dad. The mountain he died on. Said he wanted to go back. Was planning a trip in the spring. Pay his respects. He wasn't losing his sight for him; *that would be fucking stupid.*

'Snowdon. If he was going anywhere . . . probably there. Fuck knows.' The last words of the sentence drift into a murmur.

The Asian waits a moment then walks calmly out followed by his silent second man.

Warren struggles in vain to maintain consciousness.

A few minutes later, Warren's heavyweight cellmate returns and quickly walks back out.

The wailing of alarms follows.

Nine

Jake lies in his tent, freezing, beginning to realise sleeping out alone just to make a point was a stupid mistake. Zeb, Nick and Gandalf are in the van. When he pitched the tent they'd found in the back of the old van, the sky was clear, full of stars, no wind. In his hat and gloves he almost felt warm. Getting in the tent was exciting. He was having some fun at last. He felt grown up.

The roar of the wind against the side of the tent woke him up ten minutes ago.

He lies in his bag, looking up at the thin nylon roof. The wind remoulds the shape of the tent as it stalks the outside. Jake moves to the centre. The wind hits the tent harder, pushing it close to his face, flapping and rustling the thin material. He starts to shiver. He's not sure if it's fear or cold. He settles on a little of both. He pulls his jacket over him, puts his hat back on and curls up into a ball. The wind continues to batter the tent.

'Fuckoff.' He knows it won't make any difference. As if in reply, the wind pushes the tent further in, now an inch from his face.

'FUCKOFF!'

It abruptly stops. He moves back to the side in an attempt to find more warmth. His shivering increases. He should go back to the van – but he doesn't. After another fifteen minutes he drifts into a half sleep.

The fire in the disused restaurant comes into his mind. The memory warms him. Images of Nick, Zeb and his mum move around, making little sense. He falls further into sleep.

His eyes snap back open as the wind hits the tent again bringing the now wet nylon on to his face. It feels as if the wind is deliberately fucking him around. He shouts at it to fuck off again. Once again it stops. He lies there, afraid, unable to move. Rain falls loud. No chance of sleep now. He gets colder. He sits up, looking for more clothes. He looks ahead and sees the tent zip is half open. He curses himself. As he zips it shut he notices a pool of water on the floor. The base of his sleeping bag is soaked. The freezing water has reached his feet.

'Shit.' He reaches into his rucksack and takes out two Mars bars and quickly eats them. The sugar warms him and wakes him fully up. The rain falls harder, forced into the side of the tent by the continuing wind. He tries to get back to sleep. After ten minutes holding his eyes shut he opens them and looks up. The rain is dripping through the tent roof. The tent is slowly collapsing under the weight of water and wind.

He sits back up and starts to peel the wet sleeping bag off him. He puts his boots on over wet socks and slides his raincoat over his head. His trousers are dry.

He crawls out of the tent on to the soaking wet ground outside and stands quickly up. Blood rushes to his head.

His vision blurs. He steadies himself and looks around. He can just see the van through the rain. He turns and looks at the tent. The centre is caved in. The pegs have been dragged out of the ground. He looks around for some rocks, hammers the pegs back in with a big rock and puts rocks on the pegs. A lone cow stares at him, chewing.

'What you fucking looking at?' Jake scrambles back into his tent, then his bag and pulls his hat over his eyes.

Ten minutes later the tent starts to cave in again. He repeats the journey out of the tent, finding bigger rocks to hold the pegs down.

It works.

After another hour he finally falls into a shivering sleep.

When he opens his eyes, all is silent outside save two birds singing to each other. The wind and rain have stopped. The rocks held.

Jake zips open and looks out. The sky is blue, warm March sunshine covers his face. The smile that breaks out is automatic. He crawls out of the tent, stands and looks around, hands on hips, taking in the scene. Behind the tent is the lake, a good half a mile across, stretching a mile into the distance. To the left is a track that leads to one of the easier routes up Snowdon – so Nick says. The mountain itself is a further three miles ahead and can be seen clearly. It's the first time he's seen a mountain this big, a real mountain with snow. Just like in the books Nick used to read him.

He squats down near the tent and takes in the cool, clean air, proud to have survived the night.

* * *

By the time they've had breakfast it's almost twelve.

'Help me with the tent, bro,' Jake yawns.

'I'm taking Gandalf for a proper walk, do it yourself.'

'Give him a hand, Zeb. We need to get moving. Gandalf can walk all he likes when we get on the track.' Nick feels the hangover of emotion. Remnants of the memory of his father. The continued, grinding irritation of Jake. The need to keep moving; keep them happy, making out like it's all OK. The indecision. The looped anger and guilt at having taken them with him. All of it wearing him down and out. 'Come on, Zeb, help out will you?'

Zeb reluctantly follows Jake to the tent.

As Nick finishes putting the bedding away two women in hiking gear walk up the small road towards him, both good-looking, both fit, proper walkers. They smile as they approach. Nick stops what he's doing.

'Going up?' he asks.

They stop, look at him then the van.

'Sure, we're going up,' the taller, younger of the two replies.

'Where you from?' Nick asks.

'LA.'

'Three hundred and sixty-five days of sunshine.' Nick brightens a little on the inside. He could do with this, take his mind off things.

He steps forward, offering his hand up to the older of the two.

He decides to keep his real name to himself.

'Tony, good to meet you.'

'Hey. Candy. Nice to meet you, Tony.' She reaches out a tanned hand. They shake.

Nick walks over to her friend, the one he likes the most, and shakes her hand. It's younger, gentler. He finds it hard to take his eyes off her.

'Lisa, hey, how you doing?' She looks him in the eye a moment then looks away. She is less confident than Candy. It makes him like her more. Nick leans back, overdoing cool, almost missing the side of the van. Both women laugh at him.

'Know the best way up?' he asks, straightening himself out.

'Sure.' Candy smiles warmly at him. 'We've been up three times since Sunday. We *love* this mountain.' Candy is older, stronger-looking, like she can take care of herself.

'So do I,' he replies, looking up at it. 'Used to come here with my old man . . . dad.'

Candy takes off her pack and pulls out a bottle of water.

'My kids are taking Jake's tent down.' Nick points to the lake.

'Neat, both boys?' Candy looks in the direction of the lake.

'Boys, yeah. Jake stayed out last night, for the wilderness experience.'

'What happened to your face?' Candy asks.

Nick automatically touches the hardening scab around his nose. He decides the truth will do him good with them.

'Dog bite.'

'You should watch where you put your face.'

'Story of my life.' He winks at Candy and walks to the van to make space for the tent.

Jake and Zeb saunter back with the tent, talking, heads down. Gandalf is biting Zeb's laces. They don't notice the two women until a few yards from the van. Jake looks up first, sees Lisa and blushes from neck to brow.

'So you're the adventurer. I'm Lisa, this is Candy.' Lisa offers up a hand to Jake. They shake. Jake is speechless. He shakes Candy's hand. Zeb steps forward and juts his hand out.

'I'm Zeb and this is Gandalf.'

'Well look at you and your little dog.' Lisa bends down and strokes Gandalf. 'Like in *Lord of the Rings*, right?' she asks.

'Yeah, I'm reading *The Hobbit*, look.' Zeb takes out the battered copy of the book from his jacket and shows it off to her.

'Cool name for a dog.' Candy squats down and ruffles Gandalf's ears.

'Candy and Lisa are gonna show us the way up.' Nick smiles at Zeb as he puts the tent into the van and shuts the boot.

The weather is clear, a few white clouds floating free among the blue. The track starts off easy enough. Zeb runs ahead with Gandalf. Jake is on his own, too shy to speak. Lisa, Candy and Nick are walking together talking, not taking in the mountain ahead. Jake looks up and is blown away by the beauty of it. He listens to Nick's false laughter, watching the routine unfold. He hates that he changes the way he speaks when he's around women; all women except his mother. He knows Nick fancies one of them. He hopes it isn't Lisa.

'Jake!' Zeb screams. 'Come on, tosser, race you to that rock!'

'No chance.'

Zeb runs on with Gandalf.

Nick shouts after him. 'Easy, kid. We ain't in a hurry.'

'No but you are.' Jake jibes under his breath as he walks past.

'Wass that, kid?'

'Nothing, just saying how cool it is . . . the mountain.'

Nick continues talking, mainly focusing on Candy. Jake knows how this works. Nick focuses on the one he likes least to get the attention of the one he likes more. So it's Lisa. His heart sinks. He's watched him do this so many times. To his irritation it works. He listens carefully.

'So, Tony,' Candy asks. 'What do you do for a living?'

Jake turns and shoots Nick a look. The false name says it all. Nick has no intention of making a real connection with either of them. Just use and discard. Nick winks at him and continues the charade.

'Buy and sell classic cars. Few Cadillacs, some Italian, some English.'

Jake shakes his head, quickens his pace and catches up with Zeb.

'Tosser's told them his name is Tony.'

'That's not his name. Thas a shit name.' Zeb chucks Gandalf's toy into a small tarn.

'He fancies Lisa.'

Zeb pulls a twisted face. 'Think he's gonna snog her?'

'Probably more than that.' Jake kicks stones off the path as he walks.

'You fancy Lisa too. You got no chance,' Zeb laughs at him.

'Piss off.' He shoves Zeb off the path.

'Bloody do. You went all red when you shook her hand. You always go red when you fancy someone.'

'She's fit. Wouldn't kick her out of bed for eating biscuits.'

'Ey?'

'Last one to that boulder's a tosser *and* a knob.' Jake sprints off ahead.

'Hey that's not shittin' fair . . . which bloody boulder?' Zeb doesn't wait for an answer and sprints after him.

It takes two hours to reach the summit.

Nick stops by the trig. point, out of breath, bent over, hands on knees. He looks down across the low-lying lakes and hills. Jake walks up to him taking a crumpled cigarette out of his top pocket.

'Got a light?'

Nick obliges. 'How you doing?'

'All right.' Jake takes a long drag on the cigarette and sits down. 'You were right.'

' 'Bout what?' Nick wipes the sweat from his face.

'It's cool up here.'

'That can't've been easy.' Nick puts his hand on Jake's back, rubs it a few times then awkwardly removes it. 'Did I hurt you yesterday? I'm sorry, kid . . . you really fucking wind me up sometimes.'

Jake decides to save Nick from his awkwardness. 'No sweat.'

Silence falls between them.

Nick looks around. 'Used to come up here with Granddad, two or three times a year.'

'He sounded like a right wanker.'

'He was better out here.' Nick pauses for a moment. 'The war fucked him.'

Jake knows this story. 'What's your excuse?' His question isn't barbed. He genuinely wants to know.

'War . . . with him.'

'He ever talk about it . . . the war?'

'Not when he was straight.' Nick looks away.

Jake hands Nick the half-smoked cigarette. Nick rarely talks about his dad. Jake doesn't like the emotion he can see Nick trying to hide.

Zeb plays manically with Gandalf and Candy, chucking the ball too close to the edge. Lisa is quietly taking photos. Nick checks her out. Jake follows his line of sight. 'Fancy her?'

'Good tits,' Nick replies, smiling to himself. He brings his attention back to the view and hands Jake the cigarette.

'She's nearer my age than yours.' Jake does his best to hide his jealousy.

'She's old enough.'

'Why do you change when you're around birds?' Jake asks. Nick looks at him. 'Does she know all you want to do is shag her?'

'Probably.'

'What if she doesn't?' Jake picks up a small handful of

stones and starts chucking them, one by one, down the scree.

'Like you said, she's young. She'll bounce back. Yanks are tough, like their cars.'

Lisa walks over to them. Jake blushes.

'Neat view, huh?' She looks around, hand on hips.

Nick looks her up and down. 'Damn straight.'

She jabs her knee into his back. 'I mean down there!'

'Let's see how close we can get it to the edge!' Zeb shouts at Jake, hopping up and down, Gandalf at his side. Jake gets up and walks over to Zeb, takes the ball out of Gandalf's slobbering mouth and chucks it.

'Easy guys,' Candy shouts out. 'I'm sure you don't wanna lose this cute puppy down the side of the mountain.'

'He's OK, ain't he, Jake? Smart all-terrain pooch. Chuck the ball, blood!'

Jake hurls the ball across the rocks. It bounces several times before coming to a stop a hundred yards from the edge. Gandalf leaps after it, yapping.

Candy and Jake watch Zeb run after Gandalf who refuses to give up the ball.

'Your father's quite a ladies' man.' Candy waits for a reply.

'That's why Mum left him,' Jake wants her to know.

'I wondered where she was at.'

Zeb comes back with the ball and hands it to her. 'Are you gonna hang out with us?' Zeb asks, out of breath, ready for more.

'Want us to?'

'Yeah, you're cool and Jake fancies Lisa.' Jake kicks Zeb. Zeb kicks him back, takes the ball and throws it. Gandalf sprints after it.

'Does he now.' Candy smiles at Jake. 'Well you got taste. Sadly she's taken . . . mind you he's a few thousand miles back home and, well, between you and me . . . a bit of a dork.'

Candy takes out a flask, sits down and drinks. She hands it to Jake.

Nick and Lisa head over. The four of them watch Zeb and Gandalf run tirelessly around the summit.

'Where you staying?' Nick asks.

'We're camping down near Betwis-a-Curd,' Lisa replies.

Jake politely corrects her. 'It's Betws-y-Coed.'

'They got some weird names in Wales.' Lisa sits down.

Zeb hurls the ball. It flies over the edge. Everyone stops as Gandalf bounds after it. The scrawny puppy tries to stop himself at the edge, scrabbling around in scree and dust for a moment, then tumbles forward out of sight. No one moves, except Zeb who runs towards the edge full tilt.

'Shitting GANDALF!!' He keeps running, stumbles over the edge and disappears.

Nick stands bolt upright, hand over mouth. He sprints towards the edge.

As he reaches it, Zeb pops his head up and beams at him.

'SUCK . . . errrs!!!' Gandalf runs back over, ball in mouth, towards Jake.

'You little fucking . . .' Nick shouts at Zeb.

'Leave him, Dad,' Jake shouts. 'He's only winding you up.'

Zeb darts Nick a look and shouts 'Boo!' as he runs past him. Enraged, Nick picks up a small rock and hurls it at him. It misses.

'Hey!' Candy shouts, 'Go easy.' Zeb's face turns from laughter to concentration as he avoids Nick's attempts to grab him. Jake can see something is wrong. Nick slumps to the ground, exhausted. He puts his head in his hands.

Zeb stops near Jake. 'Is he crying?'

'Dad doesn't cry. He's messing, tryin' to trick you so he can give you a kicking.'

'No he is . . . he's crying.'

Candy walks over to Nick and puts her arm round him. Zeb stands tight to Jake's side.

'Probably just doing it to get her to put her bloody arm round him,' Jake whispers to Zeb.

'He looks proper upset. I was only joking. I didn't mean to make him cry.' Zeb is becoming distressed, bottom lip quivering, trying to hold back tears.

'You didn't make him cry, bro. It's not your fault. He's just being stupid and fucked up.'

Jake sees Nick shaking his head, like he wants to be left alone. Something about it looks real. He feels scared. Jake knows in this moment he's in charge. It's the first time he's felt this kind of power. He doesn't want it. Not yet. But he takes it, for Zeb's sake. He continues to stare at Nick who has now lit up a cigarette, two good-looking women consoling him. Jake experiences a skin-crawling cocktail of anger, sympathy and jealousy. He rests his hand on Zeb's shoulder and keeps his eyes on his father, and Lisa.

Ten

Jake lies in his tent, eyes wide, listening to the footsteps of Nick and the American girls arriving back from the pub. The girls giggle, trying overly hard to keep quiet. A rush of jealousy fires up his back. He rolls over. Zeb is asleep next to him. He wanted to sleep with Jake because he was freaked out by Nick's breakdown. Gandalf snores erratically.

Jake and Zeb both knew Nick would be getting drunk the moment he invited the girls to the pub. Jake knew it was for more than getting them into bed. That was how Nick dealt with his shit. He and Zeb both hate him when he's pissed.

Jake slides his hand down his pants, closes his eyes and pictures Lisa in his mind. He hears the van door open, Nick and the women clamber in.

After a good while, Jake slides into a resentful sleep.

The sound of the zip wakes him abruptly. Zeb remains sound asleep. Gandalf sits up looking at the dishevelled, drunken face of Nick peering in.

'Hey, kid, what you up to?'

'What do you mean what am I up to! I'm fucking asleep!' Jake kisses his teeth.

'No you ain't.' He laughs, raising his finger to his lips.

'What do you want, Dad? You woke me up.'

'Come out here a sec. Shhh.'

'I'm sleeping. Go away . . . you're pissed.'

'Yess . . . I'm pissed, so are the girls. Come on, you ain't got school in the morning, we can all have a lie-in.'

Jake reluctantly gets up and puts on his trousers, jumper and hat and scrambles out to the small porch. He slides his boots on, leaving the laces undone. As he stands he realises what is happening. Nick is standing silently next to Candy who is smiling warmly at Jake, giggling a little.

'Candy says she wants to give you a birthday present.'

'It's not my birthday.'

'Yes it is,' Nick insists winking at him. 'Soon.'

'Did you just wink at your son? You lying jerk, it isn't his birthday!'

'Yes it is,' Nick protests, '. . . soon. Ain't it, kid?'

Jake is speechless.

Candy walks over to him and takes him by the hand. 'Come on, birthday boy. Let's go see the stars.'

Jake doesn't speak and doesn't object. She leads him down to the river. He trips on his bootlace, stops, does both laces up and takes hold of Candy's hand again. He looks back over his shoulder as Nick heads back to the van.

'Your pop sure has got a lot of energy for someone his age.'

'How old did he say he was?'

'Thirty-nine. Said he had you young. Why?'

'Don't believe what he tells you, specially when he's drunk.'

'I'll take that as sound device . . . I mean advice.'

Jake can see Candy is trying not to look as drunk as she is. They continue to walk through the wet grass towards the river.

'What are we doing?' he asks.

'Going for a walk, with a stunning lady from LA down to a cute river in Wales beneath the shtars. Good with that?'

'What did he say to you?'

'About what?'

'Me.'

'What would he say?' Candy leans down and rips a handful of grass up, then rubs it over her face. 'Oh my god you have to try this, this is amazing.' She thrusts the grass at him. He shakes his head.

'Too cold.'

'Oh come on.' She stops, stands in front of him and rubs the wet grass over his eyes and face. She looks at him for a moment, takes hold of his hand and continues walking towards the river. Jake wishes Candy were Lisa but he doesn't want to let go of her hand. They reach the bank of the river and head for a tree hanging over the water. Candy lets go of his hand and clambers on to the lowest branch. Jake follows and sits too far from her. He pulls up his collar. Candy seems unaware of the cold.

'Come closer. You can keep me warm.' Jake slides in towards her.

'Gotta girl back home?' she asks.

'Kind of.' Jake breaks off a dead branch, snaps it into smaller twigs and begins to chuck them into the water.

'She pretty? Bet she is. Good-looking guy like you.'

Jake nods.

'What colour is her hair?'

'Brown.'

'Damn, I'd love brown hair. And I bet it's long and straight.'

Jake nods again.

Silence falls between them for a while. Jake begins to loosen up, feeling more comfortable.

'You don't seem to get on too good with your pop.'

'He irritates the shit out of me.'

'So did mine when I was your age.' She slaps her forehead with her palm. 'Sorry, I didn't mean that to sound the way it came out.'

Jake shrugs his shoulders, continuing to lob the small broken twigs into the water.

'He isn't so bad.' Candy looks up at the stars.

'Who?'

'Your dad.'

'You don't know him.'

'I got good instincts. He's a little mixed up but hey, who isn't. He loves you guys. Talks about you all the time.'

'Can we talk about something else?'

'Put your arms around me.'

Jake is unable to hide his surprise.

'Don't be scared, here.' She takes both his arms and puts them over her shoulders. 'Now show me how you kiss this pretty brown-haired girl back home.'

Jake's heart thumps into his chest.

'I . . . I'm not . . .' Candy leans forward and kisses him softly on the lips. His shock leaves him. She puts her hand round the back of his head. He begins to tentatively kiss her back. He can taste and smell the alcohol and cigarettes on her breath. He carries on. She pulls slowly back, kissing him twice on the lips by way of a full stop.

'Well that girl of yours sure is lucky. You kiss good!' Candy wipes her lips.

'Can we do it again?' Jake asks, clearly embarrassed.

'Let me catch my breath . . . tiger.' Jake feels aroused, awkward and unable to look her in the eye.

'Did he make you do this?' he asks.

'Who?'

'Dad.'

'Too much tequila. Not with you, babe.'

'Did he make you take me out here?'

'What kind of a girl do you think I am! Got a mind of my own, you know.'

'How old are you?' Jake asks, feeling angry, more confident.

'You should know never to ask a lady her age.' Jake takes out a cigarette. She rests her hand on his knee. 'You're cute, you know that?'

Jake puts the cigarette into the corner of his mouth, breaks off another piece of branch and repeats the ritual of snapping and chucking.

'Is Dad screwing Lisa?'

'You like her, huh?' He shrugs. 'Not sure what he's doing but if it's anything like what we . . .' She breaks off. Jake shoots her a look.

She squeezes his leg harder. He wants to move it away

123

but doesn't. 'Come on, hon. We're just having some fun here, good times, no need to get uptight, keep it groovy, hey.'

Jake wants to kill Nick.

'Can I have sex with you?' he asks.

'I'm not sure that's in the plan, honey.'

Jake shrugs and chucks the last of the twigs into the river. He hears a screech of laughter coming from the van. Candy looks back up the field then back to Jake.

Jake slides off the branch back on to the bank, puts his hands in his pockets and heads back across the field.

'Hey! Wait up, soldier.' Candy jogs unsteadily after him and puts her arm round his shoulders.

As they reach the site they're greeted with Zeb's face peering out of the tent, palms supporting chin, smiling. Gandalf next to him.

'You two been snogging?' Zeb asks.

Jake says nothing. He crawls back into the tent.

'Night you guys.' Zeb watches Candy intently as she heads back to the van.

Zeb wakes, mouth dry, eyes half stuck together. He's cold. Gandalf is sitting on his chest. He looks over to Jake who is sound asleep. He pushes Gandalf off, sits up and unzips the entrance. He wants to see Nick but is still unsure about being around him. He slides quietly out of the tent and looks around. He hasn't seen the camp in daylight. It stretches down to the river and is shielded by high hedges on all three other sides. He casually unzips and pisses in the middle of the field, humming to himself. He looks over at the van weighing up what to do next.

He heads tentatively over. The curtains are drawn. He knows there are no curtains on the windscreen. His heart beats a little faster. He creeps round the front and steps up on to the chrome bumper. His feet find a secure place to push up from. Gandalf starts nipping his ankles.

'Piss off.' The dog takes this as a signal to bite harder. 'Ow! Piss off I said!' Zeb kicks him. The dog gets the message. Zeb hauls himself up on to the bonnet and peers through the windscreen. He sees Nick asleep at the wheel, dribble on chin and cheek, hair sticking out in a hundred directions. Zeb reckons he looks like Sideshow Bob and laughs then stops. He looks past Nick to the back, squinting to see if he can spot either of the women. He can't make out anyone and gives up the stealth routine. He thumps on the window hard, several times. Nick jerks awake, bashing his head on the side window, looking around confused.

'Morning! Which one did you bonk? Where are they? Where's Candy? Where's Lisa?'

Nick opens the door and stumbles out.

'Fuck me.' He squats down and holds his head. Zeb jumps off the bumper and runs round to the open door. He clambers in and looks around. The van is empty. He leans back out.

'Where are they?'

'Who?' Nick covers his eyes with one hand, holds his head steady with the other.

'Candy and Lisa, dufus!'

'Went back to their hostel. Keep your voice down will you.' Nick is doing his best to stay still.

This is the only part Zeb likes about Nick getting drunk. He knows he's got the upper hand when he's hungover. He may get nasty or stupid when he's pissed but when he's hungover he's easy to deal with. Gandalf takes hold of Nick's shirt in his teeth and pulls.

'Get the wizard off me for fuck sake. I need a brew. Stick the kettle on, kid.'

Zeb runs to the back of the van, opens it up and takes out the kettle and gas stove. Nick heads unsteadily down to the river. Gandalf follows.

Zeb watches his dad as he splashes himself with water shouting at the cold of it.

Five minutes later he heads back up to the van. Zeb pours the water and stirs the bags around with skill.

'Did you bonk Lisa last night?'

'I'm not sure that's any of your business, sunshine.'

'Tell me . . . I bet you did. I won't tell Mum . . . promise.'

'Mum doesn't give a shit any more.'

'Or Jake.'

'He might.'

'Was she a good snogger?'

'Candy?'

'You snogged Candy! Thas dissgusting.'

'Both actually.'

'You snogged them both!!'

'Something like that.'

'Errr . . . you are rank!' Zeb pulls a contorted face.

Nick lights a cigarette and takes the tea from Zeb. He sits on the passenger seat of the van, door open, looking across at Jake's tent. Zeb sits on the base of the door frame at Nick's feet.

'How was Jake?' Nick asks.

'When?'

'Last night when he came back to the tent.'

'Pissed off as usual.'

'He say anything about Candy?' Nick slurps on the tea.

'No, but I know he snogged her. She could be his mum.'

Nick smiles to himself and takes a drag on his fag. Zeb sips his tea while stroking Gandalf. He looks up at Nick, seeing if he's still soft with the hangover, still approachable.

'Dad.'

'Yes, kid.'

'Why did you cry yesterday?'

'You scared me.'

'I didn't mean to.'

'I know.'

'You don't normally cry when you're scared . . . you normally shout or break things.'

'I'm sorry, kid. Really.'

Zeb wants to keep talking but he doesn't know what to say.

'Your granddad died when I was your age. Up there.' Zeb follows his line of sight back up the summit of Snowdon. 'It was an accident. I thought it was my fault.'

'But it wasn't your fault was it?'

'No. But I did want him dead. Prayed hard for it. Thought god was doing me a favour.'

Zeb can see Nick holding tears back. He hopes he doesn't cry again.

Jake emerges from his tent and heads down to the river. Nick and Zeb watch him.

'What happened to him?' Zeb asks.

'Tripped over, smashed his head open.' Nick is tight-lipped.

'Thas nasty.' Zeb watches Nick closely. His father's eyes glisten.

'If anything like that happened to you it'd be my fault and I don't know what I'd do, kid.'

'Nothing's gonna happen to me, Dad, I got super powers and I'm really strong.' Zeb shows Nick the muscles on his arm. Nick clears his throat, smiles down at him, finishes his tea and gets up. Gandalf barks.

'That fucking dog's driving me mad. Come on, I got a plan, shake off this hangover.' Nick heads down to the river, Zeb in tow.

Jake sits on the same branch he and Candy sat on the night before, carving into the trunk.

'Hey, kid.' Nick walks up to him.

'Piss off.' Jake doesn't look up. He carries on carving.

'Sleep OK?'

'Not up for it, Dad.'

'What you up to?' Jake doesn't reply. Nick looks down at the trunk. The letters 'L' and 'I' are gouged into the bark. Jake continues on without looking at Nick. Zeb watches the river, tossing Gandalf's toy from hand to hand. Nick looks at him.

'Don't even think about it, we'll never get him back.' He brings his focus back to Jake. 'We're going on a boat trip.' Zeb looks up at Nick, beaming.

'Boat trip! Boat trip! Ooh ahh. Yes, mister.' Zeb draws his elbow into his side, clenches his fist and punches the air. 'Ha!'

Jake continues carving.

'How was last night?' Nick asks.

'How was Lisa?' Jake's neck and face redden in anger.

'We're heading off in half an hour. Put your tent away. We'll go into town and get a fry-up.'

Nick heads back up to the van.

Zeb climbs up on to the branch and sits close to Jake. Jake continues carving, finishing off the letter 'S'. He gives up and stops. Zeb looks down.

'LIS? Who's LIS?'

'Lisa, you doughnut.'

'Thought you snogged Candy. Make your chonking mind up. What was it like?'

'None of your business.'

'Tell me . . . pleeease.'

Jake breaks into a thin grin. 'She was all right.'

'She was well old.'

'Twenty-eight isn't old. Dad is old. She was cool.' Jake clicks his penknife shut. 'She had great tits.'

Zeb is scared of the bent, raggedy man standing by the boats. His face is covered in deep, black pock marks. His baseball cap looks like he's had it on for a hundred years and his dungarees are covered in dirt, oil and the fading red of what could be Ribena or blood. He stares into the water like he's waiting for something to happen. Zeb falls back behind Nick as they approach, keeping a close eye on the man. Nick walks up to the boats, checking them out. Gandalf sniffs at what Zeb thinks must be dog piss on an old boat. Jake has his eye on a single kayak.

'We're not open,' the boatman grumbles in a deep Valleys accent, still staring at the water.

'We can wait.' Nick looks around, whistling.

'Not for two weeks you can't.'

Zeb tugs on Nick's jacket. 'Dad.'

'Hang on a sec, kid.' He persists. 'It's all money. We only want them for a few hours. How much do you charge for the one boat? Something big enough for the three of us.'

The man keeps his eye on the water. Jake walks up to the bank and looks down following the man's line of sight into the deep pool of fast-moving brown water.

The man repeats himself. 'Like I said, not open for another two weeks, 'til the start of the season.'

Zeb tugs at Nick's coat again, whispering to him, 'I want to go, Dad. Don't want to canoe any more. Don't like him, he smells.' Nick places his hand softly on Zeb's head, reassuring him into silence, then walks over to the man and talks to him up close. Jake and Zeb are too far away to make out what he's saying. The man takes his eyes off the water a moment, looks at Jake and Zeb then turns to the boats.

Zeb and Jake walk up to them cautiously.

'You can have one of these two, both if you like.' The boatman points to two of the more battered-looking boats. A single kayak and a two-man canoe. He jabs his finger at the canoe. 'She lets in a bit of water. There's a bit of Tupper to bail her out. Won't sink.'

Zeb walks cautiously over to the canoe, looking back to check with Nick that it's OK. Nick nods. Zeb clambers in almost tipping it over. He picks up the oar from the inside wall and starts to paddle the air.

Nick turns back to the man and takes out a small wad of cash. Jake watches him. Nick clearly gives him more than the trip is worth. The man counts, nods and heads back to the small hut behind the boats.

'Know how to paddle?' Jake asks Nick.

'No . . . but you do so you can show us.' Nick and Jake pull out the canoe, once Zeb has got out of it, and Zeb pulls out the kayak. The three of them haul the boats to the bank. Jake hides his excitement.

'I'll get our stuff. Zeb, give us a hand.' Nick and Zeb head to the van. Jake looks down into the spot that had so much of the boatman's attention. He gradually makes out the shape of a boat on the river bed. The sight of it makes him shiver. He turns and pulls his kayak to the edge and waits for Zeb and Nick.

Jake relishes the feeling of the water underneath the kayak. He likes that he doesn't have to share the feeling with anyone. Nick and Zeb are a few yards ahead. Zeb is struggling to coordinate his paddle strokes with Nick's.

Jake shouts up to Zeb, 'Slow down, bro, way too manic. Watch Dad . . . copy him.'

'I'm pissing trying!' Zeb is clearly struggling with the size of the paddle.

Jake paddles a little faster to get himself closer to their boat. 'Hold it closer to the wide bit at the end.' Zeb slides his hand down and starts to get more control of his strokes. 'Nice. Look at you now, proper paddler, blood!'

Nick keeps looking ahead and occasionally to the side, at the bank. Jake stops paddling and allows himself to slip back. He keeps the kayak straight, looking back downriver at the lines of massive, leafless beech trees on the far side. He puts his paddle down beside him and puts his hand into the water. His fingers go numb in an instant. He keeps them submerged for another minute, then picks the paddle back up. He watches Nick and Zeb get smaller, enjoying the distance, the silence and the feeling that he can stop any time he likes.

They continue on for another hour, Jake keeping a good distance behind. Nick spots a small stone beach and paddles towards it.

'What we doing, Dad?' Zeb asks.

'Lunch.'

'Yes!'

The boat scrapes along the stones. Nick jumps out and pulls the rest of it on to the shore. Zeb and Gandalf hop out. They look downriver watching Jake slowly paddle up to the shoreline.

'Come on, slowcoach!' Zeb shouts.

Jake paddles gently up to them. 'Ain't nothing wrong with slow, you should know that, spaz.' Jake speeds up his paddling and heads for the beach. 'Torpedo style!!' The boat scrapes on to the stones and he jumps out. 'What's for lunch? I'm starving.'

'Liking the water, kid?' Nick smiles at him.

'Wicked.' Jake grins.

Nick hands out the foil-wrapped sandwiches and sits down on a soft verge and opens his own.

'I'm gonna make a fire,' Jake announces.

Nick nods. Jake takes a bite of his sandwich, gets up and heads into the thin strand of trees.

'Where we going next, Dad?' Zeb asks, mouth full of cheese and bread.

'North.'

'Where north?'

'Dunno. Lake District?'

'I miss Mum.'

'We'll call her later. Need to charge the phone.'

'Can she come and meet us in the Lake District?'

'Don't think she'll be up for that, not with me about.'

'Maybe you could go somewhere for a day and we could spend a day with her?' Zeb takes another bite out of his sandwich then inspects the bread and its contents.

Jake comes back a few moments later with an armful of wood.

Nick looks up at him. 'Got some kindling?'

'Not much. Plenty of this though.' Jake takes out a wad of dried newspapers from inside his jacket and his lighter.

'Check out the boy scout.' Nick finishes off his sandwich.

Jake clears an area and lays a ring of pebbles down in a circle. Nick and Zeb watch him build the fire.

'Dad says Mum can come visit us in the Lake District,' Zeb tells Jake.

'Ain't exactly what I said, kid. We can talk about it.'

Gandalf picks up a stick in his teeth and drops it at Zeb's feet. Zeb chucks it into the water.

Jake lights the fire, leans down and blows into the flames. Zeb sits closer and starts poking it.

'Stop fucking about with it Zeb, you'll put it out. Watch how a master makes fire.'

Zeb sits back reluctantly and does as he's told. Nick

takes out a flask of coffee and pours the three of them a cup each. He rolls a joint, sits back and watches Jake, pride easily visible. The flames rise. Jake picks up some larger pieces of wood and hands a few to Zeb.

'Wood has to be bone dry, you can tell by snapping it and listening to the way it sounds.' He brings a twig to his ear, snaps it, nods and puts it on the fire. Zeb copies him. 'If it's the tiniest bit wet it'll put the fire out. Start-up's always a bitch.'

Jake continues to snap the twigs and small branches with Zeb following his lead. The fire builds as does the heat.

Jake gives Zeb his orders. 'Get some more wood, bro, we'll make it big.'

'Looks big enough.' Nick gets up and moves closer, holding his hands out, warming the palms.

'I want it bigger,' Jake responds.

'Your call, kid, it's your fire.'

Zeb heads off into the trees for more wood.

Jake and Nick squat, facing the fire, staring into the flames, calm in each other's company. Nick hands Jake the joint. Jake looks at him a moment, then reaches out for it. Rain spits down on to their heads and hisses into the flames. It starts to come down in a mist but not enough to dampen the fire. Nick pulls up the collar of his jacket. Jake takes a single drag on the joint and hands it back. Their eyes connect for a moment. Jake gives Nick a nod then brings his attention back to the fire.

Emily walks over to the mirror. The bags under her eyes have lengthened and darkened. She looks worn. Jake and

Zeb have been gone three days. It's happened before. Nick is consistent in his irresponsibility at least. Two nights without sleep and her nerves are frayed beyond sensible thought or decision. She has never felt quite so powerless or angry. She straightens her hair and wipes the tears from her cheek.

She picks up the phone and dials Sally's number. It rings once before answering.

'Em? That you, babe? Christ. Thought you were gonna call at nine?'

'I managed to get back to sleep for an hour. I'm here now.'

'What's happening? Has he called?'

'Not a bloody word. I can understand a day, that's almost normal, but three days is wrong, I know it. I keep feeling like I'm gonna throw up.'

'That wanker been round again?'

'No. I'm not opening the door to anyone unless I know they're coming round.' Emily sits on the stairs.

'Call the police,' Sally insists.

'Not yet.'

'Why the hell not? Seriously, babe, you have to do something. As they say, "Shit ain't right." '

'You don't need to tell me.'

'You don't even know if they're OK. You should visit Warren.'

'I've put in for a visit. I'm going to Pentonville this afternoon.'

'If you don't hear back from him or the kids by the end of the day I'll call the police.'

Emily wipes the tears from her eyes. 'Jesus Christ I'm

gonna fucking kill Nick when I see him.' Emily pauses for a moment. 'Come round, sis. Frank's at work. I need you to help me get myself together.'

'Get the kettle on, girl.'

Zeb sits in the bow of the boat rowing, focused, tongue sticking out. Gandalf sits behind him staring insanely at his toy, waiting for it to do something. Behind them, Nick looks about, joint in his mouth, a smile on his face. Jake is further back in his kayak, taking his time.

'How long 'til we get back to the scary boatman?' Zeb asks.

'Your pace? 'Bout half an hour. Tired?'

'Nope. I'm superhuman.'

They continue on for a few more minutes then Zeb stops and looks back at Nick.

'Need a piss?' Nick asks. Zeb nods. 'Can you wait?' Zeb shakes his head. 'Do it over the side but be careful.' Zeb puts down his paddle and starts to carefully undo his trousers. The boat slows down.

Jake glides up to the side of the canoe. 'Pissing again, star?'

'Piss off,' Zeb replies.

'Got that right, piss off the side of the boat,' Jake mocks. 'You need to see a doctor, mate.'

Jake drops back, staying close to the rear of the canoe. Zeb stands up unsteadily.

'Easy, kid.' Nick stops paddling and lets Zeb get his balance. The boat steadies and Zeb starts to piss.

'Ahhh yess!'

Gandalf puts his paws on the edge of the boat and looks

down at the steady steaming stream as it hits the water. His weight tips the boat slightly forward and Zeb starts to lose his balance.

Nick tries to counter it. 'Get down, kid.'

'But I haven't finished.'

'Get down or you'll go in.'

The boat rocks more. He starts to piss over his leg and trousers. Jake bursts out laughing.

'You dirty bastard!' he shouts at Zeb. Zeb looks over to him, still trying to do his zip up, still trying to rebalance, slightly panicked.

Nick raises his voice. 'Sit down, Zeb, for fuck sake!'

Zeb stumbles forward and puts his hand on the side to stop him going in. His soft palm slips on the piss-wet wood. He falls head first into the water. Gandalf barks three times and jumps in after him.

'For fuck sake!' Nick stands up, the boat rocks, side to side, he sits back down, looking back to Jake. 'Fuck, Jake, get over there, he still can't fucking swim.'

Jake paddles quickly across to the rippling water. Zeb is out of sight. Gandalf is circling, barking repeatedly.

'ZEB! Fuck. ZEB!' Jake dips his paddle into the river searching around in the water. It hits something solid, soft and moving. 'He's down there,' he shouts back to Nick. He feels something grab the paddle. He knows it's Zeb.

A few seconds later the weight on the paddle eases. Jake freaks.

'Fuck do we do, kid! I can't fucking swim,' Nick shouts, panicking. He paddles over to get close to Jake looking at his son for instruction. In a single movement, Jake flips his kayak and slides out of it into the murky, ice-cold water and begins looking. He swims down. Seconds pass. His heart hammers in his chest. The searching strips him of oxygen. He swims in broad strokes feeling ahead, blinded by the murk. Nothing but empty water. He pushes up and rises to the surface. Gandalf is right by his head, barking.

'Fuckoff, Gandalf!' He looks at the bank and sees that they are moving. The current is stronger than he thought. Nick is trying to steer the canoe closer, eyes wide, looking utterly helpless.

'Not too close, Dad,' Jake shouts up at him, breathless. 'Grab hold of the kayak, keep it over there. Don't wanna mash my head.' He dives back down and carries on his search. He wonders how long it's been. How long could Zeb survive without oxygen? How long in the cold? All the pieces of information he'd gathered on his school trips clatter into his head. He's not losing his brother. He ignores the exhaustion and cold and swims down deeper. He quickly hits the bottom, blindly feeling around in mud, gravel and rock. He moves forward; his hands reach the edge of what must be a hole; a deeper part of the river bed. Instinctively he swims further down into it and reaches the still shape of what he knows is his brother.

Eleven

Despite his heavy-set frame and height, Milton walks into Betws-y-Coed unnoticed. He prides himself on his quiet footfall. He prides himself on his work.

He heads for the nearest café, enters, orders a full English and sits himself down. He opens up his guide book and looks at the list of B and Bs and hostels. Most are ticked off, a few left.

He waits another five minutes for his breakfast to arrive.

The steep stone steps leading to the log cabin are wet and slippery. Milton steadies himself, heads up and through the main doors.

A small man walks out of the back office and greets him.

'Looking for a room?' the man asks.

'Just the one night, yes . . . please.' Milton looks around.

The man looks down at his bag. 'Not here for the walking then?'

'Just passing through, heading north.'

'Bloody cold up there. Still got four foot of snow in Scotland.'

'Sounds magical.'

'Twenty-five pounds a night.'

Milton takes out his wallet and pays cash. 'Busy?'

'Not really, for the time of year. Got an old couple, retired, fitter than I'll ever be, a young feller and a couple of Yanks. Good lookers.' He winks at Milton. 'I'll show you to your room.'

The young man, Candy and Lisa sit in the communal kitchen eating pasta. Milton walks in and makes himself a cup of tea. Lisa eyes him up.

Candy leans forward, whispering. 'You are unbelievable! Eat your food, girl.' The young man looks over to Candy and smiles.

Milton walks over to the table. 'Mind if I join you?'

'Sure,' Lisa replies. 'Sit yourself down.'

An awkward silence falls on the table for a moment. Milton sips his tea.

Lisa keeps a sly eye on him for a while then breaks the silence.

'You don't look like a walker.'

'I walk, just not mountains. Not often anyway.' Milton smiles at her.

'Strange place to stay if you don't walk,' the young man says. 'There are much nicer places around than this dump.'

'Not really into the upmarket stuff. Waste of money. Prefer things to be more . . . homely.' Milton puts his cup gently down.

'Well you'll get that here,' Candy laughs.

Milton feigns puzzlement.

'Let's just say it's a little rough round the edges here.' She takes a mouthful of pasta. 'So, business or pleasure?'

'Looking for some friends. We were supposed to meet back down near Brecon. Got there late . . . missed them.'

'Lady friends or men friends?' Lisa asks. Candy kicks her under the table.

'Man. I think his boys are with him.'

'Hey we know those guys! We saw them last night . . . damn, this is a small country.' Candy sits up.

'Well isn't that a coincidence. They still here?' Milton asks.

'No,' Lisa chips in. 'They're headed up to the Lake District.'

'I wanted to catch him before he gets there. He can be a little slow in getting where he's headed . . . and hard to find.'

'We're meeting up with him and his kids in Windermere in a couple of days,' Candy continues. 'Said he was gonna take them on a boat trip on the way up.'

'Which river?' Milton is aware this is probably one question too far.

'The Dee, I think. We had a look on the map . . . he seemed undecided.'

'Glad I bumped into you, good job I'm not into posh hotels, ey.' Milton smiles warmly at Candy and Lisa. 'I'll be getting to bed. Early start. Hopefully I'll catch him up before he changes his mind again.'

Milton finishes his tea, says goodnight and leaves.

* * *

Jake drags Zeb to the shore. Nick follows behind in the canoe, paddling furiously, eyes fixed on the limp body of his son. He doesn't see Gandalf paddling ahead. He runs into the dog, pushing him under before the animal has time to make a sound.

Nick looks down. Gandalf's face bobs, blood pouring from mouth and nose, and sinks back down again. 'Fuck.' Nick is beginning to feel cursed. He continues rowing hard to the shore. He sees Jake hunched over Zeb, pushing down frantically on his chest. He opens his mouth and blows into it. Nick jumps out of the boat and runs over.

'Fuck's happening!?'

'Fuck does it look like! Trying to save my brother's fucking life!'

Jake pushes down on to Zeb's small ribcage trying to get the water out of his lungs. It begins to trickle out of his mouth and nose. Nick is reminded of Gandalf. Utterly distressed, he paces up and down, hands holding his head, eyes fixed on Zeb's blue-white face, his wet hair matted to his small skull. Jake continues his resuscitation for another ninety seconds.

Zeb finally splutters and convulses and chokes up several pints of dark water. He starts gasping for air.

'Attack.' Jake takes out Zeb's inhaler from his jeans pocket and pushes several shots into his mouth. He rolls him on to his side and rests his hand on his back rubbing it, calming him. Zeb starts shivering with cold.

'You're cool, bro. Easy.'

Nick bends down, moving the hair from Zeb's face.

'Jesus fucking Christ, kid, you frightened the life out of me.'

Zeb sits up slowly, bewildered, shivering uncontrollably. Nick takes off his jacket and wraps it round his shoulders. Zeb looks at Jake then at Nick, then at the water. Between the chatter of teeth and waves of shivering he manages to get out two words.

'Where's Gandalf?'

Vincent sits on the veranda of his house staring down into the garden. The sun behind the trees and buildings has disappeared. He feels the chill hit him. He walks back into the house shutting the garden doors behind him. The fire in the living room is almost out. He walks over to the hearth, picks up a large pine log and drops it into the embers.

He sits down on the sofa, resting his head back. He sees several cracks in the ceiling, tuts and closes his eyes.

A few moments later his mobile rings. He answers it, eyes closed.

'Fucking useless, cunt of a phone.'

'That you, Milton?' Vincent asks.

'The very same.'

Vincent opens his eyes and looks ahead into the fire. The wood has taken. Flames lick under the wood.

'How's it all going?'

'It's freezing out here and this log cabin is a joke. You're not paying me enough.'

'Paying you plenty. Any luck?'

'Some.'

'Enlighten me.' Vincent sits up.

'Had a stroke of it in Betws-y-Coed.'

'Nice part of the world.'

'If you're into shit-cold rain, mud and mountains. Met a couple of Yanks in the hostel; they talked a lot. Turns out Geneva's done us a favour and been putting it about . . . with the pair of them by the looks of it.'

'Small world. Where is he?'

'Heading up to the Lake District. Cunt's doing a grand tour . . . with his kids. Fucking halfwit has taken them with him.'

Vincent leans forward and picks up a half-drunk glass of Scotch.

'What are you going to do about them?'

'No idea,' Milton responds flatly.

'No bodies. Just a little damage for Geneva and the money. Where are you?'

'Couple of miles outside Windermere. Going in tomorrow. A man and two kids'll be easy to remember.'

Jake and Zeb walk through Windermere looking in the shop windows. Jake stops and looks at the display in a camping shop. Zeb continues walking uninterested.

'Wait up!' Jake shouts. Zeb stops but doesn't turn around. Jake brings his attention back to the window and the sheath knife.

Zeb hasn't spoken more than a few words in two days. He's had nightmares through the night. Nothing has worked to make him feel better. Jake's tried to distract him at every turn, cheer him up, make him forget the river and Gandalf. He knows he's failed and feels shit about it. Nothing usually fazes Zeb. He bounces back. But Jake is worried. He knows he should get them back to London but despite nearly drowning Zeb still wants to stay.

144

'Check this out, blood, this is a beauty.' Jake waves him over.

Zeb turns lethargically and walks to the window looking in. Jake points at the largest of the three knives on display. 'Whadda ya reckon? Cool one or what.'

Zeb says nothing.

'Come on. I'm getting us one each.' Zeb looks up at him suspiciously. 'Nicked some money from Dad. He won't miss it. Make us even for shagging Lisa. If we're out in the middle of fucking nowhere we need knives.'

Zeb nods.

They head into the shop. An old man stands behind the counter sizing them both up.

'Can I help you?' he asks in a broad, Brummy accent.

'We'd like to buy some knives,' Jake responds, politely. 'Two knives, the ones in the window.'

'Would you now.' He stares down at them both. Jake feels himself getting angry at being scrutinised.

Zeb pulls Jake's jacket. 'I don't really want a knife.'

'Yeah you do, you've always wanted a knife.' Jake brings his attention back to the shopkeeper. 'The two in the window, we'd like the two sheath knives in the window . . . please.'

The shopkeeper walks out from behind the counter and gets the knives. Jake takes out a wad of five-pound notes and gives the man thirty pounds' worth. The knives are wrapped in a brown paper bag and handed to Jake.

'Don't know what you're intending with these but you be careful. They need looking after, sharpening, taking care of . . . think of them as your children.' Zeb gives him a weird look. 'Treat them with respect.'

'I'll remember that when I'm gutting the next rabbit,' Jake replies brightly.

Jake and Zeb stand in the alley checking the knives out.

Jake looks at his proudly, angling the blade into the sun. Zeb shields his eyes.

'Wanna be blood brothers?' Jake asks.

'We already are, you plonker. You got my blood and I got yours.'

'But we haven't done it Comanche style.'

'What's shitting Comanche style?'

'I cut my thumb, you cut yours and we press 'em together . . . we'll be double blood brothers, for life.'

Zeb looks at him suspiciously. 'I don't wanna cut my thumb.'

'You scared?'

'No.'

'Then do it.'

Jake draws the tip of the blade across the top of his thumb. A drop of blood beads out followed by a thin line of red.

Zeb looks at it wide-eyed then up at Jake. Jake twists his wrist to stop the blood dripping to the ground.

'You cut my thumb then I'll do it.' Zeb holds his breath.

Without hesitation, Jake takes hold of Zeb's hand, turns it palm up and draws the blade along the fingerprint of his brother's undersized thumb. Zeb squeezes his eyes shut.

Before Zeb has a chance to see it, Jake presses their thumbs together.

By the time he pulls his away, both cuts have clotted. Without speaking he takes out a tissue, tears it in half, wraps one round Zeb's thumb, one round his.

'Sweet one, bro.' Jake smiles at him. 'Now we're proper blood brothers innit. We stick by each other no matter what. Don't tell Dad and don't let him see, promise?'

Zeb nods then puts his tissued hand into his pocket.

Jake takes his belt off, loops it through the back of the sheath, puts the belt back on and tucks the knife into his back pocket.

'Now you,' he tells Zeb.

Zeb attempts to copy Jake. He gets halfway before he gives up. Jake completes the looping for him.

'Looking the part now, bro. No doubt.'

Zeb gives him a half smile. 'I want Gandalf back.'

'I know, bro. Nothing we can do about it now.'

'I wanted to bury him.'

'River's got him now, blood.'

'I'm hungry.'

'Come on, I'll get us a pasty.'

'I want to talk to Mum.'

'So do I. We'll call her after on Dad's mob.' Jake leads the way.

'Why haven't you got a mobile like Dad?'

'Too tight to buy me one.' Jake takes out his wallet. 'But we'll get us one, pay as you go innit, you can call Mum as much as you like.'

They head back out on to the high street. Zeb follows quietly a few paces behind.

Jake sees Milton walking towards them and is frightened. Nick has told him to always trust this feeling. He doesn't know him, doesn't know why he's scared but the feeling is strong enough for him to take Zeb by the jacket and veer them on to the other side of the road.

'Oi!' Zeb complains. 'What you shitting doing?'

'Schtum,' Jake commands. They cross the road. Milton checks them both out. He keeps walking and keeps looking until they reach the safety of the other side of the street.

Nick sits by the lake shore looking out across the water, a handful of stones in his palm. He skims them on the water one by one, watching the line of mountains reflected in reverse ripple with each impact. He chucks the last one, watching it bounce three times before it sinks.

He stands and heads back into town.

As he walks down the main high street Nick notices the heavy-set frame of a man, alone, looking into the camping shop window, hands behind his back. Milton. Something about him gets Nick's attention. Paranoia? Caution. Both. He knows there is always a possibility of this; the threat of danger. And he always trusts his instincts, like his dad told him. He notices the man's clothes first: too smart for the time of day. Immaculate trousers, jacket, shoes. Cosmopolitan; a London look a long way off from the nature-loving hiker's gear. The familiar twist of warning in Nick's gut confirms something is wrong about this man. He turns his fear into action and carries on walking. He heads into the off-licence and walks to the counter.

'Half a bottle of Scotch, cheapest you got.' He hands the money over and puts the bottle into his back pocket. As he walks out he takes another quick look down the street.

Milton is gone. He turns left and walks back up the street up towards the bakery and shops. The sun breaks through the grey, hitting his face, boosting his confidence. He knows he has to act quick and he knows he has to stay away from the kids.

As he turns the next corner he sees the back of Milton walking tourist slow, towards a quiet street. Nick slows down looking for a shop to turn into. He finds an alley, walks down and heads into a second-hand bookshop. The bell on the door rings as he closes the door behind him. The smell of damp mouldy books fills the shop. It's empty save a teenage boy on a stool reading a thick leather-bound book. Nick walks between the high bookcases and picks up a book. He tries to read.

The bell on the door goes again a few moments later. Nick keeps his eyes fixed on the blurring words on the *Biology of Bees* in his hands. He hears the soft pad of shoes on carpet and looks up. Milton stops at the top of the aisle, looks at Nick and smiles. After a few moments' silence he turns and walks out of the shop.

Nick knows he has to leave the shop some time. Knows he has to confront the situation. Now's as good a time as any. He puts the book back and walks out. The teenager's concentration momentarily breaks as he watches Nick leave.

Nick stops outside the shop, looking straight ahead at Milton, weighing up his best move. By the look of him Nick reckons he could outrun him. But the man's found him here. Likely he'd find him again. He's not police. This is connected to the robbery, to Warren, the dog. Nick knows it in his bones. He hasn't taken that much money or killed a dog on the job for a long time. Nothing else to warrant this kind of visit; to go to these kind of lengths. How the fuck he found him isn't important right now. Only how he's going to get out of this situation with the least amount of damage. Nick looks up the alley.

'Nick.' Milton takes a step forward, hand outstretched. 'Milton. We haven't met, but I think you know of my boss.' Nick takes a step back. Milton continues. 'Vincent . . . Cracknel. I believe you've visited him . . . the once.' Milton pauses a moment. 'Nasty-looking injury you got there. Dog bite?'

'No idea what you're talking about, mate.'

'No need to be unfriendly. We can do this easy and quick. You give back what you've taken, give me a formal apology for the dog and we'll say the matter's done.'

The offer sounded reasonable to Nick, except for the money. He could give it back, keep going north. He'd find someone else to rip off. Milton waits for a response.

'Know what?' Nick rubs his forehead. 'I get this a lot.'

Milton cocks his head. 'And that is?'

'Mistaken for somebody else.'

Milton drops his holdall, takes two steps forward, pulling out a thin strip of electrical flex. He grabs for Nick's neck. Nick steps aside. Milton reaches back, grabbing Nick by the throat, forcing him against the wall. He wraps the flex round Nick's neck. Then rams his shoulder and hips into Nick's chest and stomach, winding him, forcing his arms to drop. He tightens the flex. Nick's vision blurs and his legs buckle. He feels the scab on his nose split and break open.

'I was hoping you'd say that. Coming all this way for a

simple handover and apology would've been . . . a waste of my time.'

Nick chokes. Blood from the dog bite runs into his mouth. He brings his hand to his back pocket and slides the bottle of Scotch out. The cheap glass breaks first time. Nick head-butts Milton forcing him to let go then he brings the broken bottle up to his neck.

Milton looks at Nick nervously. 'Easy now, Nick old china.'

Nick pulls him towards the jagged glass. It pierces his throat deep enough for blood to trickle.

Nick talks low and clear. 'Now. Best you head back down country. Forget you ever saw me . . . save some face.'

Nick takes hold of his shoulder, flips him round, forcing his face to the wall, bringing his arm behind his back. He jabs the glass into the back of Milton's neck, takes a single step back, lifts his foot up and jams it into the base of his spine. Milton lets out a grunt, dropping to the pavement. He attempts to get up. Nick brings his foot up again and slams the sole of his boot into the back of his head. Milton's face hits the wall. The impact knocks him unconscious. Nick looks up the alley. Holidaymakers walk past, oblivious. Nick bends down, bringing his ear to Milton's face. Still breathing. He takes out his wallet, removes the cash, and chucks it on the floor. He continues to go through his pockets and finds a set of car keys. He wants the man to crawl home. He also wants him back in London quick as possible, away from him; away from the kids. He puts the keys back into Milton's pocket, turns him over. His eyes flicker open and shut for a few seconds until fully conscious. Nick wants to grind the bottle into the undamaged areas of his face. He resists. He feels eyes on him and turns to see the teenager looking through the bookshop window, mouth open. Nick raises a single finger to his lips. The teenager closes his mouth but keeps staring. Nick brings his attention back to Milton's dishevelled body.

'Here's what I want you to do,' Nick tells him, calmly. 'Go back to your employer and tell him I'm sorry about the dog, really, I like animals, they just keep dying on me. It isn't malicious, certainly isn't personal. Just bad luck. It was an accident. Fucking thing was on its last legs. Man should be reported to the RSPCA for putting a dog that old on guard duty. Far as the money's concerned . . .' Nick takes out fifty pounds' worth of five-pound notes and stuffs it into Milton's top pocket '. . . that should cover your petrol.'

Nick walks back up the alley, heart pumping. He takes out a tissue and dabs the bite and the blood. He feels better. He needed the release; all that tension, fear . . . stress. It's over now, out of his system.

He needs to find the boys.

Jake and Zeb sit outside the bakery, backs against the wall looking at the people and cars going by, tucking into large Cornish pasties, taking no notice of the rain and the cold.

Nick walks up to them. Jake sees him first and knows something is wrong. Zeb stares ahead, miserable.

'Hey, kids. Got me one?'

'They sold out, last ones,' Jake replies.

'Bollocks. It's not even one o'clock.' Nick walks into the shop.

He comes out a few minutes later with a paper bag in

his hand. He takes out a pasty and hands Jake the bag. Jake looks in and smells the cream buns. He hands one to Zeb. Jake looks at Nick's trousers and sees flecks of red.

'What's that?' he asks.

'What?'

'On your trousers?'

Nick looks down pointlessly rubbing it, like it'll disappear. 'Ketchup.' Zeb looks up disbelievingly. Nick sinks his teeth into the pasty, nodding approval, looking straight ahead at the people and traffic. 'Girls'll be here this afternoon.'

'I want to speak to Mum,' Zeb asks through a mouthful of pasty.

'I know you do, kid. Soon. Soon as I charge the phone.'

'You keep bloody saying that,' Jake snaps. 'Why do you keep lying to us, you're always fucking lying and I know that isn't ketchup. What the fuck happened?' Jake chucks his half-eaten pasty on to the pavement. An old couple look down at him with disgust. He stands up, wipes his hands on his trousers and walks off.

A seagull swoops down and takes up the discarded pasty. Zeb chucks a bit of crust at its head then moves close to Nick.

Nick puts his arm round him and carries on eating. He would like to think what just happened was the last of it. That he'd made it safe for his kids; they could carry on up country and have a good time. Get as far as Wester Ross. But he knows he's kidding himself. Denying the reality of what is starting to happen. What he feared the most, convinced himself would never happen. The regret at buckling and giving in to Zeb's pleas to come with him is now driving into him like broken glass. He sees the damage he did to Vincent's dogsbody in his mind. The adrenalin of triumph has worn off. The regret and remorse rise in him. He looks down at Zeb and smiles his best bullshit smile. If he can keep this feeling of dread from Zeb, keep him from having to see any of what he does to keep them safe, he'll be content. If not content, his conscience will be a little clearer. That's what a father does: protect his kids from danger. And he knows, as much as he delays the inevitable, what he's done, through his weakness and fear, through his love for his kids, has put them directly in line of danger. All he can think of doing right now is keeping going. Zeb moves in a little closer to him, takes a bite of his iced bun, takes the cherry off and chucks it at another seagull. He hits it straight in the eye and watches gleefully as it flies up to the rooftops cawing and jeering, shitting on a passing bus. Zeb chuckles to himself and breaks into the first smile in days.

Twelve

Emily walks through the prison gates. She shudders at the memory and smell of the place. To her, HMP Pentonville looks like all the other outdated Victorian prisons in London: Wandsworth, Wormwood Scrubs, Brixton. Always smelling, looking, feeling the same. Everything – the same. Trash mothers and dirty, pissed off kids. Agitating lifeless neon strip lighting; the screws with the same miserable pale faces. One of them usually checks her out without shame, nudging his mate, schoolboy sniggers like she doesn't notice. They have as much chance of getting her into bed as the murderers, thieves and rapists on remand. Inside the thick brick walls it's all the same to her.

Her visits to Nick over his two sentences were always a mix of excitement, disappointment and humiliation. Each time the next visit came round she had put the pain and stress of the previous time out of her mind. She'd wake up on the morning of the date on the VO, full of the kind of buzz Zeb clearly still had for birthdays; the kind of excitement Jake had had for the first ten years of his life. She was almost grateful to be back in touch with something she'd lost way before she met Nick.

She would get up, get dressed, make herself look beautiful, not a tart, not like the majority of girlfriends, wives and mothers that share the queues for reception. She'd get on the bus, enjoy the stares and smiles of the better-looking men on their way to their nine to fives. Walk confidently towards the prison main gates, still smiling, seeing Nick's face in her head, him striding into the visiting room towards her, proud to have the best-looking girlfriend in the yard. That's what he told her and she believed him. She would keep smiling, through the first set of security doors, smile stuck fast to her face. But each doorway took her back to the previous visit and how she would always feel walking back out. The dread would rise again and she would tell herself he was obviously the wrong sort; she needed to leave him. Her sister hated him. Her mother didn't even want his name spoken out loud. But wherever she saw him, prison, hospital, drunk, stoned, she couldn't help wanting him. Sitting in the easy silences, looking at him, loving him. Fancying the pants off him even in the standard-issue cheap denim jeans, blue and white striped shirts and black boots. Nick knew how to make the shittest clothes look good. However good he made her feel, it was impossible for her not to feel seedy, sitting in the stench of sweat and bleach and rolling tobacco. Impossible not to feel affected by the women around her crying, mascara streaking down over-made-up faces. Children clinging on to the legs and arms of dads not due out till they themselves were adults. These memories, hitting her through all the senses as she walked through yet another door, always reminded her of her anger at Nick, her rage at his uselessness as a lover and a father and friend. By the time she walked through the last gate to the visiting hall the memory and reality of where they were in their relationship smacked her sharp in the face once again. Just how she'd felt after she'd said the last goodbye, kissed him the last time, let him squeeze her tits one last time before the screws moved her on, back out into the reality of London. This memory would surface as the prison visit conversation petered into silence, slipping into long stares and groping hands up her pre-ordered thigh-high skirt. As she walked away from the hall she'd swear that would be it. The big iron gates slamming behind her were the full stop on the letter she would start composing on the bus on the way home. The letter she never sent however much she promised she would. She'd get home and by the evening she would start missing him again. The letter for the next visit would arrive and she would feel like a child getting a Wonka gold ticket. And the wait for the next visit would begin. The twisted cycle would start up and put her back in the loop she knew she would never be able to break as long as he was in prison. This wasn't something she would do to him, even if she wanted to. She could never leave him in his cell with no hope of having a life when he was released. She was grateful his sentences were never more than a few years.

The worst part of the visits was taking the kids. Zeb was always OK until it was time to part. Jake was always harder. Hiding his hurt beneath anger made it doubly difficult. Nick never seemed to be bothered by it. Not on the surface. But she knew he was. She could see it in the way he held his lips tighter and whiter as he said goodbye.

She'd waited till his last release. Having seen the damage

his time inside had done to the boys, having buried the anger at him for letting the family be split apart yet again, full of promises of it never happening again. Of getting a decent job, something on the right side. Although she looked him in the eye and said she believed him, wanted to, she always knew that, with the best will in the world, he was full of shit. He would never really be able to change, not unless he really wanted to and she knew he didn't. He wasn't ready. He was still a kid choosing to stay stuck in an emotional no man's land. The damage was done, the family split and her decision to leave him was made. He just had to step over the line one final time and that was it.

He was out for six months from the last sentence when he came home with a suitcase of cash, tipped it on the bed and waited for what he'd hoped was a round of applause, a kiss, a shag and some new underwear for him to wank over.

She had managed to stand up, without a word, walk out of the bedroom, down to the kitchen and sit at the table to wait for him to come down.

It took him two hours but he finally walked into the two a.m. kitchen like a man going to the gallows. She told him that was it. He was out. He had money. She knew damn well he was shagging at least one much younger girl and that he'd be fine, he wouldn't be alone, not in the flesh at least. She was taking the kids and there would be no argument. No courts, no lawyers. She knew he would agree to this. She knew he would do anything to stay out of another court appearance, whatever the charge. She gave him every other weekend. He listened, nodded and did as he was told. She was amazed he didn't fly into a rage and hit her as he had before. The violence of a petulant child. He walked back upstairs, packed one suitcase with money, another with clothes, and walked out into the middle of the night.

She was proud of herself. It didn't stop her crying for the next six days, but she'd done it. Dealing with the aftershock of Zeb's reactions was easy by comparison to having to go through another series of prison visits and explanations. Jake didn't seemed bothered, if anything he was happy just to be around her and not both of them, relentless rucking, fucking and fighting.

She walks through the final gate to the visitor holding area. She does her best to keep herself to herself, eyes to the ground, hands clasped in front of her holding her mock Prada bag. A younger woman standing next to her looks her up and down.

'Come to see your old man?' she asks, fag in hand, gum in mouth.

'No, just a friend.'

'That's nice. You sure 'e's just a friend? Look like you're going on a date, luv.' Emily smiles and says nothing. The young woman continues. 'Hope my mates visit me if I end up inside. Not sure they will, fuckers.'

'Hate all this bloody hanging around.' Emily tidies her hair.

'You'll get used to it . . . I mean if you're planning to come regular.' She winks at her.

'No. Just the once.'

The young woman shrugs. They're called along. Emily falls into line behind her.

* * *

Even the prisoners look the same. She definitely recognises two of the screws. She walks towards an empty table. A small boy of about eight runs in front of her and sits in the seat before she can get to it. He rests his chin in his hands and grins up at her. He reminds her of Zeb. She looks around and finds another table further down the end of the visiting hall. She puts her bag on the table and sits down.

She waits another twenty minutes for Warren to arrive. She recognises the excitement in her, the anticipation. She passes it off as a default to visiting Nick. Automatic.

Even at fifty yards from the door to her table, she is shocked by the state of his face. He walks up to the table, relaxed, clearly happy to see her. He leans down. She feels herself wanting to reel back in repulsion. She stops herself and lets him kiss her. She smells the witch hazel behind the bandage covering his eye.

'What the hell happened!?' She hears the rise in her voice, quickly bringing the volume back down.

'Nick.' Warren sits down.

'Nick? Is he in here?' She realises it's a ridiculous question.

'He fucking should be.'

'What's going on, Warren? He's taken the kids. Has something happened?'

'You could say that. You're not the only one looking for him.'

Emily covers her eyes with her hands, holding back her tears.

Warren touches her hand. 'Thought you were over and done with him.'

'He's got the kids.'

'And?'

'He took them for the weekend, last weekend . . . haven't heard a fucking thing since.'

'They'll be back.'

'They should've been back five days ago.'

'He called?'

She shakes her head. 'His mobile's switched off. Sally reckons I should call the police.'

'Not sure that's a good idea. Much as I'd like him to take some of this punishment.'

'Do you know where he is?' Emily takes out a bar of chocolate and offers him some. Her hand trembles.

'Had a feeling this wasn't a visit to see how I was getting on.'

'I am interested in how you are, Warren. You know I am. *And* I need some help. I need to know where he is.'

'No idea. Could be up in Snowdon. Kept banging on about it.'

'Why the hell would he go to Snowdon?'

'Wanted to go back to where his dad died.'

'Still banging on about that?'

'Can you get us a tea?'

'I'm sorry. Sure. Biscuits?' Warren nods. 'White and three?' He smiles at her, sits back and takes a drag on his cigarette.

She reaches the hatch. The young woman from earlier is paying for teas and cake. She turns, sees Emily and smiles.

'Like 'em rough then.' She winks at her again and walks on before Emily can reply.

Emily sits back down. If she'd walked past Warren in the street she wouldn't have recognised him.

'Have you been to the hospital . . . are they looking after you?'

'They're not that interested in patching up rucks.'

'Tell me the other guy came off worse?' Emily stirs her tea and hands Warren a pack of Bourbons.

'There were two of them. Didn't get a look-in.'

'Who were they?' Emily prays they weren't looking for Nick.

'He came here first . . . before this . . . visited me.'

'Who came here?' Emily is confused.

'The prick we ripped off. Couldn't believe it. Obviously got his hands in too many pies. Came with a plain clothes. Thought we were ripping off another low-level wanker. We seriously overshot our reach with this one. Fucker had some front . . . give him that. He was the one sent the cunts into my cell. Had a nasty feeling about him, moment I saw him.'

'What did he want?'

'Nick . . . his money back. We fucked off a bad one and I got a kicking for it.' Warren shakes his head.

Her heart doubles its beat. 'Did you say anything about what Nick said . . . about Snowdon?'

'I've got a line, Em. That or lose the eye completely . . . they won't find them. Snowdon's a big place.'

'That doesn't help.' Emily is caught between panic and anger. She can't look Warren in the working eye.

'I have to call the police,' she blurts out.

'Like I said, not a good idea.'

'For you, or Nick? I'm not having some nutcase chasing after my kids. They can do what they like to Nick.' She doesn't mean it.

'Nothing will happen to the kids.'

'You obviously think *something* will happen.'

'No one hurts kids.'

'What the hell's that supposed to mean?'

'However fucked up things get, no one hurts kids.'

'That does not reassure me, Warren. I have to call the police. The bastards could've caught up with them already.'

Warren looks at her blankly.

'You really don't give a fuck do you?'

'Bollocks. I love your kids. I think you're overreacting.'

If his face wasn't so wrecked she would slap it. 'You can be as much of an arsehole as Nick at times, you know that?'

'But you can't help loving us, ey.'

'For fuck sake!' She hears her voice loud in the room and lowers it again. Visitors and prisoners on the nearest tables look at her.

'Em, you're winding yourself up, you need to calm down.'

They fall silent for a few minutes.

'We killed his dog.' Warren looks down.

'What? Whose dog?'

'The guy who came with the police. Nick buried the fucking thing in the guy's garden.'

Emily pushes back the chair and stands up.

'Where you off to? We got another forty minutes.'

'I have to go.'

'You'll only have to wait for the rest of them to finish.'

'Fine, I need some time to think. I'm sorry about your face, really. Hope it gets better soon.'

Emily leans down, kisses, turns and leaves.

She doesn't look back.

'Come and check these out.' Nick takes Zeb's hand and they walk to the small marina at the edge of the Windermere lake. Zeb is quiet.

'Which one would you have?' Nick points at the boats.

'Boats are shit. When can I call Mum?'

'Sure.' Nick crouches down and picks up a handful of pebbles. He starts to skim them across the water. Zeb watches him closely. He doesn't join in.

'Now.'

'Sure, in a minute.'

'Promise?'

'Promise.' Nick looks down at him.

Zeb looks up. 'You said you can't break a promise, ever.'

'We'll call her as soon as I've skimmed these stones.' Nick gets more bounces with each throw. Zeb picks up some stones and joins him.

'Dad?'

'Yes, kid.'

'Why you got blood on your trousers?'

Nick stops and looks at him. Zeb carries on skimming, not having much luck.

'Some prick tried to take my wallet.'

'You said it was ketchup.'

'I didn't want to freak you out.'

'In the town?'

'About half an hour before I met you at the pasty shop.'

'Was he bigger than you?'

'Much.' Nick feels bad, eyes on stones hiding his growing guilt.

'Did you nick that money you had in the suitcase?'

Nick stops skimming. 'Won that on the horses.' He knows Zeb has spotted the lie. Zeb falls quiet.

They bring their attention back to the stones. Nick can feel Zeb watching him closely, trying to copy his technique.

'Dad.'

'Yes, kid.'

'You said always trust the feeling in my tummy when I'm not sure about someone or scared of them.'

'Yep.'

'I've got it now.'

'I'm not with you?'

'I don't believe you about winning the money on the horses or the man stealing your wallet and I'm scared.'

'You've been listening to too much of Jake gobbing off.'

'Why do you tell us fibs all the time?'

Nick takes time to compose his answer, still skimming.

'Sometimes it's best not knowing everything. I'm protecting you from the monsters.'

'Stop teasing.'

Nick picks up another handful of smooth stones and hands half of them to Zeb.

'Do they want it back?' Zeb asks.

'Who?'

'The people you nicked it off.'

'Nobody likes having stuff nicked off them.'

'Are they coming after us?'

'Nobody's coming after us, kid.'

'Did the man you bashed want his money back?' Nick drops the last three stones back on the ground.

'Time to call Mum.' Nick takes out his mobile phone.

'Can we get another dog?' Zeb asks.

'Not right now, no. Maybe a goat when we get to where we're going.'

'I miss Gandalf.'

'He was a good pooch.'

Nick scrolls through the numbers and calls Emily.

No answer.

Emily sits in the small windowless room trying to find something to look at. The heating is up too high and she's sleepy with it. She looks at the grey walls, yellow floor and door with its angry mish-mash of dents, scratches and flaked paint.

After the best part of thirty minutes a uniformed WPC and a plain-clothes officer walk in. They sit down in silence, opening up files, getting themselves organised.

'Right then, Mrs Geneva.' The policeman looks through his papers.

'Peters. Miss.'

'Got you down here as Mrs Geneva.'

'We're not married.'

The WPC sits just behind the officer.

'I'm DC Willis, this is WPC Fletcher.' Emily nods at her. 'About your kids,' He looks back into his file. 'Says here they should've been back five days ago.'

'He hasn't done this before, not this long, not without telling me.'

'Why didn't you come to us sooner?'

'Ever hopeful.'

He raises his eyebrows.

'Sorry,' Emily continues. 'Nervous. Hate these bloody places.'

'Do you have recent photos of your children?' He looks at her sympathetically.

Emily reaches into her bag and puts four photos on the table. 'Take your pick. They're all taken in the last few months.'

He inspects them, takes two, passes them to the WPC and hands the other two back to her. 'I take it you want this out of the news for now?'

Emily is shocked by the question.

'It's a standard question. Don't worry. If they're gone for more than a week you'll be asked if you want to call a press conference. If you don't, we will.'

'I'm sure it's not that serious.' Emily knows she's kidding herself.

'Most of the time it's nothing to worry about. Sometimes it is . . . we have to follow procedure.'

'What's the first thing that happens . . . after this?' Emily asks.

'We type this lot up and Fletcher begins making the calls, to all the places you've already told us he may be at, all the regions. We'll start with Snowdon and work our way up around the main motorways.'

'I'd like to head up there myself, with my sister.' Emily expects him to advise her against it.

'Can't stop you doing that, might cost you less to stay down here till we get some news. When we find them we'll bring them back to London. Nick won't be going home. This is a breach of his parole, he'll be spending some time with us first.'

'I have a feeling he might be heading up to Scotland.'

'A feeling?' he asks.

'Where we used to live. He was always pissed off about us moving back down here. Always going on about moving back there. Said as soon as he got the chance he'd take the kids up there. Seems now he's got the chance. I wouldn't put it past him.'

'Whereabouts in Scotland?' Willis asks.

'Wester Ross.' Emily sits back, feeling awkward.

'That's a big area.'

'I'll show you where we lived.'

Willis pushes a pile of papers in front of Emily, she signs and looks up at them both.

WPC Fletcher stands. 'I'd head home, get some rest, we'll be in touch in the morning.'

'For all the sleep I'll get.' Emily forces a smile.

The three of them head out into the brightly lit corridor.

Sally sits waiting for Emily in the chaotic main reception area.

Emily walks back into her flat and slumps down on the sofa. Sally heads into the kitchen and puts the kettle on.

'Got any biscuits?' Sally shouts.

'In the cupboard by the sink.' Emily rests back against the sofa, closes her eyes and massages her forehead.

Sally walks in a few moments later, tray in hand. She puts it down and hands Emily her tea and a plate full of biscuits.

'Didn't have you down as a Jammie Dodger muncher,' Sally jibes.

'They're the kids'. Usually gone by now.' Emily takes three, sips her tea and dunks a biscuit.

'You've done the right thing. I would've told them Monday.' Sally sits down.

'He looked dreadful.'

'Had it coming to 'im I guess.'

'He ain't so pretty now.'

'Bloody freezing in here.' Sally gets up and clicks on the wall heater.

Emily takes another biscuit. The phone goes. She jumps out of her seat and snatches it.

'Mum? It's me . . . Zeb!'

'Zeb? Where the bloody hell are you! You keep cutting out.'

'In the Lake District. We've been camping, canoeing and up a big mountain called Snowdon.' He pauses a second. 'Gandalf's dead.'

'What? Who's Gandalf?'

'My dog. He was my dog. He's dead and I nearly drowned.' Emily sits down, legs shaking. 'I saw a dead cow too and her baby calf.'

She does her best to control her anger. 'Where's Dad?'

'In the pub.'

'Are you on your own?'

'No. Jake's here. He keeps trying to set fire to the food sign. Ow! Stop bloody kicking me, arse bandit!'

She keeps the panic down enough to speak clearly. 'Are you OK, Zeb?'

'Yeah, I'm good but I miss you lots, a bloody lot. I nearly drowned. That's how Gandalf died.'

'Jesus Christ, Zeb, what are you talking about?'

'It's OK. I'm all right now. Not going near a shitting boat again.'

Thoughts fly through her head. Instinct tells her to hang up and get in the car.

'Can you put Jake on?'

She hears a scuffle on the phone and what must be Zeb kicking Jake.

'Mum?'

'Jake? Is that you love? Jesus fucking Christ, Jake, what is going on? Where are you? You have to come home right now!'

'Chillax, Mum. We're OK . . .'

'Don't bloody chillax me, have you got any idea how bloody worried I've been? You have to be back in school. What the hell's going on?'

Jake's voice retains a forced calm. 'Dad said he told you we were gonna be back a few days late.'

'Not a bloody word. Dad's in trouble. I want you to come home at once!'

'Dad's always in trouble. He got into a fight.' More scuffling. 'Zeb piss off, stop fucking poking me!'

Emily forces herself not to scream down the phone. 'I want you and Zeb to come back home right now. Can you get back down here on your own, with Zeb? Have you got enough money to get a train back?'

'I can always nick more.'

Zeb is trying to get hold of the phone.

'Dad said something about going up to Scotland.'

'What? Don't be ridiculous.' She can feel any vestige of control slipping from her. 'I want you to come home right now. Jesus, Jake. Get yourself on a train.'

'I need to keep an eye on Zeb and he wants to stay up here.'

'Jake. *I'm* telling you, you have to come back. If you don't get on a train first thing tomorrow morning the police will have to come and get you and arrest Dad, he's fucked up his parole.'

'Why's he fucked up his parole?' His voice moves away from the mouthpiece. 'Fuck sake, Zeb, if you don't stop trying to set fire to my trousers I'm gonna thump you.'

'He's abducted you.'

'What?'

Emily can hear Jake's tone change to anger. She knows she's lost him.

She continues, 'He took you out of London. You should've been home five days ago. He's broken our agreement and as far as the police are concerned that's abduction.'

'Dad hasn't abducted us, Mum, he's a twat but he hasn't bloody kidnapped us.'

'I want to speak to Mum!' Zeb whines in the background. 'This is shitting boring. I'm gonna set fire to your trainers if you don't let me speak to her.'

She can hear Jake struggling furiously with Zeb. 'If you touch my fucking trainers, blood!' Jake shouts, 'I'll kick your chuffing head in.' Emily holds the phone away from the shouting.

'Jake, please, come home.'

'If Dad does anything stupid we'll come back, promise. It'll be cool. Don't worry.'

'Jake, please, you have to come . . .' She hears the rustle of clothes on the other end of the line.

'Mum?' Zeb is doing his best to hold back his tears.

'Yes, hon, I'm here. You mustn't set light to Jake and you must stop fighting. I've told you, he's bigger than you and he'll hurt you. Zeb, you have to tell Jake to bring you home at once or we'll have to come get you.'

'Yeah! Come see us. We can walk up a hill-mountain. I love you big as King Kong.'

'I love you too.' Emily is unable to hold back her tears. 'You must come home. Tell Jake I want him . . . tell him you want him to bring you home . . . on the train, tomorrow.'

'Dad said . . .'

'I don't wanna hear what Dad said.'

'Jake's gonna buy a pay as you go so we can call you every day. I'm gonna call you tomorrow and every day.'

The line goes dead. She knows Jake has ended the call. She looks across at Sally, tears in her eyes. 'Jesus Christ sis, we have to go up there. I'm gonna kill him.' Emily crumples into a heap of tears. Sally comes over and puts her arms round her.

Thirteen

Vincent sits uncomfortably on the sofa looking down at his overstretched stomach. To him it looks like he's carrying a child he'll never birth. He wonders if it's the cancer. It wouldn't have got down so far from his lungs. Not yet. Muscles turned to fat are the sum total of the work he did on his body for all those years. The training, the food; early nights. His regret and resentment grow exponentially, day and night, along with his apathy, his shame at having bottled it so early on in his career. He couldn't get back in the ring after the fight with the Australian. Stage fright his coach called it. He knew it was cowardice plain and simple. What he would give for a decent outlet for this frustration. Release from the shame of so much wasted life. Something to reconnect his boxer's hands to. Something to batter. Death creeps closer by the day, leaving him with a toxic sense of urgency. A need to do something that might possibly make sense of who he is.

The purple box of liqueur chocolates sits as a divider between him and his wife. The odd couple stare at the large television, blinking, half awake. Simon Cowell and Louis bitch at each other like two spaniels on heat. Vincent's wife roars with laughter and the sound irritates the shit out of him, as always. She reaches down, fumbles into the box and picks up two dark chocolates without looking. Delicately, she pops one after the other between her lips. Hamster heavy cheeks, she chuckles at the poor jokes.

'Tea?' Vincent asks flatly, staring blankly above the TV at the wall.

'Too late for tea, sweets. G and T time. Besides, milk makes me fat.'

Vincent walks across the warm carpet on to the tiled floor of the kitchen, the ceramic cold on his feet. He curses forgetting his slippers and fills the kettle. She continues to roar at the screen in the sitting room, finishing off each burst with a snort, like a pig. As he waits for the kettle to boil he looks around at the units, at the sheer size of the kitchen; the massive American fridge; industrial-sized gas cooker; paintings of horses and hounds on the walls. They have never, nor will ever, have enough friends to cook for, to justify a space this big. He resents every inch of the décor. None of it his choice. All of it accepted to shut her up and stop her shagging men younger and fitter than him.

From dirt-poor Fulham to nose-in-the-air Maida Vale he thought he'd made it. He thought the money would do it. A good source of income after the boxing promise faded. Worked harder than he should to make up for the lack and loss of pride. Broke more laws than was sensible. Accepted the seedier side of Peckham Rye's underworld with open arms. All to fit out this house. A cold humourless space. The only warmth coming from the fire, the TV and the occasional wife swap dinners. His resentment towards the woman sitting on the sofa vibrates inside him. Constant, low level, always there. A background noise he's become used to. His only respite from this resentment are the fantasy beatings he conjures and metes out on her daily. But even these have started to lose their relief of late. He almost killed her with a pillow in bed last night; just to shut her up. He'd just as soon burn the house to the ground and claim the insurance and let the flames take her.

After ten years of it, he knows the therapy-speak back to front. Knows it in his head but feels none of it in his body, no emotion he could name or feel or make sense of. He's reeled out a thousand tear-jerking facts about the history of what made little Vincent into the nasty villain he became. He's written down the words that would sell a hundred thousand copies of yet another gangster's misery memoir: the savage, deprived childhood; the cliché of relentless beatings from a father whose own life was as much of a nothing as his own; no mother for back-up, no affection, no love. The loss of pride from a failed sporting career and subsequent spiralling low self-esteem. The fear of getting caught, time in prison. The comfort of violence. All that sleep lost over his tragic life, all this shit, this house, the stuff he has no gratitude for, no connection to whatsoever. The only time he ever properly feels alive? When he's inflicting pain or taking a life.

What's the big deal? He's been ripped off before. Many times. Part of the territory. He does it to them; they do it to him. Most of the time he gets it back. When he doesn't he lets it go, eventually. But this one has got to him. Jasper's death was painful, the money stung but there is a desire for a bigger resolution here that's got deep under his skin, beyond work, beyond redemption for a dog that was dying anyway. This one has eaten its way into him like the cancer in his chest. Nick Geneva has become more than a thief needing to understand the invisible boundary line of his house, his patch, to be forced into apology, remuneration and respect. Nick is the straw that has broken the straining back of his shit-for-nothing life and his desire to finish it on his own terms. The diary of his life written for his therapist, tucked away upstairs for his retirement to an unnamed Hebridean island, will be burnt.

The kettle whistles. He makes the drinks, gives in, opens the drawer and slides the butcher's cleaver into his back pocket. He heads back into the sitting room, places the tray on the coffee table and hands her the drink. He notices the empty chocolate box, a thin line of chocolate smeared like a streak of shit just above her ruby-red lip. He walks behind her and begins to massage her shoulders, staring ahead, above the TV. She picks up her drink, sips it and returns to twisting her hair round her fingernail, all the while eyes locked on to Simon and his judgment of the latest deluded wannabe.

'I think he's handsome, don't you? Like the way he dresses. I think he's noble. Got some dignity about him.'

Vincent doesn't respond. She says it like she's having a go. Like this is the kind of man he should aspire to being. Vincent knows it's his money she wants to fuck, not his nobility. She wouldn't know dignity if it rode up on a horse and saved her from her crushing waste of a life. He continues massaging.

'That's nice, sweets . . . lovely,' she purrs. He continues, working deeper.

After a few minutes he stops and takes a step back.

'Don't stop, luv, you've got such good hands.' He draws the butcher's blade from his back pocket, stares down at it for a long second then draws it high up behind his head.

'Such good hands, luv . . . and you always make a mean G and . . .' He brings the blade sidelong, mid-sentence, into the middle of her thin, soft neck. The thin layer of skin covering the bone beneath pops and rips open along the moving blade like parting water. The force slices neatly through the gap between the two cervical vertebrae. The metal continues forward through her throat, jugular and out the other side. The wide blade exits, streaked crimson. He lets the movement of his initial swing continue freely, bringing the steel skilfully to rest on the back of the sofa. She lets out a gentle rasp. Her glass drops to her lap and rolls on to the floor. Her head tips, holds for a second. He watches in slow motion as it falls forward and lands in her lap, face up. She looks up at the ceiling blinking, mouth moving, trying to say something, still nothing interesting, he's certain of that. Blood jets from her neck; just like in the movies. He steps out of range of the arcing blood and watches it cover the sofa. He never liked the floral pattern. The room around him blazes. Sight, sound and vision crystallise: sharp, beautiful and clean. He breathes it in, refreshed, happy. He looks around.

The silence is sweet.

Walls, floor, carpets and furnishings take on a new shine. He rests his left hand on the blade and feels the warmth of his wife's blood. He takes it all in. A round of applause. Simon Cowell said something nice. Vincent raises his arms and takes in some of the small screen

177

accolade for himself. He flicks the remote to 'off'. The blood slows its pace, trickling gently on to her skirt, skin and face. Her eyes flicker for the last time. The unchewed chocolate pops out of her mouth. He picks it up and puts it in his mouth, holds it on his tongue until the liqueur oozes down the back of his throat. He closes his eyes and listens to the silence.

Job done.

Silence.

The doorbell rings twice.

He opens his eyes and walks calmly into the hall, unlocks the two Chubbs and finally the Yale. He looks at the man standing in front of him.

The yellow, blue-black bruise on Milton's face reaches from cheek to neck, front and back. His left eye neatly bandaged, white muslin stained yellow and red, his neck covered in more bandage.

'You need a drink.' Vincent turns and walks back into the hall. Milton follows, closing the door.

Milton sits down wearily at the kitchen table.

Vincent pours them both a Courvoisier.

'Where's the wife?' Milton asks.

'In the sitting room.'

A cracked rendition of Michael Jackson's 'Thriller' echoes from the TV, matched by his wife's own out-of-tune voice. The adrenalin of his fantasy is short-lived, the disappointment worse than before.

'Could've fucking told me the cunt knew how to take care of himself.' Milton takes a long sip of brandy.

'Never known you not to be able to take care of yourself.' Vincent sits down and thinks for a while. 'Looks like I'll have to go up myself.' Milton looks up at him in surprise. 'Can't let him get arrested now, can I?' Vincent sips his drink. 'Could do with a trip away. Get some space.'

Vincent Cracknel knows that is the only way to get the relief he seeks, to cauterise the fast-fading grief of his dog. Do something to remove the shame and bitterness. Bring the violence he so often does for a living to good use. Nick Geneva was making his decision to do something tangible with his life easier than he thought.

Fourteen

Zeb walks alongside Lisa, holding her hand. Candy next to Nick, Jake just behind. They head into Windermere. The shops are closing for the day, lights in the houses already on.

Nick spots the gawping teenager from the bookshop ahead of them. He knows the boy recognises him. He crosses the road, keeping a frightened eye on Nick.

Jake sees the scuttling youth. 'Who's that?' he asks Nick.

'Saw him in a bookshop earlier . . . reading a book.'

'He looks scared.' Jake continues to check him out, suspicious.

'Can't help that.' Nick nods at the teenager. Jake watches his dad interlace his fingers with Candy's. He knows Nick is looking for reassurance to support his bullshit. Nick looks nervous to him. She moves closer to Nick.

Jake watches the teenager turn the corner and disappear. He brings his attention back to Lisa, the contours of her body. He forgives her for shagging Nick. He runs through all possible chat-up lines. Things he could say to make it work. Smart things. His head is empty of ideas, but full of her naked body sitting on top of him. If he gets her drunk enough maybe she'd give him a mercy fuck? That's what Carlos called it. He knows he's kidding himself. Nick turns back to look at him.

'Where to, kid?'

'Pub?' Jake speeds up his pace to come level with them.

'Your choice,' Nick concedes.

'That one over there, that looks all right.' Jake points to a pub on the corner.

'Looks cool, real . . . English,' Candy replies.

'That's cos we're in England, dopey.' Zeb smiles up at her cheekily.

They head into the pub. Jake turns and looks around him, scanning the street. At the far end of the road he sees the teenager dart round the corner.

'Come on, kid.' Nick puts a wad of notes into Jake's hand. 'You're in charge tonight.'

Vincent looks into the empty suitcase lying open on the bed, a neat pile of clothes beside it. Trousers, hat, gloves, washbag, rope, map, money, knife. His wife walks in, cigarette in one hand, glass in the other. Vincent watches her walk to the bathroom. Without looking back she responds to the look.

'No smoking in the bedroom blah blah blah.' She runs a bath. 'Nothing about a smoking ban in here, is there.' She lifts her skirt, wobbles a little and sits on the toilet. She lets out a fart that echoes off the walls.

'Where you off to then, sweets?'

'See a man about a dog.'

'Man about a dog. What's that mean anyway? Fucking silly . . .' Her words slur.

'You're drunk.'

'Not quite the way I like to get fucked but it'll do.' She drops the half-smoked cigarette between her legs into the toilet.

Vincent packs the bag.

'I'll get the girls in . . . cat's away . . . have a piss-up, eat some chocolate, watch some of that Super 8 seventies porn of yours.'

'You do that. Have some fun.' He zips the case shut, turns and walks out.

'Not even gonna get a goodbye kiss then?'

'No.'

'Impotent little prick.' She giggles.

He turns and walks into the bathroom and raises his hand in a striking gesture. She flinches. He leans over her and takes a bottle of codeine out of the kitchen cupboard above her head.

He walks out, clicking the bathroom door shut behind him.

Jake sits opposite Lisa and Candy trying not to stare at them. He reads the menu and sneaks a look at Nick. Easy in his skin, arm draped over Lisa's shoulder. He hates his father for being so good at being cool, like it takes no effort at all. Every inch of Jake's body tries to relax and be Californian cool. Zeb's face is jammed into *The Hobbit*.

'That is so sad about your little dog and you . . . and nearly drowning . . . that is way too much.' Lisa looks sympathetically at Zeb. 'Are you OK, hon?'

'He wasn't a small dog, he was half size.' Zeb keeps his eyes in his book.

'What you having, kid?' Nick asks him.

'Burger and chips.'

'Jake?'

'Fillet steak, medium rare with French fries and a Coke float.'

'Never had that before.' Nick keeps reading the menu, smiling to himself.

'Coke float, Coke float, Coke float!' Zeb chants. Nick gives him the nod.

'So how was the boat trip then?' Candy asks all three of them. 'I mean . . . shit . . . sorry, apart from the dog . . . and the . . .'

'Good.' Jake lays down his menu and looks up at Candy. She smiles and he blushes.

'Your dad tells me you built a fire.'

'Yeah and I almost shitting drowned.' Zeb keeps his eyes in the book.

Candy and Lisa stare at Zeb.

Nick pulls him over to him and squeezes him in tight. He shakes his head at the girls. They get not to ask any more questions.

Jake feels his neck going stiff. He holds his knees tight together under the table, hoping Lisa and Candy won't notice the sweat on his top lip. He wants to be around them and yet at the same time, he doesn't. It's hard work.

'So when you guys heading up to Scotland?' Lisa asks.

'We're getting a goat,' Zeb replies.

Nick moves the hair out of Zeb's face. 'Soon. No hurry. How long you staying?'

'We're heading back to London tomorrow, Californ-I-A Wednesday.'

The waitress comes to the table and takes their order.
Zeb orders first.

Emily stands on the corner, suitcase by her feet, umbrella
in hand, shielding her from half the rain. The wind
blows the umbrella about her head. She does her best
to keep it steady. She looks at her watch, then around
at the other three corners of Fulham Broadway. The
five p.m. rush-hour traffic trundles along in front of her.
Her feet are cold. She wishes she'd brought better clothes.
A tramp walks up to her smiling, waving a bottle of cider
at her.

'Drink?' he purrs.

'No thanks.'

'Ahh come on, one little drink never hurt anyone's
looks.' He looks at the bottle, swaying on his feet. ' 'Cept
mine of course.'

He thrusts it at her again. She shakes her head. 'Really,
no. I'm waiting for a friend.'

'Suit yourself, love. Best of luck, ey, to the pair of us.' He
continues to sway looking her up and down, smiling like a
clown. A car pulls up to the kerb. Emily bends down as the
passenger window rolls down. Sally leans across and opens
the door. 'Picking up dark handsome strangers again are
we, gorgeous?' she asks as the tramp wanders off mumbling,
swigging, failing to walk straight.

Emily gets in. 'Girl has to keep herself occupied when
she's kept *waiting.*' She leans across and kisses Sally on the
cheek.

'Fucking traffic's a nightmare.' Sally pulls out without
looking, the car behind slams its brakes and hits its horn.

She gives him the finger. 'You're crazy, you know that,' she tells Emily.

'We're both a little crazy . . . yes.'

'Why can't you wait for a call from the police?'

'Taking too long . . . something's wrong.' Emily clicks her seat belt in. 'He's in trouble, no doubt about that. He's got Jake and Zeb and I'm going to get them.'

Sally slams on her brakes as they approach a red light. 'Well, if you aren't gonna change your mind I'm coming with you.'

'What?' Emily looks at her, eyes wide. 'You hate trains. Just drop me off at Euston.'

'You're right. All them creepy fuckers wanking in the toilets. I'll drive.'

Emily looks at the back seat and sees a stuffed holdall.

'You already planned it. You can't come, you've got the kids. I've booked a hire car at the other end.'

'Trevor's taking care of them. 'Bout time he took some responsibility.'

'Sal, please, just take me to the station, I'll be back in a few days and all this'll be over.'

Sally falls silent and keeps driving. Emily sits back in her seat and tries to relax.

The car heads on to the Embankment. The white lights of Albert Bridge loom up. She looks across at the reflection in the dark water and rests her head against the cold glass of the window. She'll be glad of the company.

Jake and Nick face the urinal, pissing. Jake speaks to the wall.

'Spoke to Mum.'

'Didn't think you had a phone?'

'Used yours. But bought my own now.'

'What with?'

'Money Mum gave me.'

'How was she?'

'Pissed off.'

'Did you tell her where we are?'

'Zeb did.'

Nick's stomach lurches, followed by fear, then anger. His paranoia has doubled since the fight. The last thing he needs now is Emily.

Jake stares ahead at the small white tiles. 'Why'd you lie to her?'

'You know what she's like. She'd never let me take you out of school.' Nick feels himself tiring of the front he's holding up.

'Don't get it,' Jake asks.

'What?'

'Is it like a disease or something?' Jake's voice is calm, level.

'What?' Nick knows Jake has him on the back foot and hides it.

'Lying. Is it like kleptomania or being an alkie?'

'I do it to keep us safe.' Nick zips up.

'From what?'

'I've fucked up. I want to make it better for us.'

Jake nods in sarcastic agreement, shaking off the last of his piss.

Nick continues, 'I want us to have a laugh.' Jake shrugs. 'I've fucked it up and want you both to have some good memories . . . of me . . . us. Not just the shit.'

Nick heads over to the mirror and checks his hair.

'Is someone after us?'

'No one's after us.'

'Take that as a yes then. Great. Nice job, Dad.'

'No one's after us, kid.' Nick is exhausted.

'I bought Zeb and me knives, just in case.'

Nick doesn't know why he's shocked by this but he is. It was OK for him to have knives as a kid, but not for Jake and Zeb. He likes that Jake is taking care of business, proud of him, but he can't help feeling his control slip.

'If there was anyone after us I'd take care of it.'

'Zeb's scared. Thinks you're lying so we can keep having a good time. He's not stupid.'

'Neither of you are stupid. Everything's gonna be cool, kid. Just focus on what's happening now. Come on, let's drink.' He slaps Jake on the back.

They head back into the pub.

Zeb is sitting in between Candy and Lisa, reading his book as they silently plait his hair.

Jake sits down opposite looking at Zeb. 'You look like a girl.'

'He looks cute,' Candy retorts. 'Hey, *you'd* look good with a ponytail, come here.'

'No ta. That's for poofs.'

'That's for us girls to decide.' Candy slides over and takes hold of Jake's hair. He tries to resist but then quickly gives up.

'You guys are coming out with us tonight. We're gonna have us a goodbye party.'

* * *

Jake heads to the bar. It feels good, money in pocket, alcohol buzzing. His first round. Feels like he's waited a lifetime for this. He knows to hold his money in his hand, let them know he's waiting. He watched Nick do it for years. He feels confident.

The barman treats him well. No ID needed.

As he heads back to the table he sees Nick and Candy head to the loo. He knows Nick doesn't need another piss. Confidence is replaced by disappointment. He sits down.

Zeb and Lisa sit eating in silence.

'Easy, soldier. You'll give yourself stomach cramps!' Lisa warns Zeb. He stops eating for a moment, looks up at her blankly then continues. 'How's the steak?' she asks Jake.

'Too much blood.' Jake looks at the chunk of red, dripping meat on the end of his fork, plucking up the courage to eat it.

'You think that's rare you should see the steaks we get back home. Wipe the steer's ass and slap it on the plate!' Lisa mock-slaps her thigh. Zeb sniggers at her. Jake attempts a natural smile.

'What's a steer?' Zeb asks through a mouthful of food.

'Like a cow, only bigger.' Lisa looks sympathetically at Jake. 'Wanna send it back, get them to cook it some more?'

'No it's OK.' Jake puts the meat into his mouth and begins chewing.

'No need to be proud, hon. Steak ain't cheap. Here.' Lisa takes the plate from him mid-mouthful, gets up and walks over to the waitress. Jake watches her talking to her. The waitress nods. At the moment Lisa let go of his plate, Jake convinces himself he's in love.

'Is Dad shagging Candy?' Zeb's question breaks Jake's spell.

'Eh?'

'Dad . . . is he shagging Candy, now, in the bogs? Bet he is. Proper nasty.' Zeb puts in another mouthful of burger, eating noisily, mouth open.

'Probably having a spliff,' Jake replies, watching Lisa as she walks back to the table.

'If he doesn't come back in the next minute I'm gonna eat his chips,' Zeb promises.

Lisa sits down. 'There you go, told her to burn the bitch top and bottom. Be about ten minutes.'

'Thanks.'

Lisa looks at Jake for a moment before she speaks. 'Candy says you like me?' Zeb spits out a mass of half-chewed chips on to his plate and starts laughing hysterically.

'Piss off, twat.' Jake kicks him. Zeb kicks him back.

'That's cute. You're cute. I'm flattered. You'll have no trouble getting yourself a girlfriend soon as you're good and ready.'

Jake blushes, picks up his glass and drains it. Zeb calms himself and brings his attention back to the last of his food.

'You guys should come over to the States sometime,' she continues. 'Girls over there *love* English guys. I'll introduce you to my little sister. She is totally gorgeous and smart. She'll make you laugh your ass off.'

Zeb perks up. 'I'll come. I want to go to Disneyland.'

'Sure, hon, you all can come. Here.' Lisa takes out a pen and paper from her bag and scribbles down her address and hands it to Jake. He folds it carefully and puts it into his jacket pocket. Nick heads back to the table looking pleased with himself. He sits back down and begins eating his chips.

Zeb scrutinises him. 'You've been shagging Candy.'

'Hey!' Lisa pushes Zeb. 'That ain't no way to talk to your pa.'

'I'm used to it,' Nick replies. He brings his attention to Zeb. 'We were having a little smoke. Here.' He pushes the half-smoked joint across the table to Lisa without looking at her. She takes it. Candy walks back to the table a minute later, hair ruffled, a small streak of lipstick smeared from one corner of her mouth. Zeb watches her as she sits down.

'Hey. How's the food?' She looks at Jake's empty space on the table. 'You musta been hungry!'

'He's not a blood man, getting it cooked some more.'

'You think that's rare. Back home they wipe—'

Zeb completes her sentence. 'Its shitty bum and stick it on the bloody plate. We know . . .' Candy nods and starts eating.

Jake looks around the bar. The place is full, mainly tourists. Easily identified by their oversized cameras, hats and loud voices. The rest look redder-faced, more weathered, local. In the far corner he sees the teenager he spotted earlier, trying not to look at Jake. The boy leans across to the man he's sitting with and whispers to him. The man gets up and walks over to the bar. The barman leans forward, glances over at Jake's table then hands the man the phone.

Nick is talking quietly to Candy. Zeb looks at them and pulls a disgusted face. He picks up his plate and licks the ketchup off.

Jake leans forward. 'Dad.'

Nick carries on talking to Candy. Jake knows Nick has heard him, deliberately taking his time to respond.

'Dad.'

Nick looks over to him, smiling falsely. 'What is it, kid?'

'I think we should go.'

'I'm eating. Relax. Have some pudding.'

'Whatever you did earlier . . . we have to go.' Nick automatically looks over to the bar at the man on the phone. He sees the teenager who looks away.

'Sure, we can get some pudding back at the hotel. Ladies . . . lead on. You're in charge.' Candy and Lisa gather up their coats and bags. Nick heads over to the bar, ignoring the man on the phone, pays the bill and the five of them leave quietly. Jake looks back at the teenager as they leave. He does his best to give him the bad eye. The boy sees him and looks down.

As Jake gets outside he sees Nick talking to Candy. Candy looks pissed off. He walks closer trying to pick up the tail end of what's being said.

'I'm not fucking you around. I need to get Zeb back to the hotel. We'll catch you up.'

'Sounds like bullshit, Mr Geneva.' Candy looks into his eyes waiting for a response. Nick gives none.

'I don't wanna go back to the bloody hotel, I wanna stay with you,' Zeb complains.

Jake walks up behind him and puts his hand on Zeb's shoulder. 'Come on, bro. I'll take you back, stay with you.'

'I want to stay with Dad.' Zeb is close to tears. The girls remain silent.

'State of you, bro, you're wasted.' Jake ruffles his hair.

'Let's get back. Might get a late night horror on satellite.'

'Telly's shit in the hotel. No Sky Movies,' Zeb complains.

'Yeah but it's telly.' Jake leads him away. Jake looks briefly back at Nick. Nick smiles back at him in appreciation then walks over to Candy.

The hotel room is clean but naff, a cigarette burn in the carpet the only evidence giving away the true seediness and history of the place. Jake looks around. He can't believe Nick would stay in a place like this. Nylon sheets, floral lampshade, shocking pink curtains and bashed-up TV. Zeb switches it on. There's a sickly smell of air freshener covering up ancient dirt and sweat. The van or tent would be ten times better.

'I hate sleeping on shitting hotel beds.' Zeb jumps on the bed and bounces up and down manically on it. 'Nasty people been sexing on them. Rank blood, I'm telling you.'

He continues to bounce. Jake channel hops on the remote. He stops on the white face of a *True Blood* vampire, blood-soaked teeth, slicked-back hair. Zeb stops mid-bounce, staring rigid at the screen.

'Fucking cool.' Zeb jumps off the bed and sits on the floor, as close to the screen as he can get.

'Sit back a bit, bro. You'll fuck up your eyes.'

'I can see sweet from here, blood.'

Jake gives up, sits on the bed and starts to roll a joint.

They watch the episode unfold into death, a blood-letting.

'Fucking COOL!' Zeb smacks his fingers at the screen.

Jake happily smokes his joint.

There are three loud knocks at the door. Zeb stays hooked to the screen. Jake stares at the door. 'Who the fuck's that?' he asks Zeb.

'How should I know, probably Dad.'

More knocks. Jake walks over and brings his ear up close. Three further, irritated knocks.

Jake takes a step back. 'Who is it?'

'Manager . . . from downstairs. Can I talk to your father?'

'He's in the bath.'

'There aren't any baths on this floor.'

'Shower . . . he's in the shower.' Zeb looks up from the screen at Jake.

The manager continues, impatience rising in his voice, 'Well, can you get him . . . I need to speak with him.'

Jake takes a step closer to the door. 'Can you leave him a message . . . I'll give it to him when he's out of the shower.'

'Are you smoking drugs in there, sonny? Can you open the door . . . I'd like to speak to you face to face.'

'I'll get my dad.' Jake pads across the carpet, pulls Zeb up by the arm and heads over to the window. He puts the joint into his mouth and quietly undoes the latch. They climb out on to the narrow balcony. They climb down. The continued knocking on the door fades along with the prolonged hiss of another vampire death.

They jump down on to a small roof ten feet below the window, then on to a wide wall and finally into the main garden of the hotel. They land quietly on the grass.

'What the piss are we doing, bro?' Zeb grabs hold of Jake's hand looking for reassurance. 'We're gonna get into bad bad trouble. Why didn't you let him in?'

'We're not supposed to be in the room without Dad . . . and he smelt the spliff. Dad can deal with him when he gets back.'

'Where are we going?'

'Fuck knows. Where did Dad say he was going?'

'By the boats.' Zeb's eyes are on the spliff. 'Can I have some?'

'No you fucking can't. Here.' Jake takes out a cigarette and hands it to Zeb. Cheeky fucker.'

'Dad gave me some,' Zeb protests.

'Bollocks did he. He'd never give you spliff, you're just a kid.'

'So are you.'

'I'm fifteen. I'll be leaving home in a few years.'

They walk down a side alley, doing their best to stay out of the street lights.

'No you won't,' Zeb protests.

'Wanna bet. Soon as I can, I'm off, mate.'

'I don't want you to go.' Jake sees Zeb is upset. He feels bad, kneels down and lights his cigarette for him. Zeb coughs. A couple walk past them. Zeb cups the cigarette in his hand. Jake ushers him on and they head for the quay.

'He did,' Zeb mutters a few minutes later.

'Your lying's getting good, blood.'

'He gave me a toke on his spliff when we went to Spain. Said I wasn't to tell anyone. Said he was giving it to put me off. Made me feel rank . . . and sick.'

'Still don't believe you.'

'Swear on Gandalf's life.'

'He's dead, bro.'

'Then I swear on your life.'

Jake shakes his head in disbelief. Zeb takes another toke on the cigarette, coughs violently for a minute, looks at it in disgust then hands it to Jake.

'That one. She's cute!' Lisa points to a small rubber dinghy tied to the pier. 'We can row her out to her momma and take her for a spin.'

'You don't take boats for a spin. You sail them.' Nick pinches her arse. She pushes him back.

Nick weighs up the situation. After a few seconds looking around he walks along the pebbled beach and on to the small wooden pier. He takes out a small knife and cuts the dinghy from its mooring and climbs in. He steadies himself then begins the slow process of paddling by hand back towards the girls. They laugh at him.

'Fucking cheapskate could've left the paddles,' Nick grunts.

'And made your life easier!' Candy picks up some pebbles and starts chucking them at the dinghy. As Nick comes up to the shore he sweeps his hand into the lake and draws up a handful of water, spraying them both. Candy and Lisa run to the water's edge, grab the dinghy and try to tip it over. Lisa jumps in. Candy is speechless with laughter, finding it difficult to stand up straight. She eventually manages to get in. The three of them hand-paddle towards the bigger boat moored a few hundred yards from shore.

Nick ignores the distant barking at first.

Candy stops and looks back to shore. 'What's that?'

'A dog.' Nick tries to ignore the warning in his gut.

'Nice doggy!' Candy leans too far out of the back.

'This one don't sound nice.' Nick's heart beats faster.

'Oh come on, hon, *all* doggies are lovely. You jus' got to stroke 'em right.'

Nick looks back to shore trying to trace the barking. He hears the rapid padding of paws on wood and looks towards the pier. A large bull mastiff runs along the slats. On the other side of the pier in a small boat is a man with a torch pointing directly at them.

The dog jumps from pier to beach and sprints for the water's edge. Torchlight scans the dark, momentarily blinding Nick. The dog launches himself into the lake and starts swimming towards them.

'I've called the police!' the torch man shouts across the water. 'Piss around on my watch. Go on, Tyson! Good lad!'

Nick paddles harder towards the bigger boat. His hands turning numb. Candy and Lisa follow his lead.

The dog swims faster than they can paddle. It snaps at the back of the dinghy. His teeth sink into rubber.

Nick moves to the back of the dinghy. The dog's teeth are stuck. It snorts and growls trying to free itself. Nick hesitates a moment then leans down, pushing reluctantly down on top of its head. Its teeth are forced deeper in. It tries to shake its head free. Air begins to escape. Candy and Lisa continue to paddle towards the boat, panicking. The dinghy begins to deflate, the back end disappearing beneath the black water. The dog growls, splutters and whines trying to free itself. Nick moves to the front of the dinghy. They reach the boat. Candy scrambles up on deck, Nick and Lisa follow. Nick looks back to see the half-sunk dinghy. Torchlight panic scans the water. The torch man begins to row furiously for the sinking dinghy. Nick, Candy and Lisa look on as it submerges, taking the dog down with it.

'I don't fucking believe it,' Nick mutters under his breath.

The man reaches the spot where the dinghy was and jumps in shouting the dog's name.

Nick turns to Lisa. 'Know how to sail this fucking thing?'

'No can do, hon. I ride horses and jocks, boats are out of my jurisdiction. Candy's the girl.'

Nick looks over to Candy steadying herself against the mast.

Candy gives Nick a sobering look, raises one hand in a gesture of 'wait' then stands straight and walks to the back of the boat. She opens up a box, and pulls out a coiled rope and sail.

'Here.' Candy chucks Nick the rope.

The man surfaces, scratched and cut by Tyson's panicking paws and claws.

Lisa cheers and applauds.

Nick rests his drunken head on the boat rail in relief.

'Hey!' Candy shouts across at him. 'Get the cabin door open. We need to get to the wheel.'

Nick looks up and picks up a mooring pole. He walks over and jams the hook into the door. It opens easily. He heads down and looks around. He finds a torch. Lisa walks in behind him and slides her hand on to his balls.

'Hold that thought.' He smiles at her. They walk back on deck and help Candy with the sail.

The torch man reaches the shore, gets out of the water. He stands staring at them, breathless. Tyson is silent.

Candy leads Nick and Lisa through the hoisting of the sail. The light breeze slaps into the canvas a few times before Candy pulls it tight. Nick walks to the bow, leans over and hauls up the anchor. They begin to move slowly into the darkness of Lake Windermere.

Jake and Zeb walk down the lane towards the lake. Jake is smoking his last cigarette. Zeb is quiet. His collar and jacket are done up to his neck, teeth chattering.

'Cold?' Jake asks.

'No.'

'Don't be a twat. I can hear your teeth.'

'I want Dad.'

They continue walking down until they hit the pebble beach. Jake notices the torch man and his dog standing on the pier, talking into his mobile phone.

'Down.' Jake pulls Zeb to the ground with him.

'What?'

'Some old geezer and his dog.'

'What kind of a dog, is it big with teeth and stuff?' Zeb tries to stand up and look over.

'Yep, it's a big dog . . . nothing like Gandalf.'

Zeb pushes Jake. He hears a noise behind them and stops. He looks around but sees nothing. Jake follows his line of sight.

' 'Sup, blood?' Jake holds his breath to hear better.

'By the boats out of the water.' Zeb points.

Jake is unable to make anything out. He squints then hears movement, like an animal in a bin. Out of the dark rises a figure, he knows it's a kid, maybe a teenager, and wonders if they've been seen. Then two more. One behind a dry-docked boat, another from behind a large pile of plastic crates.

Jake looks at Zeb and puts his finger to his lips.

'I'm shitting scared, bro.' Zeb moves in close to Jake.

'Quiet.' Jake notices the taller of the three figures holding some kind of weapon. They're walking directly towards them. 'Come on, bro, we have to go.'

Zeb doesn't move. 'We have to stay here or they'll see us.'

'They already have, now fucking run!'

Jake and Zeb sprint in the opposite direction, trying to stay low to the ground. The three figures break into a run. One of them shouts out, 'There they are . . . fucking smash 'em!'

Jake runs ahead, dragging Zeb along with him through the boatyard, up the ramp back to the road. 'You gotta run faster, bro!'

Without responding Zeb picks up his pace and runs alongside Jake. Their pursuers run faster. Jake tires first. He feels his lungs straining and curses the cigarettes. The dope in his system turns his legs to mud. Zeb begins to run on ahead. He looks back and sees the pursuers right up behind Jake. He shouts out a warning. Before Jake has time to turn, the kid with the weapon swings out, catching Jake on the back of the legs, easily knocking him to the ground. The other two catch up and jump him, flailing punches and kicks. Jake looks up into a blur of arms, legs and spit. He recognises the boy from the pub, a manic glint in his eye as he brings down a soft punch on to Jake's head.

'Fucking country wanker. That all you cunting got,' Jake baits him. His friend smacks Jake square in the jaw. Panicking, Zeb runs ahead, faster. Tears fill his eyes. He stops, looks ahead, terrified, desperate to get away, then he turns back to the three figures raining punches and kicks on to Jake. Zeb looks around him. He runs over to a scrap heap pile and pulls out a lump of wood small enough to run with. He charges at the three kids, screaming, wood raised above his head. One of them breaks away from Jake and stands his ground. Zeb takes a swing. The kid catches the wood easily in his hand, pushing Zeb away from him, forcing him to the ground. Zeb tries to get back up but the kid jams his boot into his stomach, winding him. The kid laughs at him. Jake grabs the biggest kid by the bollocks squeezing them so hard he feels the small testicle collapse in his hand. The boy falls silently to the ground. The gawping teenager looks down at his mate. 'What the fuck you done, you wanker!'

'Something like this, prick.' Jake picks up the bigger kid's discarded weapon and whacks into the back of the teenager's legs forcing him to drop to his knees. Jake turns to look at the third kid, boot still on Zeb's chest. 'Take your country boot off my brother, you useless cunt.' Without hesitation he lets Zeb go and runs back towards town. The gawping teenager looks at Jake wide-eyed and terrified.

Jake narrows his eyes. 'I saw you. Shouldn't grass people up, specially not my dad.'

'I didn't . . . I . . . was . . .' The teenager trembles. Zeb gets up, walks over and kicks him hard in the balls. He drops to the floor, coughing. He pulls himself up and tries unsuccessfully to drag his groaning mate along with him.

He quickly gives up and limps back in the direction of town.

Jake feels his back pocket for his knife. Gone.

'Can't see a fucking thing.' Nick holds the mooring pole out in front like a medieval lance.

'This was your idea.' Candy holds the wheel of the boat lightly in her hands keeping it moving in a straight line. 'That old man's probably called the cops.'

'Fuck 'im.' Nick keeps looking ahead.

Lisa sits next to Candy looking down at the waves as they break against the hull.

'I don't care where we're going, this is the coolest night we've had since we got here.' Lisa high-fives Candy.

Nick takes out a plastic bag from his pocket and chucks it to Candy. She opens it up and smiles broadly at him.

'Oh . . . my . . . god.' She sucks her finger and dips it into the bag.

'Kept it for a goodbye hit . . . and a thank you.' Nick smiles at them both.

'We're the girls who should be thanking you, sweet lips.' Candy licks her finger, dabs it in the bag and puts it into Lisa's mouth. 'You are one bad little English flower.'

Nick dips the mooring pole into the water, letting it drag for a moment before lifting it back up and pointing it into the dark.

Jake and Zeb head back to town. Zeb holds Jake's hand. Jake holds Zeb's tight.

Zeb looks up at him. 'Did the wanking cunts hurt you?'

'Not much.'

'They were giving you a proper bashing.'

'We sorted the cunts out, ey.' Jake does his best to hide the pain. His ribs feel bruised, maybe broken. One of his front teeth is loose and the back of his head is grazed.

'Yeah! Fuck around with the Genevas . . . they know what they're gonna get, blood!' Zeb lets go of Jake's hand and kung fu punches the air.

'Easy, tiger. Keep quiet. Pigs find us they'll nick us for sure.'

Zeb slows his punching down. He shivers a little then looks around the sleeping town.

'Where we gonna sleep?' Zeb asks.

'The van.'

'Ah shit fucking bags.'

'You swear too much.' Jake squeezes Zeb's hand.

'You can talk! Wanna sleep in a bed not the bloody van again.'

'We can't go back to that shit hole of a hotel.'

'Dad might be back.'

'He'll be off his face . . . with Candy and Lisa.'

'Bro?'

'Yes, bro.'

'You still fancy Lisa?'

'Bit.'

'You fancy her big time, star! Saw you going red.' Zeb starts dancing round Jake poking him. Jake winces.

Zeb stops dead. 'Wassamatter?'

'Nothing. Let's get to the van. Fucking knackered.'

They walk up the high street, head on up another hundred yards and turn into a narrow row with cars parked on one side. Jake sees the van.

'You got the keys?' Zeb asks as they approach it.

'No.' Jake keeps walking.

'How we gonna get in?'

'Smash the window.' Jake walks round to the driver's side.

'You can't do that. Dad'll kill you and it'll make loads of noise and wake everyone up. You said we had to be quiet.'

'We will. Got any chewing gum?' Zeb looks at him perplexed. He rummages around his pocket then takes out a full pack of Extra. He hands it to Jake.

'Sweet.' Jake takes out a handful for himself, then some for Zeb. 'Put those in your gob and chew 'em up good.'

Zeb follows the instructions, watching Jake closely. They stand quietly chewing.

'Now what?' Zeb chomps loud.

'Spit it out.' Jake opens the palm of his hand.

'Thas rank.' Zeb plops the large, sticky ball of gum on to Jake's hand. Jake spits his out on to it. He spreads and stretches the grey mass of gum out and sticks it on to the narrow corner glass in the VW door.

Zeb watches him looking in the gutter. 'What you doing?'

Jake comes back with a small rock. He pushes it into the gum, takes his shoes off and whacks at the rock. Three quiet thuds and the glass begins to crack.

'Fucking A number 1 cool,' Zeb whispers, eyes wide as the glass cracks under the final impact. Jake pushes the glass in, reaches his hand in and opens the door.

'Where'd you learn to do that?' Zeb asks. 'Well cool. Shitting Mission Impossible.'

'Dad.' Jake climbs into the van. Zeb follows.

'He's gonna kill you.'

'Can do what he fucking likes.'

They clamber into the back. Jake slumps down on to the long seat, lets out a deep sigh and lies down. Jake closes his eyes. Zeb covers him with a duvet, then himself.

Jake listens to the wind against the side of the van, he isn't scared.

Nick sees a large shadow loom up. He holds the mooring pole tighter, expecting to come up against another, bigger boat. A shadowy outline of trees begins to form. He realises they're heading towards an island.

'You'd better steer left,' he calls back.

'Why's that, hon?' Candy asks, swigging on the vodka, following it with a long toke on the joint.

'Cos we're about to hit something . . . something big.'

Candy leans forward peering into the darkness then rears back as she realises they are going to beach the boat. She flips the wheel to the left several times. The right side of the hull hits earth and stone beneath the shallow water and scrapes along it for several feet. Nick pushes the mooring pole into the water, forcing the boat away from the shore. Lisa heads over and helps him push.

'Shall we go check it out?' Candy asks. 'We can drop anchor right here.'

'Not into it,' Nick replies flatly, continuing to push away from the island. Nick wants to get back to the hotel. He needs to get back to the kids.

Lisa smiles across at him. 'Come on, nature boy. It's our last night.'

'Build ourselves a fire, smoke a few more Js, do some Bolivian. I'll even take a few shots, email them when we get home.' Candy turns the wheel right a few times. Nick likes the way she looks at the helm, he could do with getting a little more hammered. He thinks about the kids again for a guilty second then withdraws the mooring pole from the water letting the boat bump up to shore.

Lisa jumps out first. Nick chucks her the heavier of the two ropes, she misses and it hits the water. She ducks her hand in and picks it up. Nick drops the anchor, drags it back for a purchase and eventually finds one.

Candy heads into the cabin and comes back up a few seconds later with a flare gun and jumps over the handrail.

'Proper pirate,' Nick jibes. He hurdles over the side, catching his foot on the middle rail. He falls forward, holding tight to the rail. His leg and left side of his body bang against the side of the boat. He lands feet first in the water. Lisa and Candy roar with laughter.

'Very funny. Nearly ripped my fucking arm out of its socket!' He reaches back up into the boat and takes down the smaller rope and walks to shore. Lisa ties the larger rope round a jagged rock. Nick follows suit.

After a cold half hour searching and gathering wood they have a big enough pile for a fire. Candy prepares it. Lisa huddles into Nick, keeping warm.

'Don't mind me, guys. I'll just get this going with this all on my lonesome.' Candy carries on with the fire.

Lisa shrugs. 'Doin' fine, girl.'

Candy breaks open the flare cartridge and pours the powder into the centre of the fire, takes out some paper from her back pocket, puts it over the powder then piles up the kindling. 'Best you guys stand back a little. These can be a little unpredictable. Light?'

Nick chucks a box of matches over.

Candy throws a flaring match into a small gap in the fire. The powder roars up, loud and pink, engulfing the wood in light, singeing her hair and illuminating the surrounding area. Lisa coos. Nick and Lisa step forward and crouch down, hands outstretched, palms facing the fire.

'Your boys would like this,' Lisa says looking into the flames.

'Jake'll be getting stoned and Zeb'll be out cold.'

Candy looks across the flames at Nick. 'He's a good kid . . . Jake.'

Nick nods, chucking another chunk of wood on the fire. 'They're both good.'

'Kinda weird time of year to be taking them on holiday.'

'We needed to get away.'

He starts to roll a joint. Lisa takes a swig on the vodka, passing the dregs to Candy.

'What you running from, hon?' Candy asks.

'London.' Nick stares into the flames, full of regret, wishing the kids were back home.

'What else?'

'That's enough, ain't it?'

'You got that look in your eye,' Candy continues.

'What look's that?' Nick asks.

'Like something's hunting you.' Candy chucks the bottle into the fire.

Nick looks at Candy across the flames and continues to hold her gaze. His mind drifts back to Emily. They made fires like this in Scotland. He misses her; Wester Ross. He thought he had it all sewn up. Life was sweet. The images of coast, highlands, fields and the croft stay jagged but firm in his memory. The isolation broke their connection. Nick knew it was over with Emily before the kids were born. He thought Jake would fix it, then Zeb. So did she. He remembers why he's here, round this fire, with these women, this many miles from London. He's not going back.

'I don't sell cars. I break into houses for a living.'

Lisa looks up at him in surprise.

Candy smiles. 'Did I not tell you this man was bad!' The atmosphere around the fire shifts. 'Do your kids know?' Candy asks.

'Jake does. Zeb has an idea. Don't talk about it much. Not something to be proud of. Money's good but that's about it.'

Candy keeps her eyes fixed on Nick.

Silence falls between the three of them.

Nick wants to enjoy his last few hours with them, their energy and their beauty. Get it while he can.

Fifteen

Vincent sits in the motorway service station, cup of tea in front of him, panini in hand. He looks at it, mustering the will to eat. The sharpness in his chest bites into him. He coughs another round of blood into a cheap paper napkin. He takes a bite of his panini and gazes out of the main window across to the quiet motorway. Seven a.m. sunshine trickles feebly into the dingy café. An old lady moves from table to table, clearing up empty cups, looking down, tutting, wiping, rattling her trolley and frail body on to the next. Vincent watches and feels sorry for her. She reminds him of his dead mother. This in turn reminds him of Jasper and himself. He takes out his cigarettes and heads out for a smoke.

Jake is woken by the tapping on the van window. He lifts himself up on his elbows. He winces at the stiffness in his ribs and head. There's a lot more pain in his body. He looks out on to the dawn-lit street. Nothing.

The frightened face of the gawping bookshop teenager pops up, nose to the passenger window. Jake jumps back sending a shard of pain through his body.

'The fuck?' He looks over to Zeb, buried under the duvet, fast asleep and snoring. The teenager looks in, no sign of aggression in his eyes. Jake whispers at him through the broken glass hole, 'Fuck do you want, prick?'

'Come to apologise.'

'Think I'm a fucking idiot?'

The teenager lifts Jake's sheath knife to the glass. 'And to bring back your knife.' Everything in Jake's head tells him he should tell the kid to go fuck himself, yet something in the boy's face tells him he's being straight. Despite his wounds and anger, he trusts him. Zeb rolls over and murmurs something about a big dog.

'How do I know your mates ain't hiding waiting to give me another kicking?'

'You put one of them in hospital and the other one nearly shat himself he was so scared of you.'

'Makes you the brave one then, does it?'

'Just wanted to give you your knife back . . . and . . .'

'And what . . .' Jake hears his aggression and tones it down.

'Wondered if you had any spliff? Saw you smoking some, smelt it . . . Mack said we should nick it off you, get you to pay rent for being on our turf.'

'Who the fuck's Mack?'

'The one whose bollocks you mashed.'

Jake pauses. 'He all right?'

'No. His dad's looking for you. I'd keep out of his way if I were you. He's a right nutter.'

Jake looks at him through the glass, shakes his head and slowly lifts himself up off the makeshift bed.

He opens the van door. The teenager stands at the

entrance, holding the knife, handle towards Jake. Jake looks him in the eye and takes it.

'Cheers. 'Preciate it.' Jake slides over. The teenager gets in.

Jake keeps a close eye on him. 'What's your name then? And keep your voice down, brother's asleep.'

'Thomas . . . Tom.'

Jake stretches his hand out stiffly. They shake. Jake notices the sweat on his palm.

'It's all right, you're safe, mate.' Jake puts the knife on the dash.

'I wasn't the one who said we should jump you.' Tom shifts awkwardly in his seat.

'But you fucking did anyway, joined in and had a right laugh . . . 'til you got some back.' Jake lights a cigarette, puffing himself up bigger, older.

'Wasn't my idea, honest. They said I'd get a kicking if I didn't give you one. Said you owed us rent for being on our turf and you were gonna pay one way or another.'

Tom's submissive tone softens Jake. He looks at the skinny teenager long and hard then reaches into his pocket. He takes out the small bag of weed and holds it up to the windscreen. Tom looks up at it, mouth slightly open.

'How much is it?' Tom asks. 'Is it any good?'

'Blow your fucking head off, mate. Got this from London . . . well, got it from my old man but he got it from London and he gets the bollocks gear.'

'You got this from your dad?' Tom asks in disbelief.

'He didn't give it to me, I nicked it.'

'He smokes hash . . . weed?' Tom looks at Jake wide-eyed.

'Your old man a bit straight is he?' Jake jibes.

'He listens to Hendrix and lets me stay up late on the weekend and sometimes I drink his homebrew.'

'Sounds great,' Jake shakes his head. 'Country boys.' He hunches over a CD case and starts rolling a joint.

Tom watches closely. 'Saw your dad bash up this bloke yesterday . . . gave him a proper, nasty kicking. Never seen anyone get mashed up like that, not in real life. Told the lads and they said we should give it a go, said we should bash you up like that. Get rent for our turf. I shouldn't have told them.'

Jake stops rolling the joint and looks up at him, making the connection between the pain in his body and his dad. 'What happened?'

'You didn't hear? Shit.' Tom speaks quick, excited. 'Your dad came into the bookshop then this bloke comes in, looked like some kind of proper gangster, smart clothes and stuff. Then they both go out without saying anything. Proper movie stuff. I watched it all from the window. This guy put rope round your dad's neck. It was like in *The Bourne Ultimatum*. Thought your dad was gonna die in the street. Then your dad smashes this bottle and cuts the guy up bad. Couldn't believe it. Then it looked like your dad was gonna kill 'im! Cut him with the bottle all over his neck and stuff and kicked him in the face and back and left him all mashed up in the street, all covered in blood. He walked past the window and saw me and put his finger to his lips like he was telling me not to tell anyone. Nearly fucking shit myself. Never seen a fight like that, not in real life, never.'

'You're fucking with me?' Jake knew he wasn't.

'Swear on my mum's life. Saw the whole thing through the window like I was watching it on the telly.'

Jake has never seen Nick in a fight, but feels like he has now. He puts the blame for getting beaten up by the local lads squarely on Nick.

Zeb snores loud in the back.

Tom breaks Jake's stunned silence. 'That your brother?'

'Yeah. Snores like a pig.'

'Tough nut.'

'Can be.' Jake brings his attention back to the joint, licking the papers and putting in the tobacco. 'You lived here all your life?'

'Moved here when I was three. Feels like forever.'

'Like it?'

'S'all right. Better in the summer, get the tourists . . . and the girls.' Jake nods his head in acknowledgement.

'Got a girlfriend?' Jake asks.

'Nah. No one I fancy. All dogs round here. 'Cept Charlotte. She's hot. Goes out with Mack. He's a twat. You?'

'Nope. There was this American woman, we had something going.'

'Woman? How old was she?'

Jake lights the joint, takes two tokes and hands it over. 'Bout twenty-five. Proper fit. Good kisser. Great tits. Lives in LA.'

Tom nods his head in respect and takes a mouthful of smoke, doing his best not to cough.

'That'll do the trick.' Jake smiles, nodding at him.

Tom looks at the joint. 'Twenty-five. Man that is old . . . you're a lucky bastard.'

'Always been lucky.' Jake picks up his knife and draws

the blade from the sheath. He runs the tip of it along the dash, applying just enough pressure to make a mark. Just enough to piss Nick off. Tom continues to smoke.

Jake feels comfortable in Tom's company. Easier than with most of his mates back in London. Except Carlos.

'Good?' he asks.

Tom exhales smoke on to the windscreen. 'This is the dog's. How much?'

'How much you want?'

'Got a tenner.' Tom takes the crumpled-up note out of his pocket and puts it on the dash. Jake takes out a small handful of weed, puts it into an old Snickers wrapper and hands it to him.

Zeb jams his head through the gap and looks at Tom, wide-eyed. 'You're the shitting bastard who tried to bash us up. What you bloody fucking doin' in my dad's shitting van?' He looks at Jake, waiting for an answer.

Jake raises his hand. 'He's cool, Zeb. He's all right. He brought my knife back.' He shows Zeb the knife. 'Look, he brought it back and wanted to buy some weed. I just sold him a tenner's worth. Here.' Jake takes out three pound coins and gives them to Zeb. Zeb takes them, gives Tom a long hard look then looks back to Jake. 'Where's Dad?'

'He ain't back.'

Zeb pulls the duvet over him. 'Probably at the hotel looking for us.'

'He said we should always go back to the van if there was any trouble. He'll be here when he's done.'

'I should go,' Tom cuts in. 'Got my paper round. Bastard boss'll kill me if I'm late.'

'Safe.' Jake raises his fist and knuckle touches Tom's.

Tom opens up the door and slips out, stumbling a little before straightening himself out. Zeb laughs at him.

'You wanna watch yourself on that bike, mate, do yourself some damage smoking this gear.' Jake smiles down at him. 'You about later? We could go down the lake.'

'Mack's dad's gone nuts. I should stay at home.' Tom thinks for a moment. 'Fuck it. Yeah. Why not. See you down there later.'

'Be down by there 'bout five . . . we're gonna take a boat out.'

'Are we?' Zeb asks. 'I'm not shitting going in another shitting boat, ever.'

'Time to have some fun. Place is depressing the shit out of me.'

Tom nods, gives Jake and Zeb five and heads down the road.

Sally grips the steering wheel looking ahead, face strained in concentration. Emily looks at her. 'You should relax a little, sis. Must be taking up a lot of energy holding on that tight.'

Sally's eyes are fixed on the motorway ahead. 'Quicker we get there, quicker we get the kids, quicker we get back.'

'I agree but I want us there in one piece.'

Sally swerves into the fast lane. Emily can't see any traffic in the way. She holds on to the passenger door arm rest. After a few minutes Sally pulls back into the nearside lane again. Emily shakes her head in disbelief, saying nothing. She lights a cigarette, takes a few puffs then hands it to Sally. 'You got some money for a hotel?'

Sally lets the cigarette hang out of the corner of her

mouth, smoke forcing her left eye shut. She veers a little into the hard shoulder. Emily takes the cigarette back off her.

'When's the last time you had a shag?' Sally asks.

'Where did that come from?'

'Haven't had one in months. Started running last month, supposed to ease the libido. Done bugger all to ease mine. Still horny as ever.' Sally comes up close to the back of a Bedford van. She accelerates into the middle lane. A car has to swerve into the fast lane and the driver hits his horn. Sally ignores him.

'Would you like me to drive?' Emily asks.

'No. Ta. Let you know when I start nodding off.' Sally takes the cigarette back off her and hangs it out of the corner of her mouth.

Sally pulls into the hard shoulder

'What's happening?' Emily asks.

'Been dying for a piss for the last fifty miles. Won't be a sec.' Sally gets out of the car, walks over to the passenger side and squats down, her face close to the passenger window. She smiles at Emily. A passing lorry rumbles past, its driver high enough to see Sally. He blasts his horn three times. She gives him the middle finger, stands up, shakes her arse, pulls her trousers back up and gets back in.

She sits at the wheel staring ahead. They both sit in silence for a while. Emily waiting for her to speak.

'Do we know what we're getting into here?' Sally asks.

'I know what I'm getting into, yes.' Emily pulls out a flask of tea and pours them both a cup.

'Nick's got himself involved with some nasty bastards in his time.'

'That's why I have to get up there.'

'What if they're not there? What if we can't find them?' Sally sips her tea.

'I just want to get there. If they've been to Snowdon, someone will have seen them. It's dead quiet up there this time of year. We can ask around the hotels, shops. Two boys and Nick can't be easy to forget.' Sally nods in agreement. Emily takes out a sandwich from the bag and hands half of it to her.

Emily speaks with her mouth half full of bread and cheese. 'Glad you're with me. If anything happens to the boys . . . I'll never forgive myself.'

'Nick might be an arsehole but he'll kill anyone who comes near the boys.'

'Which is exactly why I'm freaking out.'

Sally starts the car and pulls out without looking.

The road is empty.

Nick lies half asleep, snow falls steadily on him. Lisa lies against him. Candy is keeping the fire going. Nick opens his eyes and looks out across the water and the sun rising behind a thin line of trees. He pushes Lisa gently forward and sits up.

'What time is it?' he asks Candy.

'Left my watch at the hotel.'

'Got anything to drink?'

'We're all out. I could get into the boat, go to the store.'

'We need to get back to the mainland . . . out of sight in case that old fucker called the police.'

Candy stands up and shakes her legs loose. 'By the way . . .'

'Yeah?' Nick stands up and walks closer to the dying fire.

'We don't need to get back in the boat.' She smiles at him wearily. 'We're already on the mainland, this isn't an island, it's the other side.'

Nick looks at the boat and the boatyard on the other side of the water then behind him at the wood. 'For fuck sake.' He kicks the fire, jumping sparks into the air. Lisa stirs. 'What time's your train?' he asks Candy.

'Nine thirty.' She moves closer to the fire.

'Bags packed?'

'Just gotta wake up sleeping beauty here, get some coffee and we're homeward bound.'

Nick walks round and puts his arms round her. She looks him in the eye, leaning slightly back to take his whole face in. She grins at him then kisses him on the nose. 'You take care of those kids, specially Zeb. He worships you.' Nick smiles at her and moves in to kiss her. She pulls back. 'I'm serious. You may be used to what you do, don't mean he has to be.'

'Let's not fuck up the goodbye. I need a morning kiss.' He leans in again.

'What you need is a lesson in parenting skills,' Candy continues. 'You should take them back home to their mom.'

'Soon.'

'Got a bad feeling about you, gorgeous. It's one thing to fuck up your own life but not your kids.'

Nick smiles tightly at her, covering his desire to slap her for questioning his parenting. He knows she's right.

'Didn't have you down as the mothering type,' he says flatly.

'You know very little about me . . . or my sister.'

'Never met your sister.'

'You've done more than meet her.'

Nick looks bemused a moment then clicks. He looks round to Lisa still sleeping then back to Candy. 'Why wouldn't you tell me something like that?'

'She doesn't like to be known as the little sister. Doesn't stop me having to keep an eye on her. Reminds me of your boys. Jake loves Zeb like I love her.'

'He's a good babysitter.' He knows this is the wrong thing to say and knows he should be back with them.

Candy tuts at him. 'That's exactly what I'm talking about. You should be back at the hotel. They could have gotten up to all kinds of trouble.'

'Come back with me, you can both say goodbye. They'd like that, specially Jake.'

'Hey.' Lisa's voice rises as she stands up unsteadily. 'What's happening? What I miss? Damn. Anyone got anything to drink?'

Candy walks over and helps her up. 'Time for our goodbyes, hon. Train to catch.'

'I wanna say goodbye to the boys.' Lisa heads over to the fire, warms her hands then turns and warms her arse. Nick kisses Candy on the forehead, walks over to Lisa, slaps her arse and kisses her on the lips.

'That it then?' Lisa asks him. 'After all the fun we had?'

'Looks like it.' Nick shrugs. 'Been great meeting you . . . both of you.'

Candy walks over to him and puts something in his

hand. 'Something to remember us by. You're not to look until we've gone.' Nick looks at them both one last time and heads off towards the trees.

In a few seconds he's disappeared from the site and their life.

Sixteen

Vincent walks through Windermere, looking lazily in shop windows, blending in. A few winter holiday-makers trundle past in their cars, taking in the stark, leafless beauty of town.

Vincent knows for sure the Genevas won't be here now. Nick would be an idiot to stay anywhere any longer than a few days, especially at the tail end of February. Too easy to be seen and remembered in a winter-reduced population.

He looks for the people the Genevas may have come into contact with, maybe spent time with. Plays the stranger passing through, telling locals he's on the way to meet a few friends up North, the Genevas.

He didn't think Nick would've made it so easy, but he has. The information flows easily, spiked with village gossip. Something to liven up the dull cold evenings.

Vincent had initially wanted this father of two on his knees in supplication, apology and regret, dead if necessary. But he was starting to like him. There's obviously more to the man than a half-cocked thief. A gathering respect was growing with each laboured motorway mile. If he met Nick in any other circumstances he'd sit him down and have a civilised conversation with him. The more time he spent travelling, investing energy, attention and purpose in payback, the more complicated it was becoming; the more engaging. The further he journeyed north the worse his lungs got. More painful, more blood coughed up. His walk has slowed to half its London speed.

He has been careful not to arouse suspicion by asking for too much detail from the locals. Nick has left a suitably bad impression on the town, as have his kids.

One conversation catches his attention above the rest. A greying, beer-heavy local, elbows on bar, looking straight ahead as he speaks and drinks is the bearer of good news. He tells Vincent about a man fitting Nick's description and two younger women stealing a boat and nearly drowning his beloved Tyson.

'Police did bugger all about it. He was the same feller seen with two boys by the wife the other day, up the high street, eating pasties.' Vincent buys the man another drink. 'Those boys should be in school, specially the scruffy young 'un. Tom got a bit too close to proper trouble. Good lad, Tom.'

'Tom?' Vincent asks nonchalantly, hiding a smile.

'Good lad, mostly. Pain in the arse when he gets into the dope and hangs round with the Clancys though. Lads that age should be out working.' The man starts to slur a little. ' 'Prenticeships, national service, bring 'em both back, country'd be a better place for it.'

Vincent nods in agreement. The local drains another glass of the single malt. Vincent raises a finger to the barman who refills the smeared glass.

'I think I've seen him around town,' Vincent lies. 'Scruffy lad, skinny, tall.'

'Nope, not Tom. Smart lad, well dressed, takes after his dad. And he ain't skinny neither, 'e's in good shape. Make a good soldier . . . farmer.' The man lifts his glass to his lips. Vincent had what he wanted. In a town this small it would be easy to find Tom. He looks at his watch. 'That the time? Must be getting to my bed.'

The local raises his glass, head drooped, eyes shut.

Vincent wakes late the following day, skips breakfast and heads into town to look for Tom. He spots a few older locals standing in a shop doorway out of the drizzle. He innocently asks them if they've seen him. They point him in the direction of the marina.

Tom sits by the water, feet dangling over the small jetty, a handful of stones in his hand. The soles of his trainers skim the water as he swings them back and forth. He is clearly bored. Vincent watches from a distance as Tom chucks them, one by one, into the lake's blackened surface. Vincent walks further down the shingle beach, looking at the boats, then across the water – the awestruck tourist. He lets Tom see him then walks away further up the beach to ease any suspicion. He can feel Tom's eyes on him.

Vincent finds a spot and sits, making out like he hasn't seen or isn't interested in the boy. He collects a handful of small flat stones and starts skimming them across the water. Three bounces; four; six. He looks over at Tom and raises his hand. Tom looks down a moment then back at him to return the greeting. Vincent's concentration is back to the water. Tom stands on the jetty and skims his own stones, doing his best to beat Vincent's number. Vincent smiles to himself. He carries on for a while then stops to take out a packet of cigarettes. He knows Tom is watching him. He puts the fag in his mouth then pats his pockets. No light. After a few further seconds searching he hears the crunch of feet landing on shingle then the slow pace of Tom coming towards him. He turns to look at him.

'Swap you a light for a fag,' Tom offers as he approaches Vincent cautiously.

'Sounds like a deal.' Vincent takes out a cigarette. Tom extends his hand holding out a box of matches. They exchange.

Tom stands silently, smoking, looking across the water. 'Most grown-ups are shit.'

'At what?' Vincent asks.

'Skimming.'

'Dad taught me when I was a kid. Much more fun doing it on the sea though, takes more skill.' Vincent takes a drag on his fag. 'Local?'

''Fraid so.' Tom kicks a few pebbles.

'Probably not as appealing here to the youth as it is to the adults.'

'Place is a dump.' Tom puts his cigarette in his mouth and his hands in his pockets.

'A beautiful dump.'

'Soon as I can I'm gonna leave . . . for London. Gonna be a writer.'

'Got somewhere to go, someone to stay with?'

'My uncle. Said I could come stay with him while I'm looking for work . . . while I'm writing my first book.'

'What's it gonna be about?' Vincent takes his scarf off, lays it down neatly on the stones and sits.

'Sci-fi detective story with vampires.'

'Sounds original.' Vincent looks around. Taking his time. 'London can be a bit of a shock to the system . . . if you're new to it.' He starts to cough, putting his hand over his mouth.

'I can take care of myself.' Tom picks up another handful of stones and chucks them, one by one, aggressively into the air. They both watch as they arc high and drop slowly into the lake.

'Thought I could take the whole city on when I moved there, till I got my first kicking.'

'I can take a good kicking . . . if I have to.' Tom chucks the last stone.

'I don't bounce back quite like I did when I was your age.' Vincent reaches into his pocket and takes out a small bag of hash. Tom's eyes widen a little. He looks furtively back across the water, disguising excitement.

'Mind if I roll one?' Vincent asks.

'Nah, go ahead, mate.'

Vincent can see Tom straining to keep his eyes on the water.

'Can't imagine you get much of this up here.' Vincent opens the bag, rests it by his side and takes out his skins.

'Some. Never much good though.'

'Ahh well, this stuff is straight from California. Join me?'

'Err . . . yeah, sure.' Tom relaxes, now watching Vincent closely, admiring his skill at rolling.

Vincent coughs erratically and hands the joint to Tom to light.

'Nasty cough, mate.'

'Cancer.' Vincent looks across the water. Tom looks at him, surprised. 'Good hash is the only thing that eases it; relaxes the lungs.'

They continue to smoke in silence. Vincent gives it long enough for the strength of the opium-laced marijuana to ease Tom's remaining suspicion. He finally breaks the comfortable silence. 'So you're heading south and I'm heading north.'

Tom nods. 'Where you going?'

'Gonna see a mate and his two kids. Have a break from the smoke, London I mean . . . not spliff. They came through Windermere a few days ago. You may have seen them?' Vincent feels Tom tense up, remaining quiet. Vincent passes back the joint. 'I can leave you some of this if you like?'

'Really?'

Vincent holds up the bag. 'No skin off my nose. Got a load of it.'

'Yeah, that'd be cool, almost finished mine.'

Vincent passes the remains of the hash to Tom.

'I've got a couple of quid.'

'Don't be silly. You haven't even got a job. I'm loaded.' He winks at Tom. Tom breaks into a childlike smile.

'You didn't happen to see them did you?'

Tom looks up. 'Who?'

'My mate Nick and his two sons?'

Tom pauses for a moment, thoughts and calculations crawling across his face.

'Yeah I know him, Jake and his brother, Zeb. Jake's a mate.'

Vincent feigns surprise. 'Really?' He leaves Tom to fill the silence.

'Said he was heading up to Scotland but I wasn't to tell anyone, had some nutter after his dad. He was proper scared.'

'Some nutter?'

Tom shrugs. 'Said I was to keep schtum.'

'Did he say whereabouts in Scotland he was heading? I'm supposed to be meeting them. As ever Nick hasn't told me where and I've lost my mobile.' Vincent smiles at him reassuringly.

Tom eyes Vincent up for a moment then speaks. 'Somewhere on the west coast. Middle of fucking nowhere he said. Somewhere near Ulla . . . Ullpool or something.'

'Ullapool?' Vincent offers.

'That's it. Said his dad wanted to get a cottage up there and get his little brother a goat. Sounds dull as shit. Jake was into it though.'

'Well I hope he manages to stay out of trouble up there . . . our Nick, he can be a bit of a liability at times.'

Tom finishes the last of the joint, drops it on to the shingle and stubs it out with his foot.

'Sweet for the hash.' Tom offers his hand. They shake.

'Pleasure's all mine.' Vincent smiles at him. They get up and head their separate ways.

Seventeen

The Genevas' journey continues without incident for the next hundred or so miles. Café stops, petrol stations, piss stops, rest stops, stops just to look at scenery. Jake and Zeb's arguments rise and fall relative to boredom. Nick does little to intervene, lost in thought, sensing the creeping heat of pursuit. Knowing there will be some kind of payback for the man he battered. He went too far. He was scared; let his fear take over. He wonders if anyone'll find them this far up? Each mile further adds doubt to his initial conviction and determination that when he left London he would get away from trouble for good. Each day away from school, home and routine, hammers home the truth of his uselessness and recklessness as a father.

The weather deteriorates as they head further north. Nick recognises some of the countryside. He's shocked by the change. Villages turned to towns, towns to soulless urban sprawls blocking much of the beauty he remembered. It drains what little motivation he has left.

He points out the spots he recognises to Zeb and Jake, gives them the stories, makes a few up. Zeb's interest is obvious. Jake hides his. Nick recognises the stretches of road driven along with Emily so many times. Memory flashes reminding him why he was so fixed on getting back. Back to the nineties. Back to what he convinced himself were better times. Mind fixed on photo memories hiding the reality of his fuck-up; showing him only the light of a blinding sun-bleached loch on a June afternoon, walking a wooded glen in autumn with Emily; Jake in her belly. His soundtrack memory: a looped Nick Drake album soft-focusing the denial and bullshit he spun to his kids and himself all their lives. He does all this to ignore his diminishing motivation and belief that they will get there in one piece.

Moving forward, winter stands still inside the relentless grey skies.

Crossing the border into Scotland offers them a brief visual respite of more snow and less people. Snowball fights; getting drenched; drying the clothes by the fires that Jake gets better and better at building. All of this down time, good time, does little to ease Nick's paranoia. The wilder the countryside, the less people they see, the less grown-up conversation he has, the more his head kicks in, obsessing about the dumb mistakes and threat of danger. The things he's done to make it so much easier to track them down. Each mile further from London, Emily, Warren, Vincent, the more out of control he feels. Fear was never something he'd given much thought to and it was finally catching him up.

He pushes the van past what he thought it could handle. Foot to the floor whenever he has the chance.

The next stage of the journey takes them up towards Glasgow. Jake and Zeb plead with him to stop in the city for a few days, check out the sights, cinemas, restaurants. Nick ignores them, taking a detour to Kilmarnock then up the coast road through Largs, Wemyss Bay and Gourock. The back route puts extra miles on the journey, but the beauty of the landscape stuns all three into silence.

Jake drives whenever the roads are quiet enough, wide enough and safe enough. Zeb teases him relentlessly for his nerves at the wheel while entertaining himself with drawings of dogs, goats and fighting dragons. When he's bored of drawing he daydreams out the back window into the unfolding countryside. Countryside that gets wilder, more isolated by the mile.

They head inland into Trossachs National Park and up through the Grampian mountains. Each day further up country fills Nick with increasing excitement and fear.

They pass through Inverness at dusk. Nick decides against the bigger roads, instead heading past Beauly Firth and on into the Highlands. The extra miles make no difference now. Being back in Wester Ross feels good.

Zeb is asleep, snoring. Jake stares out of the window watching the mountains rise and fall; the lochs drawing in and falling back into the distance, separated by fields and pine woods. He likes what he sees, getting more and more used to it, transfixed by the massive spaces around them, feeling easier and easier leaving behind the claustrophobia of city streets.

'Don't s'pose you're gonna change your mind now then?' Jake asks Nick, staring out across Strathconon Forest and the half white fields in front of it. Melting snow reveals green and brown marshland beneath.

'The more you keep your head back home the worse this is gonna be. Get into it. You might surprise yourself. You get too serious about being serious, you'll end up in serious trouble.'

'So you keep saying,' Jake replies, flatly.

'You've got your mum's sense of humour.'

'This is funny? Am I supposed to be laughing?'

'Stop shitting arguing,' Zeb mumbles through half sleep.

'You're starting to enjoy it and you know it.' Nick ruffles his hair. The van swerves a little.

'Like I have any choice,' Jake mutters.

'Horse walks into a bar.' Nick keeps his eyes on the road.

'What?'

'Horse walks into a bar and the barman says . . .'

'Why the long face.' Jake mocks the punchline. 'Very funny.' He looks back out the window.

'Come on, you know some good ones. Cracking jokes was all I could think about when I was your age . . . that and birds.'

Zeb pokes his head between the seats. 'I got one! Heard about the magic tractor?'

Jake keeps his gaze out the window.

Nick is more interested 'Nope. Go on, kill me, kid.'

'Goes down the lane and turns into a field.'

Nick looks confused.

'Magic tractor . . . turns into a FIELD!'

Nick gets it, nodding his head in appreciation. 'That's good. Like it.'

Jake rolls his eyes. 'Can we go for a walk? In that wood,' he asks looking at the line of pine trees hugging a loch.

'It's getting dark, kid, we should think about finding a B and B or something.'

'We can stay in the van, build a fire.' Jake pauses a moment. 'It'd be cool to watch the sunset through the trees.'

'I wanna build a fire this time,' Zeb insists. 'You two can get the wood.'

Nick carries on through the village of Milton. As they come to Glenmeanie, Zeb shouts out the name over and over.

'This is where all the misers live!' He writes the name down in his book.

Nick drives on through to Carnoch and pulls the car into a small lane. He gets out the map. Jake leans over.

'Loch Beannacharan.' Jake runs his finger along the blue water on the page.

They look at the loch through the windscreen. Zeb breaks the silence.

'Come on, dufus, let's get into them woods. Bet there's bears and everything in there.' He scrambles over Jake, who winces in pain, then climbs out of the passenger door and runs towards the wood. Jake and Nick follow.

Nick puts his arm across Jake's shoulders as they walk past the lake.

Jake doesn't resist.

Eighteen

'Where the fuck are we, kid?' Nick leans into the steering wheel, nose up to the windscreen, squinting at the road ahead. Sleet rains down. The VW headlamps do little to light up the road and the thin country lane gets more dangerous by the mile.

Jake has the road map open on his lap. 'If you stopped driving like a twat I might be able to see the map properly.' He puts the torch in his mouth and grips it with his teeth.

'I want a goat,' Zeb complains.

'Soon as we get past Ullapool. Stick the fucking thing in the back if we have to.' Nick squints through the windscreen.

'Goats stink,' Jake mumbles through the torch. 'We're not having one in the van.'

Zeb scrambles to the back of the van and starts to draw on to the misted back windscreen something that resembles a goat, then a tombstone with Gandalf's name on it.

Nick lowers his voice at Jake. 'Keep him sweet, kid. Make life easier for all of us.'

'Make life easier for you.' Jake brings the map closer to the torchlight. 'Half of the villages we've gone through aren't even on this chuffing map.' He slaps it down on to his lap. 'No fucking idea where we are.'

'Pass the bottle will you?' Nick asks.

Without protest Jake opens up the glove compartment and takes out the half-bottle of vodka and hands it to Nick. He takes a swig and offers some to Jake.

'Someone's gotta keep their eye on the road.'

'Spoken to Mum?' Nick asks.

'Yesterday.'

'Don't tell her where we're headed.' Nick takes another swig on the vodka.

'Why? It's not like we're on the run or anything.'

'Talk to her all you like but . . . just don't tell her where we're headed . . . please.' Jake doesn't respond. 'If it carries on like this,' Nick wipes the condensation off the windscreen, 'we'll have to stop out here the night.'

Zeb sings to himself as he continues to draw animals, skulls and tombstones on the back window. He blows on to the glass and starts over. 'I'm hungry,' he whines.

'Have some crisps.' Nick is finding it harder to control the van on the narrowing roads. He skids on a bend. Zeb is flung to the side of the van and he shouts out in pain.

'Can I drive?' Jake asks.

Nick slows down, pulls over and gets out. Jake and Zeb follow him with their eyes as he walks through the sleet to the passenger side of the van. Jake hesitates a moment then slides over to the driver's side. Nick gets in and slams the door shut.

'If you get us to Ullapool in one piece round the back roads I'll give you twenty quid.' Nick finishes the vodka, pushes a pillow against the window and rests his head.

'Wake me up when we get there. Watch the clutch . . . it's starting to stick.' He closes his eyes.

Zeb does his best to wind Jake up. 'Bet you can't get us to Ullapool round the back roads, shit for brains.'

'I can drive in this, no fucking problem.' Jake puts his foot down on the clutch then the accelerator. The wheel spins a little. The van starts to move. Zeb gets into the front seat, squeezing between Nick and Jake. He peers excitedly ahead. 'Don't crash skid, blood. That's when you slam the brakes on ice and go into a skid.'

'Shut up.' Jake keeps his eyes on the road ahead. Sleet falls harder. Jake drives slower, half elated, half terrified.

'What time are we gonna call Mum tomorrow?' Zeb pulls his duvet over his shoulders.

'In the morning.'

Zeb leans on the dash watching the road.

'Put some music on,' Jake demands.

Zeb leans over to the glove compartment, opens a CD and puts it on. The sound of Portishead's 'Glory Box' fills the inside of the van. Nick mumbles in protest. Zeb takes a pen from the glove compartment and starts drawing a moustache on Nick's face.

'Fuck sake, Zeb, let him sleep.'

Zeb ignores him and carries on drawing. Jake grabs hold of Zeb's arm trying to pull him back.

'Piss off!' Zeb hisses. Nick grumbles, licking his lips. Zeb wriggles out of Jake's grip. Jake takes his eyes off the road to get hold of Zeb to pull him back. He flicks his eyes from road to Zeb to road. He lets his foot ease on the gas. The van slows.

'If you don't leave it out,' Jake snaps, 'I'm gonna stop and give you a proper dig.'

Zeb completes the first curl on the handlebar moustache. Leaving the job half done, he slumps back in his seat, sulking. As Jake brings his eyes back to the road he sees a figure walking casually across about a hundred yards ahead. The shape is slightly hunched, steadying himself with a stick. Jake pushes his foot down on the brake.

'Crash skid, crash skid!' Zeb chants, unfazed.

Jake feels the van start to slide on the slush then the ice beneath. He pushes harder on the brake. The van begins to skid, moving slowly sideways. Jake tries to right the skid turning the wheel in the opposite direction. It makes it worse. He looks ahead through the sleet. The man crossing the road turns to look at the van as it approaches. Jake swears he sees him smile. The van slides some more. The man reaches the other side of the road and looks back to the unfolding scene.

'Dad! Dad!' Zeb shakes Nick awake. 'Jake's crash skidding the shitting car!' Nick lurches forward.

'Fuck's going on?' Nick watches the dry stone wall ahead appear and disappear as the van completes a slow motion hundred-and-eighty-degree turn. Jake finally brings it to a halt a few feet from the wall. He wipes the sweat from his top lip, turns off the engine and drops his head on to the steering wheel.

Zeb watches as the old man approaches the driver's side of the van. He takes his time, not bothered by the sleet. He taps on the glass with his stick. Jake raises his head and looks through the glass.

'He gonna bash us!' Zeb pitches in, scared.

Jake winds down the window. Deep, weathered lines cover the man's face. His long grey hair and short beard make him look like a wizard.

'Are you Gandalf?' Zeb asks seriously.

'Been called a few things in my time, never a wizard. I'll take that as a compliment.'

The old man looks at Jake who is clearly shaken by the incident. 'Everything all right? Look a bit young to be at the wheel.'

'I was teaching him to drive, no cars about, thought it'd be OK. Stupid of me,' Nick replies.

'Funny way to teach driving.' The old man smiles.

'I'm not with you?' Nick asks.

'With your eyes closed.'

'I was doing fine 'til we hit that ice,' Jake cuts in.

'You need to steer into that kind of spin, only thing for it.' The old man reaches out his hand. 'Good to meet you. I'm Alf.' He and Jake shake, then Nick, then Zeb.

'Need a lift? Bloody freezing out here,' Nick offers.

'No ta, I only live a mile or so down the road. Out for some night walking. Where you headed?'

'Ullapool,' Jake replies.

'Won't get there tonight, not on these roads. It's a good twenty miles from here. You're welcome to come and park up at my place. I'll make us some tea.'

'Sounds great,' Nick replies. 'Hop in and we'll drive you there.'

'Like I said, I'm on a walk. Drive up another half-mile and you'll see a left turn to my place. Signposted, Bywater. I'll cut across the field and see you there in a bit.' He turns off the road. The three of them watch him in silence as he heads down a small track and disappears behind a high, dry stone wall.

Nick orders them to shift over. They obey silently. Zeb jumps into the back, Jake gets out and walks round to the passenger side.

Nick starts the van up and brings her slowly round, trundling carefully forward.

They almost miss the sign to the farm. Nick reverses the van and turns in. The road quickly turns from half decent to dangerous. Zeb bounces up and down in the back, shouting. Jake holds on to the passenger door handle. Nick is forced to drive at less than two miles an hour. The track is scattered with deep holes full of water, ice and dirt. The van hits two in succession; something solid and unmoveable hits the underside. The engine lets out a screech followed by a loud banging.

'Fuck sake, Dad,' Jake shouts.

'Fucking piece of shit road.' Nick pulls over. 'We'll walk the rest. Come on.'

The three of them get out. Zeb wraps the duvet round his shoulders. Jake and Nick put on their jackets. The sleet turns to snowflakes. They stomp down the track, huddled together. Nick looks about him, across the wall to the whited-out fields beyond. He wishes they'd gone to Glasgow first. Zeb takes hold of Nick's hand.

Alf's cottage is small, an old farmhouse made up of stone and thatch. Zeb lets go of Nick's hand and runs up to the door knocking hard and fast. Jake and Nick stop behind him and wait. They wait a long time. Finally it opens. Alf stands there smiling. Zeb hesitates a moment then runs past him and heads for the fire.

'Kettle's on.' He stands aside and lets Nick and Jake in. The sitting room is sparse, with an old sofa, kitchen table and a few chairs. 'Have a seat. Hungry?'

'Starving,' Zeb replies.

'He's always hungry. If he's not pissing he's eating.' Jake sits himself down.

Nick looks around.

Alf walks over to the kitchen area, turns on the gas cooker, puts the kettle on then pulls out a large pot from under the table. Zeb walks over and lifts the lid.

'What is it?' he asks, sticking his finger in and tasting it.

'Vegetable stew, couple of days old.'

Zeb scrunches his face up. 'Got any chips?'

'Potatoes in the pot.' Alf closes the lid.

'Mind if I smoke?' Nick asks.

'Go ahead, ashtray's over there.'

Nick offers Alf one. He refuses. Jake accepts. Zeb walks back to the fire and squats in front of it.

'Nice place you've got . . . quiet.' Nick pulls his chair closer to the fire.

'Does the trick.' Alf takes out the plates and cutlery and lays them on the table. He makes the tea, puts milk and sugar out.

Nick feels awkward with the lack of conversation. 'You don't sound like you're from round here?'

'Suffolk. You're from London?'

Nick nods. 'Fulham.'

Alf stirs the pot. 'What brings you all the way up here?'

'Getting away from it all. Wanna live up here,' Nick

replies. 'Been wanting to come back since before Jake and Nick were born. Used to live in the Summer Isles with my ex . . . their mum.'

Zeb interrupts. 'We're gonna get a goat.'

'Had one myself, 'til a few days ago.' Alf stirs the stew. 'Had to stick her in the pot.'

Zeb looks at him in disbelief. 'You said it was vegetable stew!'

'Wouldn't eat her if I was starving. Just teasing. She's in the barn. She's gonna have some kids in a few weeks.'

Zeb looks at Nick wide-eyed.

'Weather's breaking tomorrow.' Alf serves up the stew. 'I'm heading up for a walk to Fisherfield Forest in the morning. Come along, if you're not in a hurry to get to Ullapool . . . place is a bit of a dive, not a lot going on, except the boats.'

Jake replies. 'We're not in a hurry.'

Nick nods. 'Sure. Could do with a stretch.'

Alf hands them their food.

They sit in silence, staring at the fire, letting the bowls warm their hands while they eat.

Nineteen

The road leading to the forest is more winding than anything they've been on so far.

Zeb leans out of the window catching snowflakes on his tongue.

Jake sits next to Alf listening to him carefully, nodding occasionally in silent agreement.

Nick concentrates hard on the road.

Alf looks up. 'Road gets nasty up here.'

Nick doesn't hide his surprise. 'Gets . . . Jesus. Didn't think it could get any worse.'

'Gets a lot worse than this . . . that's when we walk.' Alf brings his attention back to Jake. Nick brings his to the road.

Alf talks in a low whisper to Jake. Nick tries to hear what he's saying then gives up. He puts some music on. Jake turns it down a little, nodding as he listens to Alf's unfolding words.

'Road's turning to shit,' Nick informs Alf.

'Pull over there by the rocks.'

Nick follows Alf's order.

Zeb jumps out.

'Oi,' Nick calls after him. 'Coat.'

'Don't want it. Not that cold.' Alf reaches into the back, gets his coat and chucks it to Zeb.

'I'm not nursing another cold,' Nick insists.

They get out and head up the track leading to the edge of the forest. As they come over the hill, Jake stops and takes a look. He puts his hand in his pockets, scanning the area.

Zeb pokes him in the back. 'What you doing, shit head?'

'Looking.'

'Seen an animal? Is it a massive bear?!'

'Looking at the line of trees over there . . . and the light.'

Zeb looks along Jake's line of sight. 'You're shitting weird. Looks like a wood to me, with no shitting bears.'

Alf walks past and puts his hand on Jake's shoulder, points index and middle fingers towards his eyes then points them at the wood then walks on ahead.

'What's that all about?' Zeb asks, fascinated.

'Telling me to keep looking.'

'At what?' Zeb asks, confused.

'The trees, you plonker.'

Zeb looks ahead trying to find something of interest in the trees, gives up and runs ahead, picking up a stick, whacking each tree as he passes, shouting, 'Sucker, sucker sucker.'

Alf walks up alongside Nick.

'Good lads. Bright, funny.'

'Not sure if that's down to their mum or me.'

'Been apart long?' Alf steers them in the direction of a

small path. As they enter the wood the wind picks up.

Nick turns up the collar of his jacket. 'Last year. Just after Christmas. Drove me to drink.'

'And you're up here making it good with your boys?' Nick nods. They walk on a few yards further. A series of small lochs come into view. Alf continues, 'Funny time of year for bonding.'

'Been meaning to come back up here for years.'

'Were they up for it?'

'Zeb was. He's up for most things . . . as you've probably figured. Jake's taken some turning.'

'I think he turned a while ago.'

'Not sure about that.'

The path narrows and Alf steps forward, leading the way. 'It's his job to give you a hard time.'

'Could do with a break from it. Sometimes it's all I can do not to slap him.'

'Looks like it'd be a fairly even match.'

Nick is surprised by the comment. He'd known for a long time that his confidence in being able to slap Jake down when he stepped out of line had been wavering. Hearing it out loud from a stranger nailed it. His alpha dog status was slipping and he felt Jake knew it. Part of him is relieved. Part of him is proud of his eldest boy's growing strength. Blue sky breaks through the gaps between the pine trees. After another half-mile they head into an old oak forest. Wet, moss-covered boulders make it tough going. Zeb jumps up with ease and hops from rock to rock. Jake follows, more slowly but with just as much ease. Nick continues to follow Alf as he leads the way between the boulders keeping them at ground level.

'Bet this place looks amazing in the summer.' Nick looks up through the trees, sunlight forcing him to squint.

Alf continues to lead the way. 'All year round it's got some kind of magic. I come up here a lot.'

They head out of the oak wood across a field, back into the dank, cold, dark of another pine forest. Zeb and Jake run ahead, quickly disappearing out of sight. Nick feels he should call after them but doesn't. He wants to continue enjoying the silence and peace.

Twenty minutes into the forest, Alf and Nick reach a clearing. Jake and Zeb are still out of sight but they can be heard running through the trees shooting each other with sound effects. As they reach the clearing, Nick sees a well-maintained log cabin. Alf walks straight for it.

'That's a cool little gaff. Could live there.'

Alf turns back and smiles at him. 'This is the *kuti*.'

'Yours?'

Alf nods. 'Meditation space. Somewhere to come and recharge, hang out. Get some peace and quiet.'

'You don't get enough of that already?' Nick smiles at him.

'I get a lot of visitors, especially at this time of year.'

They reach the front door. Alf takes a key from the ledge above it and opens it up.

As Nick walks in he smells fresh pine resin and is reminded of his dad. Alf walks over to a burner and starts to build a fire. Nick looks around: bed in the corner, a chair, table, a small kitchen area and a pile of logs. Alf walks back out of the hut and comes in a few minutes later with a barrel of water.

'No objection to rainwater?' he asks Nick.

'None at all.'

Alf puts the kettle on the hob, loads the wood burner up and lights it.

Nick sits on the bed. 'How long do you stay out here then, on your own?'

'Anything up to a month. Depends what's happening back home.'

'That's a long time. You ever freak out?'

'Depends how you mean?' Alf pulls the chair over and sits himself down, looking straight at Nick.

Nick continues, 'Must get lonely, nothing to do, no one to talk to.'

'Sure.' Alf smiles at him, keeping his gaze fixed.

'I could do with some of that.'

'Stay a while.'

'Love to but I've got the kids, need to get moving.'

'I'm good with kids. Had three myself. They can stay with me.'

'Nice offer, cheers, but we have to get going tonight.'

'I've got a smaller cottage half a mile down the road from my place, you can rent it for a while. Give yourself a chance to catch up; rest. They could stay there. Got everything, electric, gas.'

Nick looks at him sidelong, trying to figure out if he's serious. 'You're not fucking around are you?'

'You look like a man in need. Sounds like it would do you good to get some space . . . from Jake at least.'

'Zeb doesn't like being away from me. He gets nightmares. It wouldn't work. Much as I'd like it to, believe me. Nice offer.'

'Zeb'll be fine. It's you you need to worry about. If you're no good to yourself you'll be no good to them. You'll end up making small mistakes that'll lead to bigger ones. Done it myself.'

Nick wants to believe this man can't be trusted; he's after his kids. He pictures knives cutting into Zeb and Jake's flesh. Something ridiculous to convince him not to take up the obviously clean offer. He looks around the cabin again. He feels at ease. He brings his eyes back to Alf. 'This isn't part of the plan.'

'Like Lennon said . . . life's what happens when we're busy making them.' Alf gets up and makes the tea.

He hands Nick the cup. 'I'm not interested in what you're really doing up here but if you need some rest, stay here. Come back any time you like.'

Alf stands and heads for the door.

'Where you going?' Nick asks, suddenly feeling like a child.

'See what Jake and Zeb are up to. Make sure they're not setting fire to anything.' Alf turns to Nick as he reaches the door. 'Sit a while. When you feel like getting up and leaving, stay a bit longer. This room has seen plenty, it can handle whatever you've got going on, believe me.' Alf walks out and closes the door.

Nick hears the key in the lock turn and slide back out. He stands up abruptly and strides over to the door.

'EY! What the fuck's going on?' Nick waits for a reply. He puts his ear to the door.

Alf's voice is muffled. 'I'll be back in a bit. Rest up.'

'If you touch my fucking kids I'll hang you from this fucking cabin!' He realises he sounds absurd and feels embarrassed. He knows his boys are safe; knows Alf is safe.

'This a good place, Nick. Give yourself a little time.'

'Open the fucking door!'

Nick stands, waiting for the key to go back in the lock. Nothing.

He turns and leans back against the door looking around at the inside of the cabin: steam rising from the kettle and his half-drunk cup of tea; the building flames in the wood burner; the bed. His first response is to smash the place up, burn it down.

But he doesn't.

He slides down the door, crosses his arms and lets his head drop.

Zeb sits in the crown of a pine tree looking down, listening to Jake count up to a hundred. It took him forty-five seconds to scale the tree. He keeps his lips pursed and tries to stay silent. He looks across the tops of the trees at the lochs. He can just make out the sea. The tree moves with the wind. He holds on, moves with the sway, riding it like a boat.

Jake completes the count. 'Ninety-seven, ninety-eight, ninety-nine . . . a hundred. Coming, you little fucker . . . ready or not.'

Zeb looks down at Jake as he scans the ground. He puts his hand over his mouth to hold back his snickering. To his surprise Jake starts climbing a tree twenty yards away. Zeb watches him, not moving a muscle.

Jake gets to the crown of his tree and starts looking around. It doesn't take long to spot Zeb.

Jake shouts across, 'Got ya! Man that was easy.'

'You have to come get me and tag me,' Zeb taunts him.

'Bollocks to that. A visual on a bogie's good for me.' Jake looks around again. 'Wicked view.'

Zeb shrugs his shoulders. 'S'all right.'

'Don't give me that. This is the business.' Jake makes himself comfortable in the V of a branch and leans back looking across at the loch.

'What did Alf say to you in the van?' Zeb shouts across. 'He was being weird and talking quiet. Is he a poof?'

Jake laughs and shakes his head. 'Told me about the spirits of this place.'

'What the shit's that? Like ghosts and stuff?'

'Said this place was alive, everything, trees, ground, air, water. If you look long enough you'll see it.'

'Wot?'

'The spirits.'

'You're talking shitting bollocks. You're just trying to freak me out.'

'And you're talking like Dad.' Jake pauses a moment, eyes fixed on the lochs beyond the wood. 'You've been thinking about that cow and her baby, ain't you?'

Pause.

'Maybe.'

'Dreaming about it?'

Zeb nods.

'So have I. Alf said that's their spirits, staying with us. See them in our dreams they're real.'

'Wasn't a dream, it was a shitting nightmare.'

'I was scared too, bro. Not any more though.' Jake stops abruptly. 'Shh.'

'Wot?' Zeb whispers.

'Listen.'

They hear the cracking of twigs in the distance. The footsteps get closer, then the crunching of shoes on dead pine needles.

Jake and Zeb look down and see Alf.

'Where's Dad?' Zeb whispers across to Jake. Jake brings his index finger to his lips. Alf walks to the base of a nearby tree and sits down. He rolls himself a cigarette, lights it and rest his head back against the bark of the tree.

Alf calls without looking up, 'Good view up there, ain't it?' Jake and Zeb look at each other wide-eyed with surprise. Zeb bursts into a long rasp of uncontained laughter. Alf continues smoking.

After a few minutes Jake starts to scale down the tree, hanging from the lowest branch then dropping quietly to the ground.

He walks over to Alf. 'How'd you know where we were?'

'Heard you.' Alf passes him the roll-up.

Jake shakes his head. 'No thanks.'

'Zeb coming down?'

'Eventually. He's into his trees. Where's Dad?'

'Back at the *kuti*.'

Jake sits down next to him. 'What's that?'

'Log cabin, about a quarter of a mile back.' Alf points to his left. 'That way.'

'What's he doing?'

'Meditating.'

Jake snorts a laugh. 'Dad don't meditate; way too stressed.'

'Well he's giving it a go.' Alf takes a draw on his roll-up then looks up into the tree at Zeb looking across the forest, towards the lochs.

'Your dad seems to be running...on empty,' Alf continues.

'He's always running.' Jake picks up a stick and starts carving a groove through the dead needles into the earth below marking out a big, dark 'J'.

'You're here to look after Zeb then?'

'Mostly.' Jake keeps his attention on the unfolding letters of his name in the ground.

'You're doing a good job.'

'Cheers. Half the time I wanna hug 'im, half the time I wanna kill 'im.'

Alf nods and smiles to himself. 'Your dad's probably gonna stay up here for a few days.'

Jake looks up at him. 'How do you mean?'

'I said he could stay in the *kuti* if he likes and you two can hang out at mine, in your van or at a cottage I've got not far from my place, it's got a telly.'

'He said that was cool?'

'Yep. He needs some rest, get his head together.'

'Sounds good to me.' Jake looks back down and draws the final line of his 'E'. He looks back up the tree at Zeb. 'Hey, bro!'

Zeb looks down. 'Wot?'

'Dad's gonna stay in the woods for a few days do some hippie shit. We can hang at Alf's.'

'Where is he?' Zeb sounds unconvinced.

'In Alf's hut back in the wood.'

'He say we could?'

'Yeah.'

'I wanna see 'im.' Zeb starts to climb down the tree.

Alf stands up. 'No problem. Let's go.'

Zeb lands on the ground with a soft thud and the three of them head back the way they came.

Nick sits on the bed looking at the door. He gets up and paces across the worn cabin floor. He notices a dip in the boards smoothed by pacing. He sits back down gets back up and walks over to an old mirror next to the wood-burning stove. He looks at himself properly for the first time in days. His beard has turned from stubble to a face full of whiskers. His nose is all but healed, a soft scab of blood good enough to pick. He rubs his chin and stares into his eyes. Thin red veins streak across the greying whites. His pupils are dilated. He knows he's exhausted. His legs feel weak from driving. The walk to the cabin has left his knees feeling wobbly. He tenses his thighs, relaxes them again then walks back over to the bed. He stares at the door again, silently cursing Alf, Vincent, the dog, Warren, Emily, himself. His regret for travelling so far north with such a bad plan grows by the minute. He lies down on the bed and looks up at the wooden ceiling, criss-crossed by old and new spider webs. He looks for their makers but finds none.

The bed smells damp but is comfortable. He turns on his side, supports his head with his hands and closes his eyes. Images run through his mind. The puking dying dog; the burial. Gandalf. Zeb. The river. Jake. Warren. Lisa. The boy in the bookshop. Vincent's battered messenger. Candy. The fire. Lisa. Candy's gift. He puts his hand in his pocket and pulls out her parting present. He sits up and looks at it. The prospect of something to do inside the heavy boredom excites him. He slowly unwraps it. He notices writing on the inside. He holds the paper in the flat of his hand and looks at the gift inside: a small piece of charcoal, pencil thin. The inside of the paper is blackened and smudged, the writing underneath obscured. He looks at the charcoal, bemused. He lays it gently down on the bed next to him. He slowly smooths out the paper on his knee and reads the words.

March 2010

Hey handsome. Lisa and I will be in LA by now in the heat and sun and you'll probably be in Scotland in the snow with the boys. You're quite a man Nick Geneva. I thought all the English guys were gonna be uptight or just plain stoners – you're neither! You guys made our trip – for real. You're probably wondering what the charcoal's for. It's from the fire, the one we had on our last night. I whittled it down a little while you were asleep. It's for writing. My pa used to do it when Lisa and I were kids. We'd sit round the fire the whole night telling stories and when we left in the morning we'd all take some charcoal home to whittle and write down the things we all wished for with it. We called them black wish sticks. So here's yours, gorjus.

Write down some stuff for you and the boys, stuff you want, then chuck it into a river and wait!

Don't be pissed off but will you do something for me? If the boys want to go back to their mom, let them. They're great kids but their life with you isn't always so easy, no

matter how much fun Zeb thinks he's having. Don't mess
them up like you were. Don't take this the wrong way.
I'm worried about Jake, the boy's going through a lot of
changes!

So write some stuff down and make the magic happen,
babe.

You've got my number. Give us a call sometime . . . and
if you're in the U S of A, drop by!

Big squeeze for you.

C

XX

PS Give yourself a break for a while and keep it in
your pants!

Nick stares at the crumpled paper for a long time. After
a few minutes the words start to blur. He relaxes his
focus. A tear hits the blue ink and runs. He stands up and
walks over to the mirror and looks at himself. His eyes
are redder. He keeps looking at himself waiting for
something to happen, for more tears, for his face to change.
The sadness hits him in waves, rising up from his guts into
his throat.

He hears muffled voices outside the cabin door,
wipes his face and waits for the key to click into the lock.
The voices outside the cabin door. The door opens. No
key.

Alf walks in first, followed by Zeb who runs in and
jumps on the bed. Nick is speechless.

'Hey, Dad. Been hanging out medivating, 'av ya?' Zeb
picks up the letter and the charcoal, examining them both,
chimp-like.

255

Jake walks in last. 'Not medivating, you plonker, meditating.' He looks around the inside of the cabin and nods approvingly.

Nick looks at Alf, clearly pissed off, happy to disguise his sadness. 'What the fuck's going on?' Zeb and Jake stop what they're doing and look at Nick.

'I'm not with you, Nick. How was your sit?' Alf asks.

'Fuck the sit. You locked the door.'

Alf shrugs and looks at him bemused. 'Now why would I do a stupid thing like that?'

'I heard you lock the door.'

'Place can fuck around with you after a while but you've taken no time at all to get into it. I'm not an arsehole, Nick, I wouldn't lock you in . . . what would be the point in that?'

Nick looks at Zeb and Jake, blank-faced. He starts to question the memory of what he heard as Alf left. Alf seems one hundred per cent straight. The door wasn't locked. Nick's head keeps looking for a reason to deck him, tell him to fuck off and move on to Ullapool but he never manages to find anything in his instincts that backs up his paranoia and suspicion.

'You losing it, Dad?' Jake asks, a poorly concealed smile on his face.

Nick sits down on the bed next to Zeb.

'What's this?' Zeb holds up the charcoal.

'A black wish stick.' Nick rubs his forehead trying to ease the confusion.

'Black witch stick. Wass that? Is it evil like voodoo? Can you put spells on people with it and make them explode?' Zeb looks at it like it's an alien.

Nick corrects him. 'Wish stick. From the fire Candy, Lisa and I were sitting round the night before they left. She says we can write wishes down with it.'

Zeb reads her note. 'On this, can I write something on this? I got loads of wishes, bike, airgun, bow and arrow, goat, wizard.' Zeb turns the paper over and starts reading the blackened, tear-smudged ink. Nick looks over to Jake then to Alf.

'Yukspastic! That is rank!' Zeb holds the note at arm's length. 'It's a nasty shitting love letter!!' He hands the letter to Nick, jumps off the bed and runs outside, charcoal in hand.

'So . . . wanna stay?' Alf asks Nick.

'Not sure what I want to do.'

'Sounds like you're staying.' Nick stands up and walks over to Jake, puts his hands on his shoulders.

'You up for hanging out with Alf for a few days?'

'Sure.' Nick pulls Jake into him and puts his arm round him.

'Hey, Zeb!' Nick calls out.

'What?' Zeb doesn't come back in.

'You OK with hanging out with Jake and Alf for a few days?'

Zeb remains outside. 'What for?'

'Think I'm gonna stay up here for a bit, get some peace and quiet . . . and some rest.'

Zeb mumbles from outside, only the last word is audible to Nick. 'S'pose.'

Nick walks out but can't see him. 'Where are you, kid?'

'Here.'

Nick follows Zeb's voice round to the back of the cabin.

He sees Zeb writing something on the back of the hut with the charcoal.

He stands alongside Zeb looking at the scrawled big black letters:

PISS OFF BEARS

'What's that about?' Nick asks.

'It's a wish spell to stop you getting eaten.'

'No bears out here, kid, not even wolves.'

'Wolves!' Zeb takes out his knife from his pocket. 'Come anywhere near us I'll cut their bloody earses off.' Zeb stabs and slashes into the air. Nick decides not to comment on the knife. He leans down close to him. 'You sure you're OK with me hanging out here for a bit?'

'Yeah. Alf says he's gonna show us how to drive his tractor and said I can look after his goat and their kids. I'm a kid.'

Nick stands up again, admiring Zeb's writing, warmed by the sentiment. He smiles to himself. 'I could do with a break.'

'Are you cream-crackered?'

'Something like that, knackered, yeah. If you get scared, talk to Jake. If you get really scared, come get me. I'm only about an hour's walk from Alf's place.'

'If I get really scared I'll run here and be here in ten minutes, super swift.'

'Come on, toe-rag, it's getting dark.'

They head back round. Alf is showing Jake how to throw his knife.

Zeb stops in his tracks. 'I wanna learn that!'

Alf looks back at Nick. 'You ready then? Plenty of

canned stuff in the cupboard. If you're feeling brave there's a gun in the back, you can shoot yourself dinner.'

'Give me the key so I can lock myself in,' Nick asks.

'Sure.' Alf hands Nick the key.

Nick gives Zeb a hug and a kiss, walks over to Jake and hugs him again. 'Don't drive the man mad. I'll be back by Wednesday.' He hands Jake the mobile. 'Just don't tell her where we are.' Jake nods.

Alf, Zeb and Jake head back up the track. Nick stands, watching them. Zeb turns three times to wave and give him the double thumbs up. Jake turns once and waves at him. Alf continues walking ahead without looking back.

Twenty

Warren walks into the brightly lit courtroom, half asleep, unshaven, his greasy six a.m. breakfast refusing to settle in his stomach. His damaged eye still aches, still leaks. The court clerk gives him a look that makes him want to punch her. He resists. Most of the people in court are sitting at desks heads down buried deep in paperwork. Those standing are either police or prison guards. Piles of paperwork line the desks, some as high as the heads of the clerks behind them. Warren knows he is more a piece of paper than a human being to these people. He's led to the empty dock. He sits down behind the scratched Perspex partition. The bench is hard on his arse. He looks around, enjoying the sight of the two women, dressed smart, both ignoring him. The magistrate sits comfortably in his chair, reading through what Warren knows are his notes. He looks for the slightest reaction. Signs that will give him a clue to which way the man will ask him to turn when he leaves the dock. Right, out into the street, or left, back down to the cells and a day's wait to be shipped back to prison. If he's lucky he'll get a new one, out of London. He touches his wound, feeling the soft sting of pain, liking its familiarity, reassuring himself it's not rotting. He smells the tip of his finger and wipes it on his trousers.

The magistrate looks up. 'Mr Sykes?' The prison guard gets up, directing Warren to do the same. He rises.

The magistrate calls out his full name, his address and asks for his plea.

'Guilty.' Warren looks down to the ground. Wishing the whole process over. He now needs a shit. His brief gets up and begins the procedure and the bullshit of putting in for bail. Warren isn't confident. This process takes eight minutes. The magistrate follows Warren's brief's reasoning, nodding, from time to time, looking back down at his notes.

The brief finishes. Warren is asked to sit down.

Two minutes later he's asked to stand again.

'Mr Sykes, this isn't the first time you've been before me or indeed many of my colleagues. I would for that reason alone be inclined to refuse your application for bail. But it seems the main assailant for this crime is currently running free and with your guilty plea I'm inclined to believe your intention to come back to this court, or the Crown Court, and follow through with your due punishment. So I'm granting you bail.'

Warren feels his knees buckle slightly with gratitude. He smiles at the magistrate.

'Thank you. I appreciate it.'

'Indeed.' The gavel cracks down on the circle of wood.

Warren is led out of the dock, to the right.

Nick lies in bed looking up at the ceiling of the hut. Alone with his thoughts he misses his dad properly for the first time in years. It surprises him. He's eaten too many tinned beans and feels rough for it. Three cups of coffee, two cigarettes, no spliff, no booze. His legs twitch with irritation through lack of exercise and alcohol. Too much sleep. He looks at his watch. Alf and the kids left just over fourteen hours ago. He slept like shit. Nightmares hammering away at him until the dawn came crawling in through the small window and the cracks and slits in the cabin walls. Same place the wind pours through which never stops. It only speeds up and slows down depending on how close to sleep he is, like it's fucking with him. His neck aches from the draught coming in from more directions than he can count; he tried to, better than sheep he thought, just as useless. It was cold, even with four blankets. He reckons it would be a good idea to head back a day early, he gets the point of being here. He feels rested. He's had enough, he's clearer about everything now.

He'd go out for a walk but something is stopping him. A voice tells him he's scared. He tells the voice to fuck off. He reads Candy's note again, gets halfway through, stopping before he gets to the bit about Jake and Zeb. He puts it back in his pocket, sits up and looks around the hut. The familiarity of the place is already beginning to wind him up. He looks over to the door, then at the key he's been holding tight all night. He walks slowly over to the door, puts the key in the lock. It turns half a cycle then stops. He twists it back then forward again. Same thing. He begins to panic; tells himself to calm down then starts kicking the door. He quickly knackers himself.

'Easy now. If it's bust we kick it in, no problem. Try it again.'

He turns the key back then anticlockwise again. It sticks again. He looks around the cabin, goes to the cupboard and takes out a thin tin of sardines. He pulls the lid back and off, flattens it out with his foot and takes it to the door. He inserts the aluminium strip and slides it up and down and gently back and forth.

The lock clicks. The door opens.

He steps out and breathes the air in. It feels cold in his lungs. Cold enough to snow again. He looks up. The sky is the right kind of grey. A sliver of fear moves through him as he imagines himself being snowed in, unable to get back to the kids, unable to get food. He imagines his stick-thin body crawling across the floor for the door, dying at the threshold. He laughs at himself. He wonders if he's kidding himself into thinking Jake would come before he copped it.

He looks around, taking in his surroundings. The cabin is encircled by trees on all sides. Mainly pine trees, big, high, thick trunks. Round the sides and back of the cabin he sees what looks like newly planted oaks and chestnuts, some protected by brown plastic cylinders; some of which have been split by outgrown trees. There is one large oak to the left of the cabin.

'You're a beauty.' He walks over to it and stands underneath it. He looks up into the bare branches. It's been a long time since he's climbed any trees. He checks out the low-lying branches, working out if he could make it. The lowest branch is out of reach. He goes back to the cabin and gets a chair.

He pushes it down in the hard ground to steady it, steps up on it, grabs the nearest branch and hauls himself up.

His arms are weak. He fails the first time, and the second. On the third go he manages to hook his foot up on the massive branch and haul himself up. He smiles to himself with pride.

'Not bad for an old cunt.' He looks up at the next group of branches and begins to work out the best, safest route. He reaches up to the next branch, recalling the best techniques bit by bit.

After ten minutes cautious climbing he looks down. His legs shake when he sees how high he's climbed. He looks up. Snowflakes begin to fall towards him. He lets one land on his tongue then continues climbing, feeling good, carefully reaching up with arms and legs like a monkey . . . he remembers. Within another two minutes he's up in the crown of the tree, breathing heavy, feeling amazing. He imagines what it must be like up there in the summer, hidden by a mass of leaves looking out, unseen by anyone below. He looks east towards Alf's place. He makes out the small area where he thinks they walked from; confirmed by a thin wisp of grey smoke.

He misses the kids. And he doesn't.

The wind is stronger at the top. He looks down at the wood and lake and at the ocean beyond. He has never seen anywhere as beautiful, not since he was in Scotland with Emily. He misses that time and her. He shuts it out of his memory. He wishes he had someone to share this with. Candy comes to mind. He convinces himself she was just a quick fuck, but she left something more with him. Not just the gift. Her face has stayed with him.

He reaches into his pocket and pulls out the charcoal,

now broken into three pieces. He puts two of them back in his pocket then looks around for a surface flat enough to write on. He has no idea what he's going to write. The top of the tree spreads out into four main branches, two of which look lightning-struck, the main branches long gone. The silver-grey surface looks good enough.

He edges across to the largest flattened surface and wraps his left arm round its stump. He holds the tip of the charcoal in his right hand and looks across the lochs, waiting for inspiration. Nothing.

The snow begins to fall harder. He looks down at the cabin and sees that it's begun to settle on the roof. He looks down at his hands, pale blue and trembling. He curses himself for forgetting his gloves and hat.

'Make a wish. Bollocks. The fuck am I supposed to wish for? House in the country and enough money so I don't have to worry any more?' He shakes his head, thinking.

'Bout sums you up don't it, mate. Money and property. Fuck all about the boys.

He looks around him. 'Turned out pretty fucking grim, ey Dad?'

He flashes back to Snowdon, the walk, his father falling, the silence, a lack of anything worth remembering. He'd promised himself the day he held Jake in his arms at the hospital that he wouldn't turn out to be the arsehole his dad had been. He'd be gentler, kinder, show them a good way to be. But he'd turned out pretty much the same, if anything, worse. At least his dad made an honest living. He wonders if he made the same promise the day he had held baby Nick in his arms. He holds the charcoal in his shaking hands. The snow falls faster. The bark of the tree darkens under the melting ice. It occurs to him it's going to be harder to get down, more dangerous.

The kids? He felt the same, thought the same when he held Jake in his arms, looked at Emily with tears in his eyes and thought *this is it, I've fucking done it, bust the cycle and turned into a top bloke.* Emily's decision to leave him had been set in motion long before Jake was born. She'd made her mind up in Scotland, a million miles from anywhere. He was so wrapped in self-obsession and insecurities he had no idea what was going on with her. He didn't think fucking off to the pub every night had had that much of an effect, it's what all blokes did. He did anything not to be at the croft with her, facing up to the trickier, far less romantic side of their relationship. Emily put up with a lot of shit, a lot of insecurity, for too many years. He knew that.

Make a wish?

Snow settles on the thin strip of charcoal. He scratches the black wish stick into the dark grey wood.

The words come with little or no thought.

Get us home in one piece.

The words surprise him.

Home?

London was the last place he wanted to be. He would've expected a wish along the lines of *make our life in Scotland a good one.*

He reads them back out loud.

'Get us home in one piece.'

The six uneven words glare back at him like a prayer.

He looks at them for a long time. The snow continues to fall and settle on him and the creaking, leafless tree.

* * *

Vincent drives along the M9 towards Falkirk. Ten a.m. light breaks through the gunmetal sky. It does little to illuminate the land and water of the lochs beneath. David Bowie trills out of the car stereo. The soundtrack over the passing images of the bleak Scottish landscape relaxes him, eases the tension in his lungs. He lets his arms relax, his hands hold the steering wheel a little less tight.

The further he gets from home the better he feels, the more he's able to breathe; the less he thinks about his wife, his dog and his own death. He is less and less interested in the money taken; more focused on doing something to mark the animal's untimely demise and, ultimately, his own fast-approaching end. A funeral of sorts. It would no doubt be marked with a final flicker of drama and violence. Something tangible to express some of the grieving that armchair remorse cannot reach. But he's capable of being reasonable. If Nick apologises, genuine and sincere, knees to floor, forehead to ground, closure will be good, fair and long-lasting. If Geneva refuses to supplicate, the memory of the damage he will do to him will act as memorial to his dead dog. Which would also be fair and long-lasting. It's a win–win situation. Either way he would want Nick to fully understand how much love he had for Jasper. Get a glimpse of his pain. He'd want Nick to experience this through the body, by blade, or hammer. He'd take his time. He wants Nick to be the full stop on a lifetime of reckless, misdirected rage. The ritual would make sense, have meaning and, if necessary, end once and for all in gratifying blood and bone.

* * *

As he comes out of a long bend he sees a woman at the side of the road, long hair, boots, skirt, sheepskin, thumb out. He's passed three hitchhikers in the last mile, two men and now a woman. He could do with a conversation, as long as she isn't going too far. Ten miles' worth of chat, no more. He flashes his lights and slows down. She picks up her bag and guitar. He can make out a smile as he pulls into a lay-by.

He rolls the passenger window down. 'Where you headed?'

She moves her hair from her face. 'Bannockburn?'

'You're in luck, jump in.'

She hesitates a moment, checking Vincent for safety. 'Thanks pal, you're a gem.'

She opens the back passenger door, loads her bag and guitar in and gets in the front.

Vincent likes how she fills the space. He's aware of the smell of his sweat. He winds the window down an inch and turns the stereo down.

'I love this one.' She leans back in her seat.

He pulls out. 'Local?'

'Just outside Glasgow. Going to see ma feller . . . weekend in the country.'

Vincent gets that the boyfriend statement is aimed at making her safe. Letting him know she's not on the market. Not a hooker.

'Where yous from?' she asks.

'London.'

'Long way from home then.'

'Furthest I've been in a long time.'

'Where you headed?'

'North-west. Far as I can get.'

'Mind if we have the heating up a bit?' she asks.

'Sorry, Hang on.' The stale air cleared, he winds the window up.

'So what's happening up west?' She looks out across the passing countryside.

'Views and clean air.' Vincent doesn't like all the questions.

'Come on . . . yous up here for more than that. You can get clean air much further down south, and nice views.' She smiles at him cheekily.

'I'm splitting up with my wife. I need some time to think and I need to be a long way from home. Here's where it's at.'

She looks at him for what feels like an overly laboured moment. 'Sorry to hear that.'

'Don't be. She's a fucking nightmare.'

'I was married once, when I was nineteen. Lasted about a month.'

'You a musician . . . the guitar?' He comes out of a long winding road and reaches a straight. He puts his foot down a little on the accelerator.

'Sort of.' He notices her scratch her nose. The best indication of a liar. It could also be nerves. Maybe she's embarrassed about her talent. 'Ma playing's all right . . . it's ma voice needs work.'

'You don't even want to hear mine.' He pushes the cigarette lighter in and pulls out his cigarettes from his top pocket. 'Want one?'

'No ta.' As he reaches down for the lighter he notices her legs.

Good legs. Wrong time of year for a skirt so short.

He rests his elbow on the inside of the door, driving with one hand; relaxed.

Warren looks up at Nick's place. He thinks on what to do. He puts his hand into his pocket and takes out a set of keys. He fingers through them counting as he goes, coming to the familiar Chubb and two Yales. Someone comes out of the house next-door. He drops to his knee and starts to tie his shoelace, not looking up.

He waits for the footsteps to fade then lets himself in. He smells rotting milk as he steps into the hall. He walks into the familiar living room. The curtains are drawn. It's in almost as bad a state as his place. Unusual for Nick. A hint of patchouli in the air forces Nick's face into his mind and along with it comes a rush of anger. Nick had finished their working relationship, their friendship, the moment he decided to leave London. Taking the kids was a mistake. Warren convinces himself he would never have done the same to him. Nick had always pushed everything too far. He looks round the room, opening drawers, cupboards, walking into the kitchen to continue his methodical search. The last room is the bathroom. He goes straight for the cistern, pulls off the lid and feels around underneath the ballcock. His fingers touch soft plastic. He pulls out the bag and tears it open, water dripping on his trousers and shoes. Inside the bag is a thick wad of twenties, under these, a large cellophane wrap of coke. He puts both in his pocket and heads for the door. His hand reaches the latch. He stops. He looks at the door for a moment. He knows Nick won't be back, not for a long time. He needs payback beyond cash and coke. Some-thing to mark the end of the friendship. He turns back and walks into the sitting room. He heads for the drinks cabinet, takes out an unopened bottle of brandy and pops the cap. He take a long swig, then another and looks around the room feeling the burn of the alcohol spread through his chest and into his belly. He walks over to the desk; the one that he knows belonged to Nick's dad, and pours the brandy over it, the carpet and the curtains. He takes out his lighter and ignites the brandy on the curtain. He stands watching the flame trail across the carpet, on to the desk. A heap of papers catches alight. The house begins to smoke and burn.

Content, he walks slowly out, locking the door behind him.

Jake sits upright in the open-topped tractor, concentrating hard, tongue poking out the corner of his mouth looking straight ahead. Alf sits next to him, Zeb stands up in the trailer holding a length of wood to his shoulder, pointing it left and right, looking for something his imagination can shoot. All three are dressed for heavy weather, coats, boots, gloves, jackets done up to chins. The snow falls steady, settling and compacting under the tractor wheels.

'Where the bastard Orcs then?' Zeb shouts out to Alf.

'Only at night, they hate the daylight . . . but then you know that.'

'Bastard Uruk Hai like daylight. Better watch me cos I'll blow their shitting heads off if they come out of them woods.'

Alf laughs to himself, keeping his eyes ahead, helping

Jake steer through the deep, frozen tracts of mud, snow and fallen trees.

'Where we going?' Jake asks.

'Through this wood then wherever you want, you're the driver.'

Jake steers them along a wide track into the pine wood. The light dips quickly. He finds it harder to see and steer round the smaller fallen trees. The tractor hits a large unseen hole. Alf and Jake leave their seats, springing two feet into the air. Zeb is thrown from one end of the trailer to the other.

'Fucking 'ell whassamatter with you, blood!' Zeb shouts at Jake.

Alf turns round to check. 'You OK?'

'No worries, lost me bloody gun though.' He takes out his knife and slashes it about. 'Have to cut 'em up good style now!'

Alf turns back to watch the track. 'Here.' He leans over and flicks the tractor lights on. The track ahead is illuminated by the wide beam of dull, yellow light.

'Didn't know this old heap of junk had headlights that worked. Cool.' Jake slips the syncromesh gears into second, leans forward, gripping the wheel enthusiastically.

Nick puts the charcoal back into his shirt pocket and taps it gently, promising not to let it break. He looks down and remembers something he'd forgotten a long time ago: it's a lot harder climbing down than up. He checks his route then lowers his foot to the nearest branch and twists the sole of his shoe on it to make sure it's safe. He lowers himself down, taking one last look at the view across to the sea. He lowers himself on to the successive wet branches a lot slower than his ascent. The snow disappears quickly under his shoes. He slides a little and slows down the descent. The snow glides past him in thick flakes. He notices further down the tree that it has settled on the bigger branches.

'Not gonna fall, mate. Nice and slow. You remember this. Like riding a bike.' The last time he rode a bike was a lot longer ago than the last time he climbed a tree. He does his best to block out the rising curses in his head telling him he was a prick to even think of climbing a tree, specially this big.

He reaches the halfway point and stops. He sits down on one of the largest branches and lights a cigarette. He can still just see above the tops of the trees. He looks out over the woods into the barren, white fields beyond.

He feels lonely, misses the kids. He wonders what Warren's doing. He hasn't thought about him for a while and feels bad for it. He convinces himself once again what he did was the right thing. Warren would've done exactly the same, no doubt. He wonders if he's managed to stay out of trouble in prison . . . or if he's out. He'll be seriously pissed off.

Nick realises this is the first time he's been properly alone in months. He doesn't want it but he knows he needs it.

Fuck it. There'll be plenty of time to stop when they get to their spot. Home in one piece? Back home, back to the place that's waiting for them further north. The perfect gaff, safe, out of the way. Somewhere no one will find them.

He stubs out his cigarette and stands. He does this

without thinking, wrapped in thought, like he's back on the ground. He doesn't reach out to steady himself. His left foot slips and jerks forward. He looks around. Awake. Both arms rise up, searching. He panics for a branch, sees two, flails and misses both. He feels himself tipping back.

'Fuck.'

True to form, what happens next, happens slowly. Just like the car crash he was in when he was a teenager.

'Fuck.' The words come out quietly, laced with terror. His left foot leaves its purchase completely. He's in the air, both legs above him as he falls back. He falls ten feet. The right side of his body hits a branch knocking the wind out of him and into a new direction. He sees another branch coming towards him. He puts his arms out in front of his face. His chest slams into it. He grabs and wraps both arms round the branch, struggling, panicking. The snow beneath cancels out any chance of keeping a firm enough grip. He feels himself slip, knowing the ground is still at least twenty feet below. He scrabbles, looking ahead into the thick pine trees. *Home in one piece?* He digs his fingers into the ridges of bark. His nails break and split. Two are ripped out. He lets out a scream he hopes everyone can hear and he's back in mid-air. His mind does its best to calculate what will happen. Break his legs, arms, skull? Freeze to death on the ground before Alf figures something's up? Maybe it would be better if he landed head first? He'll see it coming but he won't feel it. He could close his eyes. Then he'll be done with.

Thoughts increase in relation to the speed of the fall.

Alf will get the kids to Emily. He's all right. Trust him. Not many you can. He wouldn't do anything to hurt the kids. Why the fuck did I agree to stay in this shit hole of a cabin? Not like I had the fucking time.

The wind around his body increases, snow hitting his face, hands and neck. Some of it moving faster than his falling, sprawling body. Images of Zeb, Jake, Warren, Emily, Candy. That's what they said: life flashes. He thought maybe he'd see some of the better things, some nice images to go with, few beaches, mountains. Not just faces.

Then nothing.

A split second of pain.

Then black.

Twenty-one

Vincent's car moves slowly through the countryside. Nick Drake comes on the radio.

'Mind if I turn this up?' the hitchhiker asks, excited.

'Go ahead.' Save minor irritations, Vincent is enjoying her company.

'I know this one by heart.' She starts singing. He thinks her voice isn't so bad. She wasn't lying, just shy. That's why she scratched her nose.

'I learnt to play the guitar to this.' She leans into the back. 'Mind if I . . . ?'

Vincent looks briefly behind him. 'Sure, go ahead.'

She brings it to the front, clicks open the case and lifts the lid. Vincent wonders how she'll manage to play in the front of the car. It'll be a squeeze. He brings his attention back to the road.

It takes him a little less than a second to realise what the cold object is against his neck.

'Best you keep yous eyes on the road. No sense in us crashing, ey.' The tone of her voice has changed. No longer friendly. Rough; monotone.

He smiles to himself. Unable to believe he actually

trusted her. He thinks he must be getting soft. 'Brave cunt, aren't you?'

'Desperate times call fu' desperate measures. I need some money and you looks like you got a few quid to spare.'

'How's this gonna unfold?' he asks. 'Soon as we have to get out you'll have lost the advantage. Soon as I get free I'm gonna take that knife off you and do things you wouldn't want your feller to find out about.' His driving isn't affected. He has no fear of her. He just wonders whether he'll do what he would usually do in this situation. He's never been ripped off by a woman before. Not at knifepoint.

'Keep driving along here for another mile or so, you'll come to a turning for Linlithgow Bridge.' She keeps her hand and knife steady.

'Why don't you put that thing back in its box and play us a tune like you promised?'

'Promised you nothin'.'

'You do that, I'll put this down to a simple transgression, a momentary lapse of reason, a mistake, you just misjudged the situation. I'm reasonable, I like you.'

'Well you can't have me.'

'Don't flatter yourself, sweetheart. I like you, I don't want to fuck you.'

'Well I think yer a prick with too much money and too much time on your hands and I want some of the cash.'

Vincent falls quiet and keeps his eye out for the sign.

After a mile he sees it, indicates and slowly turns left. The blade remains at his neck.

The road narrows. A line of bare beech trees growing

from long, ancient, dry stone wall rises up to meet his eyeline. Two hundred yards further ahead he sees a figure, on the same side of the road. He twigs.

'See that man.' She points ahead.

'Hard to miss. That your feller then?'

'Something like that. Pull over.'

Vincent follows her instructions. As he slows and pulls the car in he wonders if running the man over might do the trick. As if in response to the thought, the blade point is pushed deeper into his skin.

He brings the car to a stop. The man walks to the driver side and looks into the window, weighing up the danger. He looks over to her and nods.

She prods Vincent with the blade. 'Wind down the window.' He follows her orders.

'Out,' the man commands. 'No fucking around.' Vincent leaves the car running and opens the door. The man grabs him by the arm and pulls him out. The blade slips away from his neck. He stands outside the car. Another much larger blade is jabbed into his back. He arches away from it for a second then relaxes into it. The mugger leans down to look into the car. 'What's he got?'

The woman starts looking in the glove compartment. She takes out a wallet and opens it. 'Not much, few twenties.'

'Don't tell me we have to go to the bank. That'd piss me right off.'

Vincent looks him in the eyes, unflinching for a long moment. 'The boot.'

The man puts hand and blade round the front of Vincent's neck and leads him to the back of the car. Vincent can see the man is hiding fear and it gives him all he needs.

'Where's the key?' the man asks.

'In the ignition. You can open it from the dash.' Vincent checks as much as he can around him. No cars have passed in the last two minutes. Nice quiet road.

'Flip the boot will you, babe!' the mugger shouts across.

A few seconds later the boot clicks open. 'Where is it then, where's the money?'

'Up in the back, over there by the wheel jack.'

'Better not be fucking me about.' He pushes Vincent forward, closer to the car and leans in. Excited by the search, the man loses a moment's concentration. Vincent reaches out and slams the boot lid on his forearm then lifts the lid back up and slams it down again, harder.

The man drops the knife and falls to his knees. A long scream starts off low in his throat, building. Vincent hears the passenger door open, the hitchhiker running to the back of the car.

'What the fuck's happening, ba—' She stops and sees him on the ground.

Vincent looks calmly at her, shaking his head. 'How's that for gratitude, ey? I pick you up, do you a favour, don't rape you, mug you or bore you and this is how you repay me. You really should be more careful who you get in a car with.'

She stands in front of him, speechless, unable to move. Vincent opens the boot up, takes out the wheel jack and cracks it over the man's head twice. He slumps to the ground. They both look down at him, waiting for something to happen, for him to move. He remains still. Blood seeps out from his skull on to the road and her boots. She turns and runs.

'Hang on, sweetheart, you've forgotten your stuff . . . your guitar,' Vincent calls after her. She carries on running. *She's fast*, he thinks, *even in those stupid boots*.

He puts the jack back in the boot, gets in the car and drives. He looks ahead at her running figure, getting smaller by the yard. He puts his foot down. By the time he gets to within a hundred yards of her he's doing forty-five miles an hour. She looks back over her shoulder several times, terror covering her face. She swerves left and right, looking for an opening into the field on her left. Vincent speeds up. She heads for a battered gate. As she reaches it the front right wing of the Mercedes clips her foot.

'There you go,' Vincent says to himself, concentrating hard, relaxed grip on the wheel. She stumbles and falls. He slams on the brakes, reverses and puts the car back into first. She lifts herself off the ground, staggering for the gate. She reaches it and begins to climb. The car smashes through the wooden slats of the gate, just missing her. The gate collapses and she lands, face first, in the frozen field. The car stops. Vincent looks at her lying in the hard mud and snow, unmoving, contemplating whether he should carry on.

He waits. She reaches out her arm, trying to push herself up, face still in the dirt and ice. He puts the car in reverse, turns it round and heads back for the Falkirk road. He drives slowly past the body of the failed mugger, satisfied by its lack of movement.

* * *

Jake drives on through the wood, feeling more confident by the minute. Alf sits quietly by his side. Zeb leans out the back of the trailer scooping up handfuls of snow and chucking them into the trees.

Jake steers the tractor out of the wood on to a wide farm track. The fields in front fall away steeply towards a cluster of houses, the lights already on.

'We can head down to the village if you like?' Alf offers.

'Drive down in this?'

'Sure. Head down this track for a mile or so . . . it'll lead to the road into Dundonnell.'

'I haven't got my licence,' Jake responds flatly.

'Wouldn't worry about that round here. Police have better things to do with their time. Besides, you're with me. Keep on this track. We can have a whisky mac to warm us up when we get there.'

'Cool.' Jake softens his grip and eases up on the gas, letting gravity do the work.

Fifteen minutes later they reach the village. Alf points Jake towards the best place to stop.

Zeb turns round to see where they are. 'What we doing here?'

'Having a drink. Alf says we can get a signal here . . . call Mum.'

'That's what I'm talkin' about, blood!' Zeb jumps down and follows Jake with the phone.

Alf heads into the pub.

Jake looks at the screen. 'Two bars, that'll do it.' He finds home in the address book, presses the green phone and hands it to Zeb. 'Stick it on loudspeaker, we can both talk. Don't tell her where we are.'

'What if she wants to come up and see us? She could come up and stay with Alf.'

'That's not gonna happen.'

They stand in silence waiting.

They hear the engaged tone.

'Why she on the bloody phone!' Zeb presses the red phone and folds his arms in a sulk.

'We'll try again in a minute.' He rubs Zeb's hair.

Zeb pulls away from him.

'What's up?'

'I want Mum to come and stay with Alf.'

'Well she can't . . . ain't gonna happen.'

'Why has Dad taken us all the shitting way up here?'

'What? You're lovin' it, blood.'

'It's a bloody stupid long way to come for a bloody goat,' Zeb moans.

'You know why. Dad wants us to spend some time together so we can get on better.'

'But you hate him.'

'I don't hate Dad, bro.' Jake does his best to sound sincere. He means what he says. 'It's not so bad up here. Dad's not being as much of a twat as normal. Thought I'd hate it but I'm having some good times, specially with Alf. You're having a good time ain't ya?'

Zeb looks down. 'S'pose. But I still want Mum.'

'Try again.' Zeb presses call again. The phone rings. His face quickly loosens and moves from sulk to excitement.

'Mum!'

'Zeb? That you? It's your aunt Sally, your mum's driving.

Where are you, love? We're worried sick. Why haven't you phoned?'

Zeb pulls a silent contorted face at her voice, tongue pushing out his bottom lip.

'Hang on,' Sally continues. 'I'll stick the phone on loudspeaker.' Pause. 'There, go on, speak now.'

'Mum?'

'Zeb . . . where are you, love? I've been trying to call you all afternoon.' Her voice sounds fluttery to Zeb, like she's scared.

'We're in Scotland in this cool village called Dundonnell.' Jake glares at him and pushes him to shut up. Zeb pushes back. 'We're hanging out with this cool dude called Alf . . .'.

Emily cuts in, 'Where the hell's Dad? This is not a bloody game, you have to come home. We're coming to Dundonnell. We're in Wester Ross.'

'Dad's in the woods in this cabin medivating.'

'Meditating,' Jake corrects.

'What? You're on your own? Jesus Christ!' Zeb can hear her barely contained anger.

Jake puts his hand out. 'Let me speak to her.' Zeb hands him the phone without objection.

'Mum?'

'Jesus, Jake, I thought you were supposed to be looking after him . . . where the hell is Nick?'

'He's taking some time out. It's cool, Mum, we're OK. Alf's safe. We've been staying at his place. He's got a telly. Zeb is cool . . .'. Jake trails off. 'So am I.'

'Sally and I are coming to get you. We'll be there tonight. You stay right there. Whatever you do stay there. Is there a pub or something?'

Jake doesn't want to tell her. 'In the village, we're going there now.'

'Wait there, Jake, whatever you do just bloody wait there.'

'I wanna say goodbye,' Zeb whines, holding out his hand.

Jake hands Zeb the phone.

'Bye, Mum! Love you big time, innit!'

'We'll see you soon, couple of hours. Stay in the pub, don't go anywhere and keep warm.'

Zeb finishes the call and stares at the mobile.

Jake glares at him. 'I fucking told you not to tell her where we were.'

'You never do what Dad tells you so why should I do what you shitting tell me?'

Jake is exasperated. He resists punching him. 'You got no fucking idea, bro. She gets here there's gonna be all kinds of shit flying. She's super pissed. This is a bad one. You know that. She's gonna fucking take us home and I don't wanna go. I ain't. You can. I'm staying.'

'I want to see Mum. She can stay and we can go walking in the woods and see the ghosts and bears and monster and shit.'

Jake shakes his head in disbelief. 'Raas boy. She ain't gonna be up for walking. She's gonna kick Dad's arse and want us to come home. You fucking did it. I told you not to tell her where we were. Your fault. Come on. I'm gonna get pissed with Alf.'

Zeb falls silent, looking close to tears. Jake heads to the pub. Zeb follows behind, head drooping in a loud sulk.

* * *

Nick moves jaggedly, minute by minute, back to consciousness but not back to light. He can't see a thing.

I'm fucking blind. How am I blind! I landed on my cunting back!

He tries to open his eyes. The lids won't move. He lies in the dark and cold and feels a lot of weight on him, like someone or something is sitting on every inch of his body. Something cold on his mouth, lips and face. He feels panic rise in him again. He pokes his tongue between his lips and realises what it is. Ice. Snow, compacted all over his body. His heart beats insanely in his chest. He pictures himself ten feet under a tomb of pure snow.

This is a fucking bad way to go. He quickly tries to move his legs. Nothing.

Arms? Nothing with the left. Fingers on my right hand. They move a little.

Now the wrist, arm, shoulder. Fuck me.

He moves the weight off his arms, raises a hand to his face and wipes the snow off. Only a few inches thick. He gently touches his eyes and realises the lids are frozen together. He instinctively rests his palms across both of them. The ice melts, his eyes open. The night is black. He tries to move his head. Stiff, cold. *Broken? Fuck. Move it.* An inch to the left, two inches to the right. *Not broken, just cold, stiff.*

'Fuck.' The words come out thin and empty. He opens his mouth and stretches his jaw and tries to sit up. No chance. He uses his working hand to move the snow off his chest and arms then rolls on to his side. He pushes himself up with his right hand. His legs move a little. The cold has reached his bones, not broken, just cold, frozen and stiff. He knows he has to get back to the cabin and get the fire going. He looks over at its rough black shape in the darkness. He moves the rest of the snow off his body, trying to get some movement and feeling back into his limbs. His left arm slowly regains sensation.

He drags himself over the cold ground.

'Fucking piece of shit tree. Burn the fucking thing to the ground. Fuck the wish stick. Home in one fucking piece, no chance.'

It takes Nick the best part of twenty minutes to reach the cabin door. He pulls himself up and slumps his back against the wood, exhausted. He looks ahead of him. In any other circumstances the view of the white forest floor, trees laden with snow, the silence, would be beautiful. Right now it shines back nothing but danger. Sensation returns to his legs and with it comes cold and pain. He shivers uncontrollably. His reach for the door handle falls a few inches short. He pushes his back against the door and pushes up from his feet. As he rises he roars in pain and slides back down again. The burning sensation starts in his right thigh and works its way down to his foot. He runs his hand down the side of his leg and feels a lump beneath his jeans.

Calm yourself. Everything's gonna be cool.

He pushes his back against the door again, using his left leg to work his way up. He reaches the handle, turns it without thinking. The door clicks and flies open. He collapses into the cabin in a heap cursing and shouting, holding his right thigh, hurting it more.

After a few minutes the pain eases enough to continue

dragging himself fully into the cabin. He kicks the door shut with his left foot and lies on his back looking up at the ceiling. The fire is still going. The orange embers reflect and flicker round the room. For the first time since he managed to open his eyes he starts to feel his muscles relax but he doesn't stop shivering. The pain in his leg is constant.

He rolls on to his side and pushes himself up level with the chair, another push and he's high enough to sit on it.

He unbuttons his trousers and slowly rolls them down. He feels the warmth of blood against his skin mixing with the cold air. He reaches the lump and pulls the darkened jean material away from his leg inch by inch, rolling it down his leg, refusing to look down.

'Cunt.' Through gritted teeth.

The cold air in the cabin chills the exposed skin. He finally gets the courage to look down. The skin is split three inches down and two inches across. The brilliant white of bone shines out between muscle and tendon. The bleeding has stopped around the opening, clotted, thick, glutinous and black. He looks around the room for something to wrap round it. He stands up and hops to the bed. He drops down, takes up a corner of sheet and tears it. He gently wraps it round the wound and bone then lies back on the bed exhausted. He exhales a single mocking laugh at his stupidity.

'Climbing a fucking tree. Prick.' He lets his weight and exhaustion sink into the thin mattress. He has no idea what he's going to do next. If he waits long enough Alf and the boys will come.

How the hell are they gonna get an ambulance up here? He wishes he'd kept the mobile.

He listens to the wind outside once more. He misses Zeb and Jake more than ever. For the first time since the beginning of the trip he starts to seriously worry about them. He does his best to convince himself that no one will find them up here. He knows it is a very real possibility. The thought of the pain he'll have to go through to get back to them under his own steam leaves him hopeless. He slams his clenched fist into the wall of the cabin and looks over to the dying fire. He readies himself to get back up again and build it up enough to stop him shivering.

Vincent's routine stops at every pub and shop along the road have begun to bore him. His well-rehearsed story now so familiar that he believes it himself, making easy friends with bored, curious locals, eager to answer any of the questions he has about the area, the mountains and the travelling father of two he's meeting 'up country'. He's stuck faithfully to the A835 to Ullapool for the last fifty miles. Taking the left fork on to the A832 to Dundonnell is partly a mistake, part curiosity, part instinct. So many of the previous locals along the way told him stories of the beauty of the Wester Ross highlands. The isolation, the lochs, the mountains and the sea. He has time to take in the beauty of the place on the way. Nick will stop eventually, not much further north he can go. It will only be a matter of time before he finds him. He has time. Scotland has grown on him. Good a place as any to die. Quiet, isolated, perfect.

* * *

Jake is on his second pint. The rough cider buzz swirls inside his head. The whisky mac was easier going. He wants to lie down. The booze has affected his knees. They said it would, the chuckling locals at the bar. He needs a piss but he's afraid to get up in case he falls over and makes an arse of himself. Zeb is buzzing on Coca-Cola and eating his eighth packet of prawn cocktail crisps. He munches them quietly, a broad sugar-induced smile on his face, looking around the pub, kicking his feet against the chair leg. Alf sits quietly, hands resting on his stick, pint in front of him. The fire in the corner fills the room with heat. The place is quiet, a few locals at the bar, a young couple in a booth sitting close to each other. Jake watches them furtively, jealous, wishing Lisa was next to him.

'Got a girlfriend?' He knows Alf has spotted him checking the couple out.

'Not really.' Jake looks away.

'Yes you have,' Zeb jabs. 'You're going out with Lisa and you snogged her sister Candy. You're a dirty bastard.'

'Nothing wrong with playing the field at your age,' Alf takes a sip of his whisky and glances over at the couple. 'Mind you, not as much as she does, that one's a bit of a bike.'

Zeb splutter chuckles into his Coke.

'So what you gonna do when you get back to London?' Alf asks Jake.

'Not sure we're going back. Well I'm not, not yet.'

Alf raises his eyebrows. 'Oh?'

'Dad says he wants to move back up here. Says he hates London.'

'And you?' Alf asks.

'What?' Jake lifts his pint for distraction, sipping slowly.

'Do you hate London?'

'I love it. Got all my mates there. But it's good up here . . . I like it better than I thought but I miss my mates, the streets and stuff.'

'You should be back down there . . . place like this is for romantics and runners, not for kids.'

'Runners?' Jake asks, confused.

'People trying to get away from something or other.'

Zeb kicks Jake under the table. Jake ignores him.

Zeb chatters through crisps and Coke, 'Mum's coming here to meet us in the pub. She's seriously pissed off but she'll chillax. She likes red wine cos it makes her happy.'

Alf looks at Zeb half surprised. 'She's come a long way for a drink.'

Jake speaks up, embarrassed. 'She's coming to get us. Should've told you. Zeb told her where we were. Told him not to.'

Zeb opens up another bag of crisps.

'No problem with me. She can stay in the cottage if she likes.' Alf smiles at them both.

'Not sure she'll be into that.' Jake finishes his drink.

'Well she won't be able to start back down any time soon, not in this. We should be getting back, before the ice kicks in again. Tractor's a bugger up hills, need some new tyres. We'll leave a note for your mum at the bar.'

Alf stands up, stacks their glasses and takes them to the bar and writes a note, leaving it with the landlady. She nods and smiles at him.

Jake manages to get up. He wobbles a little. He puts his hand on the table to steady himself.

Zeb walks over and tugs at Alf's coat. 'Jake's pissed!'

'Piss off.' Jake feels the spin ease. Two of the locals at the bar give him a knowing nod then bring their attention back to their conversation.

Alf puts his hand on Jake's back. 'You OK to head on back?'

Jake burps loudly, suppresses the next one then nods.

The three of them head out.

The snow has settled another couple of inches. Zeb gathers up enough to make a ball and chucks it at Jake who is unable and unwilling to fight back.

Alf drives them back, slowly. Jake and Zeb sit huddled in the trailer, out of sight. The wind blows the snow around their heads in mini blizzards, freezing their faces. Jake watches the lights of Dundonnell fade into the grey white of the night.

'Shall we watch some telly,' Zeb asks, huddled up close to Jake.

'I'm going to bed.'

'I'm not watching it on my own.'

'Wanna bet.' Jake turns up the collars of his jacket. The road is empty of all cars. The tractor trundles along at a steady pace. Jake looks at Alf's back, body upright to the wind and snow, unfazed.

After a couple of miles Jake looks up to the sky and sees the constant grey night-time snow shine brighter, then brighter still. A soft yellow stretches above them in a hazy arc. He thinks it looks beautiful. He hears the distant rumble of an engine and realises what he's looking at. Zeb is asleep at his side when the lights of Vincent's Mercedes pass them on the road. Alf lifts his hand and waves to the car as he passes. Vincent's headlights dip down for a brief moment then flick back up. Jake scrutinises the car and wants it.

Twenty-two

It's late when Vincent drives into Dundonnell; well past closing time. The lights in the pub are on but it should be closed.

A *lock-in*, he thinks. *Good*.

He knocks on the door, looks around the main street of the town and waits. Apart from the blackened slush-covered roads it looks picture perfect. The door opens. A stooped overweight woman looks up at him without speaking.

'I'm sorry, I know it's late, I got lost, was supposed to be in Ullapool by now.' He pauses. 'I was wondering if you had something to eat. Been travelling all day. Starving.' He mock coughs into his handkerchief for sympathy. Blood comes up anyway.

The woman looks straight at Vincent and calls out a man's name.

An equally overweight man, taller, with an alcohol-reddened face takes over.

'Says he wants some food. Bit late.' She walks back into the pub.

The man looks at him a moment then opens the door

fully. Vincent walks in, feeling the warmth of the fire on his face.

He's invited to the lock-in. The whiskies line up. It takes a while for him to catch up. The conversation comes round to Vincent's destination and his meeting with the Genevas. At first it seems to go nowhere, until he talks about the boys, and one of the stooping drunks mentions Alf and his two charges, 'in here earlier. Good man, Alf. Safe as houses, man you can trust.' Vincent nods in appreciation at the word 'trust'. 'That boy with him though, the older one, can't handle his cider.' The man shakes his head, chuckling to himself.

He had their trust. The rest would be easy. Vincent feels the whisky relax the stiffness in his muscles and chest and gets ready to leave.

Jake's head is slumped against the back of the sofa. His mouth drifts open. A gurgle fills the room and makes Zeb jump. He leans across, pushes Jake's mouth closed and brings his attention back to the TV. An American girl talks, apoplectic with terror, into a video camera in a wood, convinced she is about to die at the hand of an unseen witch. Zeb's knees are up against his chest, duvet over his shoulders, eyes wide and bright with fear. The rest of the lights in the room are off. Alf is upstairs asleep. Jake's mouth drifts open again and his gurgling kicks back in. Zeb jabs him in the side. Jake stops, opens his eyes a moment, looks around dazed, tries to focus on the TV, gives up and lets his head slump back against the sofa. The woman continues to talk to camera while running manically into the darkness of the trees. Zeb thinks of Nick in the *kuti* with a horde of Uruk Hai pouring in through a splintered door, devouring him. He shuts his eyes to make it stop. He moves closer to Jake. Jake puts his arm round him.

Zeb is determined to stay awake for his mum, no matter how late she gets there.

The camera girl enters an abandoned house. She spots tiny black hand prints on the walls, jabbering to camera as she stumbles back down the stairs in a blind, breathless panic. She heads for the basement.

'Don't go down there, you shitting numpty! Get out of the house. Never go up or down only out!' Zeb flicks a look at the sitting-room door then brings his eyes back to the TV.

Camera Girl heads into the basement. The camera tracks around the room, stopping at a man standing facing the corner, rocking gently, murmuring. Zeb jumps up and turns the TV off. He looks around the room at the shadows and cupboards and chairs, the hissing gas fire. He moves closer to Jake and closes his eyes. Images rush into his mind. He wishes he hadn't watched that, especially the last bit. He always wishes he hadn't watched the last bit.

He rests his head against the sofa. After ten minutes of frightening rerun images of girl, camera and man in corner, he falls asleep.

He dreams of woods, witches, tractors and snow. Being chased relentlessly by a giant snowman hurling boulders he skilfully avoids. Then the back of the tractor, looking up at Jake, following his line of sight back up to the sky and the yellow arcing light of the Mercedes.

He opens his eyes to see yellow light filling the room. It

comes through the curtains then shuts off. He sits up, looks at Jake then at the window. He gets up and walks across the carpet and peeks through the curtain. A Mercedes freewheels a hundred yards from the house and comes to a stop. Zeb watches it wondering if it's a mate of Alf's.

Why's he turned his lights off before he stopped?

He watches a man get out, looking around, like he's smelling the air. He thinks of the Uruk Hai that got away and the witch. His balls tighten. The man walks to the back of the car and opens the boot. He takes out a bag, clicks the boot shut and starts to walk towards the house. Instead of heading for the front door he walks round the back.

'Shitting burglar!' Zeb whispers out loud. Jake stirs.

Zeb shakes Jake awake.

'Wha . . . ? What! Fuck's going on?'

'Wake up! There's a bloody shitting burglar sneaking round the back!' Zeb continues to shake him.

'I'm awake, I'm awake for fuck sake.' Jake sits up. 'You fucking around?'

'No! Look. His car's outside.' Zeb pulls Jake up by the hand and drags him to the window.

Jake sees the Mercedes and recognises it immediately. 'That's the car that passed us on the road earlier. Maybe it's a mate of Alf's. He waved to him.'

'He's not a mate he's a bloody burglar. If he was a mate he'd come through the front door.'

'Maybe Alf leaves the back door open for his mates.'

'Let's look.' Zeb pulls Jake towards the door.

'OK I'm coming, fucksake. Chill your boots, fucking head's banging.'

They head out of the sitting room and walk down the

short corridor into the kitchen. A torch beam shines in across floor, cupboards and walls. They duck down, stay silent, breathing shallow. Zeb breaks it, whispering close to Jake's ear, 'Shitting told you. Shitting burglar. Let's get Alf.'

'Shhh.' Jake follows the torchlight. 'Alf's too old.'

Zeb's eyes widen. 'Maybe he's got a gun like Arnie and we're gonna make his shitting day.' Jake hears the fear in Zeb's whisper. 'Wish Dad was shitting here.'

Jake puts his hand on his shoulder. Zeb is trembling. 'So do I.'

The figure outside tries the kitchen door. Jake quickly pulls Zeb back out of the kitchen. They hold their backs tight against the corridor wall. Zeb remembers the basement man standing in the corner murmuring. He squeezes his eyes shut trying to force the image out. The kitchen door opens. They hear footsteps walk slowly across the lino floor then stop. Torchlight reaches into the corridor. Jake gently puts his hand over Zeb's mouth and leads him back down the corridor to the back study. As he closes the study door, flashlight floods the corridor. The floorboards creak towards the sitting room.

Jake looks around the room. He leads Zeb to the window, opens it and gestures to Zeb to climb out. Zeb does as he's told.

Jake thuds on to the snow. Zeb stumbles forward, landing face first. He doesn't laugh. Jake lifts him up and they head for the small copse of trees at the back of the house.

'What the shit do we do now?' Zeb hisses. 'I want Dad.'

'We wait.'

'But I'm freezing.'

Jake takes off his jumper and slides it over Zeb's head then pulls him close to his body. They see the torchlight beam shine erratically out of the sitting-room window then disappear then shine out of the upper landing window. Jake starts shivering. He holds Zeb closer.

'I want to go back in the house, bro.' Zeb's teeth chatter.

'We have to wait.' Jake looks up. Alf's bedroom light goes on.

Then nothing.

A few minutes later the landing light goes on. Then the sitting-room light.

'Come on.' Jake leads Zeb round to the front of the house. He crawls down beneath the windowsill and lifts his head up. He can see through the gap in the curtains. Alf sits in his armchair, back to the window. In front of him is a man sitting on the sofa with slicked-back hair. He's talking to Alf. He has a bag on his lap.

'I think it's cool. Let's go in.'

'Is the burglar still in the house?' Zeb asks.

'I think it's a mate of Alf's.'

'But why did he go into the house without turning any of the lights on?'

'No idea. Come on, I'm fucking freezing.'

They walk in through the kitchen door, into the kitchen and down the corridor. Jake knocks on the sitting-room door.

'Come in.' Alf's voice sounds strange to Jake. He changes his mind about going in. Before he has a chance to turn back, Zeb heads in. He walks in straight after him.

Alf looks at them both. He smiles unconvincingly. Jake and Zeb stand looking at Alf and Vincent. Zeb picks up his duvet and drapes it back over his shoulders.

'Hey, lads.' Alf continues to smile. 'Late night for you, ey. This is Vincent.' Jake and Zeb eye him suspiciously. 'He's here to see your dad.'

'Well he's not here,' Jake cuts in.

'Just what I told him.' Alf rests his hands on his knees and squeezes them. Jake now knows something is wrong. He wishes they'd stayed outside.

Vincent speaks. 'All right, lads. I've come a long way, it won't take long, just need a little chat.'

'He's gone on holiday,' Zeb chips in.

'You're on holiday already ... aren't you?' Vincent doesn't move.

Jake dislikes everything about him.

Vincent continues, 'When's he back?'

'Like my brother said,' Jake looks straight at Vincent, trying to look unafraid, 'he's gone on holiday, won't be back for a few weeks.'

'Come on ... Jake. Do I look like a prick who would swallow that?'

'Don't know what you'd swallow, mate ... told you, he's gone away. We're staying with Alf. Don't know where he is, gone walking or something.' Jake is pleased with the lie.

Vincent remains still and calm. Jake notices his leather gloves.

'You see ...' Vincent looks around the room. 'I think you know exactly where he is, you all do. You're just watching his back. I can understand that, look after your own. I'd do the same. But this really is in your best interest to tell me where he is . . . then I can leave, get on with my life.'

Alf looks at them both. 'Lads . . . why don't you head on up to bed, get yourself something to eat and I'll talk to Vincent.' Jake looks at him. There is resignation in Alf's eyes; tiredness. He doesn't want to leave him. He does as he's told. He'll get his knife.

'Come on, Zeb. Let's go.' Zeb looks up at Jake then at Alf and without a word, walks out; Jake follows.

Jake and Zeb stand in the corridor for a moment. Jake feels like shit, regretting bringing Zeb back into the house. And a new feeling: behind the building hangover, a fear in his belly that hurts.

They head upstairs and get into their beds.

'What do you think he wants to see Dad about?' Zeb asks.

'Probably got something to do with what happened in Windermere.' Jake knows the man downstairs is someone to be scared of, not someone to fuck around with. He reaches out and picks his knife up without Zeb seeing.

'We lied good.' Zeb smiles. 'Sucker-punched him with a good one, star. He'll piss off soon and we can go back down and see Alf.'

Jake doesn't reply. Jake listens carefully to the murmuring of dialogue downstairs. Unable to make out the words he follows the tone. Each voice speaking a moment, then a reply. He can easily make out which is Alf's and which is Vincent's. Alf murmurs at length for a while. Zeb starts to snore. Jake pushes him with his foot. Zeb turns over.

Silence for a minute until Vincent responds with what Jake reckons are a series of questions, each answered in a clipped monotone murmur by Alf. Then silence.

Movement.

A muffled protest from Alf.

Something falls to the sitting-room floor.

Jake sits bolt upright in bed. He looks over at Zeb. He knows they won't be able to get out of the house a second time. His legs start shaking. He slides out of bed and lets them rest gently on the floor, pushing the soles of his feet into the carpet to make the shaking stop. He looks straight ahead.

'Never around when we need you, Dad,' he whispers into the dark. 'The fuck am I supposed to do now?'

Silence downstairs. He puts the knife in his back pocket and makes his decision.

He gets up and walks gently across the floor hoping to remember where the creaking boards are. He makes no noise as he heads out into the hall. He peers over the banister. The sitting-room door is closed. He waits. Terrified.

Move your fucking legs, Jake. Move your legs.

Sweat runs down his back, quickly turning cold on his skin. He pulls the knife from his back pocket, removes it from its sheath and heads for the stairs, blade leading the way. He walks down one step at a time feeling like he's in a horror movie, hating every second. His heart beats out of control.

He gets to the bottom of the stairs and stops. He hears the muffled voice of Vincent again. Nothing from Alf. He walks up to the door and puts his ear as close as he can bear.

Vincent speaks from the other side, muffled but audible.

'Now you know this is completely unnecessary. What could you possibly have to gain from keeping schtum? You don't even know them. Told me yourself, only met him recently.'

Silence.

Then some kind of movement. 'Lot of trust, that Nick. To let a stranger take care of his kids while he fucks off . . . and hides. Tell me where he is and I'll stop.'

Stop? The fuck does he mean, stop? Jake presses his ear closer to the door.

He hears a muffled whine and knows it's Alf. Then a sound he can't make out.

Open the fucking door, Jake.

He raises his hand slowly and rests his palm against the cold wood. He holds it there listening to the sickening sound on the other side.

He pushes it open.

He sees Vincent's back, leaning down over Alf who is obscured by Vincent's frame. Vincent's right arm is pushing something into Alf's face.

It looks to Jake like a dentist at work and his knees almost give way. He panic-scans the room. He doesn't notice it at first, the small crimson patch at the base of the armchair, dripping like oil to the floor.

Jake's knees hold but he is paralysed with fear, holding the blade in front of him, arm shaking.

What you gonna do now . . . kid?

Vincent looks over his shoulder.

'Ah, Jake. Wondered when you'd be back down. Shame

you have to see this. Gave you a fair chance though.' He stops what he's doing and turns to face Jake. In his hand is a long, thin shaft of dark grey metal tapering to a sharp point. Jake is transfixed by it. Along half of the shaft to its tip shines a creeping dark liquid. Alf is obscured by Vincent's body. Jake dare not look round.

Alf is silent.

'Come sit down.' Vincent stands up. Jake takes a faltering step back stabbing into the air without true meaning or force. Vincent reaches calmly forward, taking the blade from Jake's trembling hand, and puts it on the table next to Alf.

'Over here.' Vincent leads Jake to the sofa. Jake jerks his head to the left to look at Alf. His mouth is taped. The tape is doubled round the stem of the lamp behind him holding his head upright. The table beside him is on the floor. His eyes open, looking straight at Jake. Jake is gently but forcibly led to the sofa. He tries to read what Alf's eyes are saying. All he can make out is an apology.

Why the fuck are you apologising? This is our fucking fault. We did this to you.

Vincent pushes Jake down on the sofa; force not aggression. 'Stay there . . . don't move an inch.' His voice is soft, controlled, calm. He walks over to his leather bag and takes out a length of rope. He begins to tie Jake to the sofa. Jake does nothing to stop him. He tells himself it's a game, like the ones he plays with Zeb. He looks over at Alf unable to believe what he sees. Alf closes his eyes. His face is marked by what look like small stab wounds. Beneath each cut, tiny frozen waterfalls of blood. His eyes stay closed, his face peaceful, unmoving. Jake thinks he looks like an old, dying Jesus.

He's closing his eyes so I don't have to look at him.

Piss leaks out of Jake on to his thigh.

Vincent ties him up with care. Looping the rope round the short legs of the sofa.

Jake looks away from Alf to the floor. The rope is wrapped across Jake's chest, the full width of the sofa and over his stiffened legs. He is ashamed of himself for not putting up a fight. Stand his ground and kick the shit out of anyone who crossed him or his mates. That's what he did back in London. He could fight kids his age easy but he made a rule not to pick on anyone younger than him. Size was never an issue. He knew a kid half his size could be crazy enough to stick a knife in him. Size clearly wasn't an issue for Vincent either, nor age. He was easily a foot taller than Jake, about as big as Warren, much bigger than Nick. He was imposing, frightening to look at, all the more because of his calm. It's clear to Jake he's done this before, many times, like it is all part of the routine. He looks at Vincent finishing off the knots, neat, tight, taking pride. Finally, he tapes Jake's mouth. He turns to look at Alf who has rested his head against the sofa, eyes still closed, face soft.

'Open your eyes, old man. Have a look at the consequences of keeping your mouth shut.'

Alf keeps his eyes shut. Vincent looks back at Jake a moment, like he's thinking, working out what to do next. Jake can feel his eyes on him. He doesn't look up.

Vincent walks across to Alf. Jake looks up and sees him straddling Alf's lap.

Vincent asks the one-word question.

'Where?'

No response.

Jake looks at Alf. *Please open your eyes. Tell him. Please tell him.*

Vincent shakes his head in disappointment. 'Open your eyes, Alf.'

Alf keeps his eyes closed.

To Jake he looks asleep, peaceful, except for the blood covering face, shirt and chair.

Vincent lifts his arm up, Jake's knife in his hand. The knife hand disappears between Vincent and Alf.

Everything stops for Jake.

He wants to see what's happening. He's glad he can't. He doesn't move. Alf's body begins to buck. Vincent hardly moves, his arm working away around Alf's unseen head.

Silence a moment, followed by the scream behind the tape, like someone a long way off, like the howl of a distant ownerless dog.

Jake shuts his eyes, swearing never to open them again.

Alf's scream fades. Jake hears Vincent get up and walk across the floor back to him.

Don't open your eyes, ever. Jake's body shakes uncontrollably. Vincent lifts his head up from its submissive droop.

'Open your eyes, Jake.' Vincent's voice is soft, reassuring, terrifying.

Jake feels him kneel down on the sofa.

'Come on, Jake. Have a look.'

Come on you fucking chicken shit, look at him.

Jake's breathing is rapid, panicking and stifling. He can't

get enough air into his lungs through his nose. He slowly opens his eyes. Alf's face and beard are covered in fresh blood. Jake focuses his attention on the smallest details of Vincent's jaw and chin, the hairs, the colour, refusing to take Alf in. His eyes move slowly up Alf's glistening face. Jake's body reacts before his mind has time to realise what he's seeing. He retches three times. Unable to get it out of his mouth, vomit forces its way through his nostrils. He begins to suffocate. Vincent leans across with his gloved hand and removes the tape. Jake gasps for breath swallowing and spitting sick, choking. His breathing returns erratically back to normal. He retches again, his upper chest and shoulders buck forward twice and he throws up into his lap.

He closes his eyes in shame and shock and starts rocking as much as the rope around his body will allow.

The image of Alf's face flashes into the black behind his eyelids.

That's not real.

Yes it fucking is and he did it with your fucking knife.

Jake keeps his eyes shut but the image of Alf's face crystallises into his mind, refusing to be anything he could make up. He pushes the image away leaving an empty space. He forces in images of Lisa; Candy; Zeb in the back of the tractor shooting Uruk Hai; Mum cooking roast dinner; Nick lying in the cabin on his own, fire blazing in the corner; Carlos through the flames in the restaurant, himself in the seat of the tractor driving across snow-covered ground through the woods, the pub, to a pint that softens up the tension, bringing a smile to his face. He wants that drink again, a spliff, anything to wipe that first image away. He layers the good times into his head, building them up into a futile collage. Each layer is ripped apart by the image of Alf and what Vincent just did with his knife.

Why did I buy that fucking knife?

He'd've used something else.

He tells himself over and over it's not real. He's not here. He's upstairs in bed, asleep. He grinds his teeth and rocks back and forth. He hears a low whine coming from somewhere near him. It turns into a roar, then he realises it's coming from him. He couldn't stop it if he wanted to. He doesn't. The good times are ripped apart by the image of Alf's face, blocking out everything else. Narrow strips of horizontal red where his aging eyelids once were. A deep, clean cut. That's what Jake saw. Eyeballs staring straight ahead at him, unblinking, pin thin streaks of blood running a couple of inches down his face, clotting; coming to a series of red full stops.

Worse than the films.

'Have a good look, Jake,' Vincent continues. 'You see there a terrible waste. All he had to do was tell me where your old man was and we could've avoided it.' He holds Jake steady. 'Keep looking.' Alf and Jake lock eyes. They keep looking at each other. The least Jake can do now is keep eye contact. The bravest thing he's done in his life.

'If you look long enough,' Vincent looks at Alf, unfazed, 'by the time I come to ask you the same question you'll be more than happy to draw me a detailed map and even lead me there by the hand . . . I promise you.' Vincent wipes Jake's blade on the sofa and rests it on Jake's trembling thigh.

Then he does something that throws everything into confusion; further terror. Vincent lifts his hand and tenderly pushes Jake's hair behind his ear, away from his face.

Vincent looks over at Alf again and continues talking.

Jake smells the puke on his lap. He holds back another retch. His legs ache from holding them still. He cannot stop them shaking. He keeps looking at Alf hoping for something to come from the old man's face to tell him what to do, what to say.

'So what's it to be, Jake, son? Do I turn your blade on to you?' Vincent looks at the knife admiringly. 'Or are you going to make nice and tell me where he is? This can be simple or horrific. I'm easy either way, believe me.'

Tears run down Jake's face. He keeps looking at Alf. Vincent leans across and wipes the tears from his cheek. Jake recoils. He wants to head-butt him. He's too scared to do anything but keep looking at Alf.

After a long pause, Jake speaks. 'He's gone to Ullapool. Don't know where, a B and B on the seafront.' He gives him just enough to make it believable.

Vincent looks over at Alf, then back to Jake. He thinks for a moment, then smiles. 'Good lad. Now you can get on with your life.' Vincent rests Jake's knife on the arm of the sofa.

He gets up. 'Anyone for a cuppa before I head off?'

Twenty-three

Zeb sprints through the woods, finding his way by the reflection of snow and the haphazard breaks of cloud and moonlight. His lungs feel like they're going to explode. He keeps running not letting up on speed, tears streaming down his face. He comes to a steep rise leading up to the edge of the wood. He tries to run up it at the same speed. His body weight holds him back, forcing him off balance. He falls back, rolling down to the base of the embankment. Snow cushions his fall. He lies on the ground looking up at the star-filled sky. His mind sees Jake on the sofa being tied down, Alf tied to the lamp and the bastard greaser looking so calm . . . happy. Zeb's breathing is out of control. He takes out his inhaler and takes three long puffs.

Fucking shit bag. Uruk Hai wanker. Dad'll sort 'im proper style.

He pushes himself up and starts up the bank to the wood, more slowly this time. He makes it to the top and looks into the trees. The light all but disappears.

Different to daytime, bloody shit scary. Nasty monsters in there. But Dad's there. He'll sort them out.

He walks forward slowly, looking for a stick. He finds a long thin branch, picks it up, takes out his knife and starts whittling the end into a point. He holds it out in front of him, wishing he had a torch.

It takes fifteen minutes to reach the cabin. The snow is thick on the ground, drifted up to the sides and deep on the roof. Zeb looks up at the chimney stack and sees a small wisp of smoke. His spirits quickly rise. He walks forward and sees the broken branches scattered at the base of the tree and knows something is wrong.

Maybe that gangster wanker's been here already? Terror replaces hope.

He looks around on the ground for clues. He sees the dented outline of a body in arms and legs splayed like a crooked snow angel. It looks big enough to be his dad. He sees something dark in the snow and bends down. Frozen blood. He hears coughing coming from the cabin.

'Dad!?' He gets up and runs over to the cabin door and stops for a moment.

Maybe he ain't in there? Sounds like him.

He knocks. Another cough.

'Thank fuck. That you, Alf?'

Zeb pushes the door open and sees Nick lying on his back on the bed. He runs over, wraps his arms round him and bursts into tears.

'Hey, hey, hey. It's me who should be crying. Look at the fucking state of me.'

Zeb hollers into Nick's chest, 'Jake and Alf, the bastard shitting Uruk Hai, gangster wanker.' He trails off into hysteria.

Nick pulls him away, holding him by the shoulders. 'Hey, what the fuck's going on?'

Zeb is unable to speak clearly through rapid breathing, jerking tears and panic. He takes out his inhaler and sucks in two more bursts. Nick lifts himself up and sits on the edge of the bed and looks at him closely.

'Remember what I said, kid, take your time. Breathe slowly.'

Zeb slowly calms himself down and begins to speak. 'There's a man at Alf's, big man, an' he's got Jake and Alf.'

'What do you mean he's got Jake and Alf? Who?'

'Bastard shitting Uruk Hai with black hair, big horrible nasty bastard Jake had rope all over him and Alf had blood on his face and tape on his mouth.' Zeb speaks so fast Nick finds it hard to keep up.

'Listen.' Nick stops him in his tracks. Zeb looks at him wide-eyed. 'I fell out of a tree and hurt myself, badly. You're going to have to help me get back to the house, quick.'

Zeb nods through rapid in-breaths and tears. He takes another draw on his inhaler. Nick leans forward and wipes the tears from his son's eyes.

'You've been brave to come up here and get me, kid, I'm proud of you. We have to sort this out. You're going to have to be a proper grown-up. Hear me?'

Zeb judders tear-filled in-breaths then nods. 'Fifteen minutes.'

'What?'

'I ran all the way.'

Nick struggles to lean forward. He kisses him on the forehead. 'Help me up.'

Zeb nods and breaks into a half smile. Nick pushes himself up off the bed. He stumbles and falls to the floor. He shouts out in pain. Zeb rushes up to him. Nick puts his hand on his shoulder. 'Give me your stick.' Zeb gets it. Nick puts the point to the floor, lifts his weight on to it. The point snaps. He jerks forward, regains his balance then breaks off the remaining point of wood.

'That's my Uruk Hai killing spear,' Zeb stutters through snot.

'Come here.'

Zeb steps up close, Nick rests his hand on his shoulder and they head for the door.

Nick winces, cursing every step. Zeb keeps his eyes fixed on the ground looking for any holes and bumps to steer Nick away from.

They head through the wood, following Zeb's incoming tracks. They move as fast as Nick can bear, half jogging, slowing for breath then speeding up again. Zeb's energy is constant, Nick's decreases with every step. Zeb is terrified Nick'll be too knackered to fight the man when they get there. He fills the silence.

'Why did you fall out of a tree?'

'I slipped.'

Zeb doesn't speak for a while, concentrating hard on keeping them moving and keeping Nick from tripping and falling.

Nick keeps his eyes on the ground. 'Made a wish up there.'

'What kind of a wish?'

'That we'd get home in one piece.'

'London?'

'Your guess is gonna be better than mine right now.'

They make their way back down the steep embankment and follow the track leading to Alf's place.

Nick can see the light coming from the sitting-room window. The closer they get the less pain he feels, replaced with rage and regret. He notices the black outline of a car a hundred yards from the house.

Nick whispers to Zeb, 'Be quiet.'

Zeb nods.

They approach the house through the small copse of trees. Nick stops a moment, looking around. He talks close to Zeb's ear. 'Come with me round the front. I'm gonna drag myself across the ground. I want you to look through the sitting-room window and tell me what's happening. 'Kay?'

Zeb nods.

They head round and reach the corner of the old building. Zeb gets down on his belly and crawls towards the sitting-room window. Nick pulls himself along the ground slowly, keeping as close to Zeb as he can.

Zeb lifts himself up and looks through the window and through the curtain. He keeps looking. Nick can see he's frozen with fear. Zeb eventually looks back down to Nick, his face panic-stricken. Zeb drops to the ground and crawls back to Nick.

Nick whispers, 'What's happening?'

'Alf's still tied to the lamp . . .' Nick can hear the fear in his voice. 'And Jake is sitting there staring ahead . . . he's . . . he's . . .' Nick squeezes his arm to reassure him.

'He's been sick . . . all over his lap . . . he looks really white. And the nasty bastard is drinking tea.'

'Kid, I want you to wait here.'

Zeb raises his voice for a split second. 'I DON'T . . .' He realises what he's done and quickly lowers it again. 'Don't want to. Don't want to stay here. Don't leave me here.'

'Listen . . . do you wanna help Jake?' Zeb nods. 'And Alf . . . I know you want to help Alf.' Zeb nods again. 'Then I need you to stay here.'

Nick hears the lock on the sitting-room window open. He drags Zeb back round the corner with him. They hear the window slide open, silence for a moment, then it slides back down again.

'You have to be quiet,' Nick whispers. 'That's the most important thing. I want you to wait here for three minutes . . . got your watch?' Zeb holds his thin wrist up to show Nick the oversized watch. 'Good. Time three minutes. When the second hand reaches the twelve for the third time I want you to creep back round and chuck a rock at the window . . .'

'But I don't have a rock.'

Nick looks around. He finds a rock the size of a cricket ball beneath the snow. He puts it into Zeb's hands and curls Zeb's little fingers round it.

Zeb looks up at him, pale with shock. 'Why is he here, Dad? Why does the shitting bastard want to hurt us?'

'I've been a prick and he wants to remind me . . . not to be.'

Zeb's teeth chatter. 'What did you do to make him angry?'

'I'll tell you later.'

'I don't want to stay here on my own. I want to come with you.' Nick can't tell whether or not his son is shivering from cold or fear. His guilt and shame are overridden by a desire to get Jake and Alf out of the house.

'I want to come with you,' Zeb repeats, pleading.

'I know you do, kid, but you have to do this. I promise I'll buy you a goat when this is done. Buy you two.'

'I want to go home.'

'Sure. When this is over you can go home . . . I promise.'

Nick looks down at his leg. He pushes himself up and starts to roll down his trousers.

'What you doin'?' Zeb looks wide-eyed as Nick rolls down the trousers revealing the bare skin and the wound in his thigh. Zeb sees the white of bone through muscle, flesh and congealed blood. He starts crying, putting his hand over his mouth to stop the noise. Nick does his best to console him.

'Get some snow and pack it real tight in your hands.' Nick picks some snow up and packs it down into his palm. 'Like this.'

Zeb follows his instructions. Nick tears off a piece of material from the bottom of his shirt and starts to load the dense snow into it. Zeb puts his lump on to Nick's then watches as he lays the snow down on his wound. He pulls the material over the top and wraps it round his leg, pulling the snow in tight.

'Why you doing that?' Zeb asks.

'I need to walk properly. Numb the pain.'

'You gonna give the man a dig?'

'That's the idea.' Nick leans down and kisses Zeb on

the top of the head. 'Stay here and keep quiet. Three minutes from when I leave, then it'll all be over. Promise. OK?'

Zeb purses his lips and nods once. He watches Nick walk upright and straight, round the corner to the back of the house.

Nick reaches the open back door. His heart beats harder. His mind pushes him forward without a plan. He walks in and sees small pools of melt water on the lino floor. He follows the trail through the kitchen. He stops at the door, turns back and takes three knives out of a drawer, puts one in his back pocket and holds the other two in either hand. He breathes himself calmer, steps across the threshold of the door and limps down the creaking carpeted corridor without stopping. He reaches the sitting-room door. He hears the chink of a cup and saucer, then a voice from the other side. Nick has an overwhelming desire to hide, like a kid, run back out the door into the snow and the dark. He stands rooted to the spot. He checks his watch. Ninety seconds.

Snow falls to the ground forming a new layer on the compacted snow beneath it. The farmyard is quiet, dark, no lights anywhere except the thin beam of white coming from the ground-floor window. Zeb Geneva stands looking at the window holding the rock in his small hand. His arm aches under the weight of it. Back home, all the other rocks he chucks land him in trouble. Nick does his best to punish him but Zeb knows he doesn't really give a shit, just doing what he thinks dads are supposed to do to shut everyone else up. But now he's ordered him to chuck the rock through the window after exactly three minutes as if Zeb's life depended on it. He looks at it, feels the weight. He looks at his watch and counts down from ten. He looks around.

Five, four . . . He strains his arm up behind his head, holds his breath, *two, one.* He hurls it. The moment before impact a violent crash echoes inside the house. Then his rock smashes and shatters the glass. Zeb wants to run up to the window to see the damage, look inside, see what's going on. He stands rooted to the spot imagining the greasy Uruk Hai bastard of his nightmares crashing out of the window face first, landing in a dead heap in the snow. But his legs tell him to run. He sprints into the copse of trees in front of the house, finds a hollow in the base of a tree, climbs in and waits. He puts his hands over his ears to stop the roar of adrenalin and fear in his head. He knows he has to do something. He looks down at the red line of the healing blood brother cut on his thumb and makes up his mind.

He waits for as long as he can before he climbs back out and heads, slow and terrified, back towards the house.

Nick stands at the entrance of the sitting room, holding the kitchen knives by his side, catching his breath; splinters of door and flakes of paint at his feet. He is confronted by Alf sitting in the chair staring up at him, unblinking.

'Jesus fucking Christ,' Nick mutters to himself. 'The fuck happened here?'

'Door wasn't locked. In answer to your question, *you* happened, Nick.' Vincent stands in the middle of the room, clearly in control of the situation, looking at Nick, waiting. 'And there's me thinking you were in Ullapool.' He looks at Jake and shakes his head. Nick is unable to hold back his tears and anger. He lunges at Vincent who steps aside. Nick swings back round bringing the smaller of the two knives across Vincent's face in one movement. The cut is shallow, deep enough to draw quick, thin blood. Vincent lifts his hand to his face, looks at the blood on his palm then moves quickly towards Nick, cracking him across the side of the head with the steel of the spike. Nick stumbles, regains his balance and body-slams him into the wall. They crash into the table, just missing Alf. Jake tries furiously to free himself, screaming at his ropes. Jumper up to his armpits, Nick feels the sting of the tip of the spike slide into the side of his stomach. He holds back the scream of pain, focusing on getting it out of him before it drives in deeper. The quickly melting anaesthetic of the ice he packed round his wound quickly begins to expose searing pain. He falls back on to the empty sofa. Jake feels a tugging on the rope round him, as if someone were tightening it. His mind flies, trying to figure out who it is. The rope judders rhythmically as Zeb's knife cuts into the binding. Vincent leans over Nick who is still trying to get back up. The pop and release of the rope forces a rush of rage into Jake's arms and legs. He grabs his knife and launches off the sofa careering on to Vincent's back, pulling him away from Nick, bundling him chaotically to the floor. He is shocked and elated at his strength, terrified at his desire for violence: out of control, savage, relentless. He sinks the knife into Vincent's leg three times in quick, shallow jabs then into his arm. He pushes the blade in, screaming into the back of Vincent's head. He lets go of the blade, stands, staggers back a little then toe-punts him in the balls from behind. Vincent groans loud and coughs up a heavy clot of cancerous blood. He collapses into a heap. Jake draws the blade out of Vincent's arm and rolls him over. Vincent smiles back at him. He lunges the spike at Jake. Nick rises, booting it out of his hand then falls heavily on to the sofa. Jake leans over Vincent, pinning his shoulders to the ground with his knees. 'Touch my family, my mate, come in here, touch me, you sick fucker, let's see how the blade feels on *your* face.' Jake raises the bloodied blade to Vincent's face and slashes open two warpaint-like gashes just below his eyes then brings the blade to his left eyelid.

'Stop.' Alf's voice is weak, trembling, close to a murmur. Everyone hears him. Nick looks over to him, trying to get up. Jake stares down at a barely conscious Vincent, blade to his eye, breathing manically. He turns to look at Alf who shakes his head in refusal.

Jake drops the blade as if it were infected. He looks down a moment then punches Vincent in the jaw, cheek and eye in quick successive digs. It stings his knuckles. He rises up off him. Vincent doesn't move.

Jake stands and looks around the room. He has to get them out. He blocks Alf from Zeb's view and walks over to him, taking him out of the room. Zeb says nothing. Jake takes him down into the kitchen and sits him down.

'Stay there, blood. I'm gonna get Alf and Dad and we're

gonna get to the hospital, get the fuck out of here. Do as I tell you, yeah?'

Zeb nods.

Jake heads out of the kitchen. 'Bro,' Zeb calls after him.

'Yes, bro.'

'You smashed the wanker up good style.'

'Good job Alf fucking stopped me. Nearly killed the cunt. He's a sick cunt, but the wanker doesn't deserve to die and we ain't going to prison. I'm not ending up like Dad, neither are you. We're going home.' Jake walks back into the sitting room. Nick is up on his feet looking dazed. Vincent's eyes are open but he doesn't move. He coughs several times, more blood trickles out. Jake feels fleeting sympathy but little regret. He unties Alf, lifts him up and leads him out of the sitting room. Nick limps silently behind.

Making sure Zeb hasn't seen the extent of his injuries, Jake soaks a cloth in a cup. He covers Alf's eyes and ties it gently round the back of his head.

'What's the matter with his eyes?' Zeb asks. 'Why have you blindfolded him with that cloth?'

'Come here, kid.' Nick raises his hand out to Zeb. 'I need you to help me get to the van.'

Zeb looks at Jake holding Alf's hand, standing unashamed in underpants and T-shirt.

'I'm not going to hospital with you in your scuzzy sicky pants.'

Jake looks down at his bare, aching legs and pants. 'Stay here, look after Alf a minute.'

Zeb steps forward hesitantly and takes hold of Alf's hand.

Jake runs upstairs.

Zeb looks up at Alf. He sees a half smile break on to his face.

'What's happened to your eyes?' Zeb asks.

'The lidless eye of Mordor found me,' Alf whispers. 'Nothing can't be sorted.'

'Why've you got a wet blindfold on?'

'You're gonna have to trust your brother, Zeb,' Alf continues. 'Do as he says. He's in charge for now.'

Jake comes back down the stairs, dressed and ready to go, holding extra coats for Alf and Zeb. He stops outside the sitting-room door. He looks in. Vincent lies on the floor looking up at the ceiling.

'S'pose you're gonna get the police on to us?' Jake asks.

Vincent shakes his head. 'Got what I came for.'

'What's that then?'

'Peace of mind. A peaceful death.'

'You're not dying.'

'Nothing to do with you, son, been a long time coming.' Vincent looks at him with clear eyes. 'Don't worry yourself, there'll be no police. You did well.'

Jake stares at him a long moment. 'Get yourself to hospital. And don't come near any of us again.'

Vincent continues to look at Jake, says nothing, smiles in resignation and closes his eyes.

Jake walks out and back down into the kitchen.

He hands Zeb his jacket. Zeb helps Alf with his coat and leads him out the back door into the snow. Jake helps Nick up and puts his arm round his shoulder.

'Can you walk?'

Nick nods. Jake helps him out. They walk out into the snow, side by side in silence.

Jake heads with Nick to the van.

'Can you drive?' Jake asks.

'Prefer if you did.'

'I'm taking the tractor. Can you?'

'Sure.'

'See you at the hospital.'

Nick nods.

Zeb helps Alf into the VW then gets in, waiting for Jake. Jake walks up to the open door.

'What you doing, bro?' Zeb asks, worried.

'I'll see you at the hospital, be right behind you.'

'No. Come with us,' Zeb insists.

'I'm taking the tractor.'

'You're shitting nuts, blood.'

'Be right behind you, blood.'

Nick pulls out slowly. The van judders. He stalls it twice before he gets it going. The wheels spin on the ice followed by the acrid smell of clutch burn.

Jake watches the van head out of the drive. He stands in the whited-out farmyard and looks around. He looks at the shattered sitting-room window, the other side of which lies the man that just tried to kill his dad.

He'll remember this place for the rest of his life.

He takes in a lungful of the morning air, bends down and picks up a handful of snow. He washes it across his face. Just like she said, it feels amazing.

He stands, takes one last look at the house and heads into the barn.

He comes out a minute later with Alf's goat on a tattered length of rope.

For Zeb.

Twenty-four

Emily leans forward at the wheel, doing her best to see through the sleet. The car slides intermittently on the compacted snow.

Sally tuts, 'No wonder it's taken us so fucking long, you're driving like Mum.' She looks out across the mountains. 'Can see why he wanted to come back. Never seen anywhere like it.'

Emily nods reluctantly.

They continue to drive for another three miles through early dawn light. The road is quiet. As it begins to bend more sharply, Emily slows down further. Sally shakes her head in despair.

Emily is finding it hard to keep her eyes open. 'Pass me a Mars bar.'

Sally gets one, unwraps it and forces more into Emily's mouth than she can handle.

As they come out of another sharp bend Sally sees the sign for Bywater. 'Not very Scottish-sounding.'

They drive past and continue on for another two miles. Emily sees a large vehicle up ahead in the distance. As she gets closer she realises it's a trailer with a tractor in front.

It's moving slower than she is. A man sits up front exposed to the driving snow.

'What the fuck is that looking out the back?' Sally asks.

'Don't know, a sheep?'

'Looks like a goat to me. Place is full of bumpkins. Overtake it.'

'I'm not overtaking it,' Emily protests.

'What, in case another car comes in the other direction?' Sally mocks.

'We're not far from Dundonnell. We'll hang back till we get there.'

'Fuck sake, sis, you'll only need to take it up to forty.'

Emily drives in silence for another mile, looking at the back of the man driving the tractor. If someone's back can look determined, this one does. The car lights reflect in the eyes of the hairy animal looking at them from the trailer. The sugar rush wears off. Her exhaustion makes it hard to concentrate.

She puts her foot down a little and pulls out.

'Hallefuckinglujah.' Sally takes out a Mars bar from her bag and opens it. Emily concentrates hard on the space between the tractor and the far side of the road. They slowly begin to pass the tractor.

Sally jerks forward. 'What the fu . . . ! Is that Jake?' she shouts, opening the passenger window, looking out. Emily looks to her left and catches a glimpse of Jake's face.

'It bloody is . . . it's Jake!' Sally shouts out of the window. 'Jake, it's Sally!'

Emily looks again, loses control of the car a moment and knocks into the side of the tractor. Jake turns quickly and angrily to look at them. Emily sees his face clearly. She puts her foot on the brake forcing the car to fall back behind the trailer. She starts beeping. Jake slows the tractor down. She pulls into the side of the road.

Jake pulls over, climbs down from the tractor and starts walking towards the car.

The snow has stopped. Nick parks the van illegally in the main hospital forecourt. He gets out and staggers, slumping back against the side of the van. Zeb gets out and helps him up. Steadied, Zeb goes to the passenger side and helps Alf out. He leads him to the main entrance. Nick takes Zeb's Uruk Hai spear and hobbles in behind them. He gets twenty yards down the main corridor when his eyes start to blur. He sees Zeb and Alf disappear round the corner. He feels himself fall. He lies on his back, half conscious.

This is as far as I go, then.

A nurse comes into his line of sight.

'Got yourself into a bit of a state there, ey.' She smiles. 'What's your name?'

The words flop out of his mouth. 'Tony . . . Nick. Nick Geneva.'

A uniformed policeman walks past, looking down at him and his blood-covered leg and hands with natural suspicion. The nurse leaves his line of sight for a moment then comes back with two male nurses and a bed on wheels. They lower it and lift him on to it.

He's wheeled down the remaining stretch of corridor to the lift where they wait.

Nick turns his head to see the horizontal image of the policeman walking down the glass corridor towards

Accident and Emergency. He continues to look down the corridor as he's pushed clunkily into the lift. His eyes struggle to focus on Zeb and Alf at the far end. Alf is sitting on a chair, surrounded by two nurses and an inspecting doctor. Zeb holds his hand. Nick blinks to clear his vision. The lift door closes. Through the two rectangles of wire mesh glass he sees Emily, Sally and Jake walk past. He wants to call out. His mouth opens. No words. He closes his eyes. The lift goes down. He lets go and lets himself relax into the stretcher bed and slides into the welcome, long-awaited black of unconsciousness.

Twenty-five

London. Three Weeks Later

Zeb walks through the first of a series of double doors, Jake and Emily are close behind. The doors close. They are held temporarily between two doors.

Zeb beams excitedly at Jake. 'Fill this up with water and make it into a massive fish tank.'

'Fill it up with sharks.' Jake smiles. He pulls out a newspaper and starts to read.

'What you reading, dufus?'

'Words.'

'I know you're reading words. What words?'

'Same old shit.'

Zeb looks at him nonplussed then takes hold of Emily's hand.

The prison officer looks at them and the family behind them through the security glass. After a delay, he presses a button. The second door opens. Zeb is first through.

* * *

They're escorted through a series of doors and holding areas.

'Too many shitting doors,' Zeb complains in a whisper to Jake. Jake nudges him forward through the final door.

They reach the visiting area.

Emily stops short of the entrance. 'I'll wait for you in that room down there.'

'You can't do that,' Zeb complains.

'It's fine, Zeb, you go ahead.' Emily smiles at him.

'You'll get bored, come see Dad. He wants to see you,' Zeb pleads. Pulling her to the entrance of the visiting hall.

'I told you I wasn't going in. Go on, you're dying to see him. I've got my book. Send him my love.'

Jake kisses her on the cheek and walks in. Zeb follows. They look around, trying to spot Nick.

No sign.

They find a table. Jake gives Zeb some money. He heads to the open hatch selling teas and coffees.

Jake sits back in his chair, feeling good, unsure of seeing Nick again. He's missed him but he's still seriously pissed off with him. He's enjoyed the freedom around the house. Zeb does what he tells him more than he used to and Emily gives him more slack than before. He thought she would get harder. He feels trusted. Good to be back with Carlos, good to be back. He misses Scotland and Alf.

He places the newspaper strategically, neatly on the table.

Zeb returns a few minutes later with a tray of teas, a pile of biscuits and a large bar of chocolate. He opens the bar and breaks off two rows and puts the lot in his mouth.

He hands the bar to Jake, grinning. 'Why'd it take so

long to get a shitting visiting order?'

'Cos they move him around so much. Think they did it on purpose . . . wankers.'

'Yeah, wankers.' Zeb chews the chocolate. 'Why's he here . . . why won't they let him out . . . he's been in shitting ages?'

'You keep asking the same questions and I keep telling you the same thing, bro.'

'But he didn't kill anyone.'

'Bust your parole, you get banged up no question.' Jake breaks off a piece of chocolate.

'When's he getting out?' Zeb asks.

'Why do you think I know everything?'

'Cos you're a shitting know it all.' Zeb looks around the room at the other kids waiting for their dads.

Jake smiles. 'When he's been to court we'll find out. You'll be an older spaz when he gets out, that's for shit sure . . . might even have a few pubes on your saggy hairless bollocks . . . if you're lucky.'

Zeb kicks his shin. Jake doesn't fight back.

They sit in silence, waiting, watching the prisoners come in the room in twos and threes dispersing to families and friends.

'You gonna write to him? Zeb asks.

'Dad?'

'Alf.'

Jake shrugs.

'I've written him a letter and done him a drawing of the goat you got me.' Zeb slouches across the table exhaling loudly. 'He wrote me one back.'

'What'd he say?'

'He went up to the *kuti* for a week to get his eyes better, innit.'

'Why didn't you tell me you got a letter, dufus?'

'Didn't ask.'

'When you write him . . . tell 'im I miss Scotland, all of it.'

Zeb nods and breaks off another piece of chocolate.

Twenty minutes later a prison guard pushes Nick through the doors in a battered wheelchair. He waves at Jake and Zeb, trying to look cool.

Zeb jumps up and sprints over, throwing his arms round his neck.

Jake stays seated.

Zeb takes the wheelchair off the guard and wheels Nick over, beaming a wide grin.

Jake gets up and scrapes the third chair away from the table. Some of the visitors look round at them.

He waits patiently for Nick to fill the space.

Zeb wheels him up to the table. He looks at them both, eyes glistening.

'Don't cry, Dad. Please,' Zeb asks in a hushed tone.

Nick takes hold of their hands melodramatically and looks at them for a long, proud moment. Jake shifts uncomfortably in his chair, doing his best to remain silent and look as pissed off as he can. He's pleased to see him. He keeps his hand inside Nick's warm grasp.

Nick looks to Zeb then back to Jake, squeezing their fingers tight.

'Back in one piece, ey?' His eyes look down to the table for a moment.

Nick spots the paper and picks it up. 'Decent paper. Makes a change from the shit they read in here.'

'Page eighteen,' Jake instructs him. 'Carlos found it.'

'What's on page eighteen, bro?' Zeb asks.

Jake remains silent.

Nick scans the page. He reads the obituary at the bottom. Jake watches him closely as he scans the short article.

FORMER 70s BOXING STAR VINCENT CRACKNEL DIES OF CANCER IN SCOTTISH HOSPITAL AT THE AGE OF FIFTY-THREE.

Having risen up from a tough life on a housing estate in Peckham to the number one middleweight boxing champion in the UK, Cracknel's short-lived stardom was ruined by the double trouble of a lost fight to the Australian 'Thunder from Down Under' and a series of court appearances for robbery, racketeering and grievous bodily harm. Cracknel's last three decades living in London were spent in and out of prison and police custody. His amassed estate derived mainly from the buying and selling of sporting memorabilia, most of which was reported to be stolen, will be up for sale at auction later this month. All proceeds will go to his wife, Sam Cracknel, age twenty-three.

Nick stops reading and looks at Jake. 'Didn't know Carlos could read.'

Jake ignores the joke.

'Told you it'd be all right,' Nick continues.

'Doesn't change what happened.' Jake leans back

335

wanting to be as far away from Nick as possible without actually leaving the table.

Zeb remains wide-eyed and silent, looking to both of them in turn.

'Nothing I can say will make any difference, kid. Besides I've said it already. You know how I feel about what happened. I fucked it up. I did . . .'

'Damn straight,' Jake interrupts.

'All I can do is be here, do the time and get back to you guys as quick as possible. Christ I've missed you . . . both of you.' Nick stops speaking mid-sentence, tears rising in his eyes.

'When are the bastards gonna let you out then?' Zeb asks.

'Soon, kid, soon.'

'You gonna get a job or carry on bullshitting and robbing and killing dogs?' Jake asks without irony.

Nick lets their hands go. He looks at Jake and smiles. 'You did good, kid. Good to stop him, good not to kill the fucker. Better man than me. I'm gonna make this up to you, both of you, soon as I get out. This has seriously done me. Easy enough for me to bullshit my way through my own life, promise to make the change, but bringing you two into it, into that kind of danger, that is unforgivable, I know that. I don't expect you to . . . forgive me. Don't think I forgave my old man for being such a prick, didn't want to, not until we went to Snowdon. Maybe in a few years, when things have cooled off, ey, kid?'

Jake looks down and shrugs. He's glad Nick is alive. One day he'll tell him that; tell him that he loves him too. But for now he needs to feel this anger and disappointment and he needs his dad to see it.

Zeb looks at him intensely. 'Mum said we can't see as much of you cos of what you did and cos your house got burned down and we haven't got anywhere to sleep now. Burnt some of my best toys, bastard fire.'

Jake looks up at Nick. 'Where's Warren?'

'Haven't heard from him, don't expect to. Mum OK?'

'She's good.' Jake eats the last piece of chocolate. 'Still majorly pissed off with you. Sends her love.'

Nick nods in appreciation. 'Send her some from me. If she'll have it.'

Jake shrugs.

Nick looks at them both for an awkward moment. His eyes glisten with unshed tears. Jake can see tiredness, regret and shame etched in his face. He watches Nick do his best to pull himself together and clear his throat. Jake feels a lot older than his father right now and he's comfortable with it.

A heavy silence falls across the table. The three of them sit in it, finding a comfortable spot within it.

Nick finally breaks it. 'So what's going on out there? Girlfriends, school, I wanna hear it all.'

Zeb speaks first, non-stop, filling him in with the news.

Jake sits patiently, smoking, drinking tea, relaxed, listening to Zeb with pride.

Hard Girls

Martina Cole

HARD LIVES. HARD LESSONS. IT'S MURDER ON THE STREETS.

Danielle Crosby had a body to die for. A body she sold to the highest bidder. But she ended up paying for it with her life.

When a prostitute's body is found lifeless, mutilated and brutally raped, DCI Annie Carr has never seen anything like it and never wants to again. Kate Burrows, retired DCI and now consultant, has plenty of experience when it comes to murder – after all she caught the Grantley Ripper and broke the biggest paedophile ring in the South East. She is determined to help put the killer behind bars. But whoever it is won't be easily caught. And when another girl's body is found, even more horrifically disfigured than the last, it's clear the killer is just warming up . . .

In a ruthless world where everyone's out for themselves, Annie and Kate must dig deep if they hope to catch a callous serial killer who knows no limits and makes no mistakes. For some, prostitution is seriously big business. But how many people will pay the ultimate price?

Utterly riveting, HARD GIRLS is a gripping and disturbing thriller that will have you hooked until the very last page.

'Cole is brilliant at portraying the good among the bad, and vice versa, so until the very end we never quite know who to trust. This is the very stuff that makes her so compelling' *Daily Mirror*

978 0 7553 2870 3

headline

You Can't Hide

Karen Rose

YOU DON'T KNOW WHO I AM.
Someone is tormenting psychiatrist Tess Ciccotelli's patients, pushing them to commit suicide, and setting her up to take the blame. But even police pressure won't make her break her oath to protect their secrets.

YOU CAN'T STOP WHAT I AM DOING.
Detective Aidan Reagan understands Tess's need to safeguard her clients but all the clues suggest that a nameless, faceless enemy is set on destroying her career, her family and, finally, Tess herself.

YOU CAN'T HIDE.
As Reagan and Tess race to stop the killer, one thing becomes clear – the noose is tightening around Tess's neck and there is nowhere for her to go . . .

Tense, taut, terrifying – YOU CAN'T HIDE is Karen Rose at her very best. Be prepared for anything.

Acclaim for Karen Rose:

'Intense, complex and unforgettable' James Patterson

'Rose delivers the kind of high-wire suspense that keeps you riveted to the edge of your seat' Lisa Gardner

978 0 7553 3709 5

headline

Vanished

Joseph Finder

NICK HELLER: The man who beats the odds.

Viciously attacked on a night out with her husband, Roger, Lauren Heller wakes twenty-four hours later to find that he has disappeared without trace. With the police investigation stalled, Lauren turns to the only person who is able to help: Roger's brother, Nick.

Nick Heller is an international security consultant. He is also ex-Army Special Forces. A man who doesn't take orders from anyone and is relentless when pursuing a lead. A man who knows where the bodies are buried. Most importantly, a man who always puts his family first.

If Nick is to find his brother, he is going to have to call on all his skills for it appears that Roger may have a powerful enemy – an enemy that will do whatever it takes to stop Nick finding him.

From international bestseller Joseph Finder comes the first pulse-pounding Nick Heller thriller.

Praise for *Power Play*:

'Grabs you by the throat and doesn't let go. Joseph Finder is one of the best thriller writers around' Harlan Coben

'Great characters, a roller coaster plot, and a hero you'll cheer for. I dare you to read the first page. You won't be able to stop' Tess Gerritsen

978 0 7553 7000 9

headline

Blood Red

Quintin Jardine

Primavera Blackstone is in Spain, comfortable with the tranquility of coastal village life. But since she first entered the dangerous world of sleuthing, it seems trouble has a way of tracking her down.

What begins as gossip about her growing friendship with the village priest turns into moral outrage. But when a powerful politician is found dead, suspicion spirals out of control and all eyes are on Primavera. Now a prime suspect, she must hunt a killer if she is to save herself and her son from a nightmare beyond their imagination . . .

Praise for Quintin Jardine's novels:

'Well constructed, fast paced, Jardine's narrative has many an ingenious twist and turn' *Observer*

'Perfect plotting and convincing characterisation . . . Jardine manages to combine the picturesque with the thrilling' *The Times*

978 0 7553 4026 2

headline

CASPAR WALSH

Criminal

When Caspar Walsh was three years old, his young mother faced a difficult choice. Her son, or her lover? She chose her lover. Reluctantly, Caspar's father became his primary carer. But Caspar's father was not classic dad material. He robbed banks. He dealt drugs. His currency was charm, deception and violence. Yet despite his unconventional, illegal lifestyle, he loved his son. Not enough to put aside the criminal world he was immersed in, but enough for Caspar to love him back, to look up to him, to emulate him.

Criminal is the story of a wild childhood punctuated by drugs, violence, abuse and the absence of a father frequently detained at Her Majesty's pleasure. It's the story of how Caspar inevitably became part of his father's world: dealing drugs, doing drugs, doing time. And of how, as a young man, he made the decision not to be a victim of his upbringing but to take control of his life, to rehabilitate himself and, in doing so, help rehabilitate others.

Praise for *Criminal*:

'An extraordinary autobiography. Vibrantly written with one of the most compelling characters in Caspar's father that I've come across in a long time. It's a masterful portrayal of the two sides of a man and demonstrates with absolute clarity how confusing love can be within an abusive relationship' Minette Walters

'A surprisingly touching, beautifully written tale . . . While peppered with hair-raising accounts of scrapes with the cops, violence and abuse, Criminal never loses its sense of optimism' *News of the World*

978 0 7553 1763 9

headline
review

Now you can buy any of these other bestselling
Headline books from your bookshop or
direct from the publisher.

FREE P&P AND UK DELIVERY
(Overseas and Ireland £3.50 per book)

Criminal	Caspar Walsh	£6.99
Don't Tell	Karen Rose	£6.99
I Can See You	Karen Rose	£6.99
Hard Girls	Martina Cole	£7.99
The Business	Martina Cole	£7.99
Vanished	Joseph Finder	£6.99
Aftershock	Quintin Jardine	£7.99
Blood Red	Quintin Jardine	£7.99

TO ORDER SIMPLY CALL THIS NUMBER

01235 400 414

or visit our website: www.headline.co.uk

Prices and availability subject to change without notice.